W9-ADI-027

YOU BELONG TO ME

Johanna Lindsey

YOU BELONG TO ME

WHEELER
PUBLISHING, INC.
ROCKLAND, MA

★ AN AMERICAN COMPANY ★

Published in Large Print by arrangement with
Avon Books, a division of the Hearst Corporation
in the United States and Canada.

Wheeler Large Print Book Series.

Set in 16 pt. Plantin.

Library of Congress Cataloging-in-Publication Data

Lindsey, Johanna.
    You belong to me / Johanna Lindsey.
       p.   cm.—(Wheeler large print book series)
    ISBN 1-56895-213-9 : (hardcover)
    1. Large type books. I. Title. II. Series.
[PS3562.I5123Y6   1995]
813'.54—dc20   95-15707
                                              CIP

For Jamie,
the daughter I wasn't fortunate enough to have—
until now.

1

Ukraine Province, Russia, 1836

Constantin Rubliov stood at the window in his drawing room, his hands clasped behind his back, watching the dust cloud in the distance slowly approaching. The window, located at the front of his house, looked out on the road that wound past his country estate and led to the Dnieper River in the east. From the second floor of the house, you could just make out the river on a clear day. From his vantage point in the drawing room, the road to the west was visible as far as the eye could see, and that was where the dust cloud was approaching from.

If he hadn't known that there was going to be a horse race today, the sight of all the people crowding both sides of the road just beyond his house would have told him. His Cossacks loved a good race as much as they loved a good fight. They were a tough, volatile, high-spirited people, always laughing, singing, or fighting—and fiercely loyal.

But they weren't exactly his, although he had always thought of them that way because they had been so long associated with his family. And they, too, thought of him and his as theirs. But Cossack meant "free warrior," and these Cossacks were certainly that. Since his great-

1

great-grandfather had given them permission to settle on his land and raise their families in peace, they had worked for the Rubliovs in whatever capacity was required. They staffed Constantin's house, they bred his horses, they guarded him and his family in their travels.

The settlement they had started all those years ago was now a thriving town less than a quarter mile to the west of his estate. The Razins, who had supplied the town with its leaders for all these years as well as populated three-fourths of the town with the many branches of their family, had grown as prosperous as the Rubliovs.

With their help, Constantin now supplied horses to the Czar's army, and thoroughbreds to aristocrats who could afford them. His sugar beet crops filled the markets of Kiev and the settlements along the Dnieper, and his wheat brought fine prices along the Black Sea coast. He was growing richer by the year since he had taken an active interest in his horses and fields. Ever since his wife had died ten years ago, he had stopped being an absentee landlord, as most of the Russian nobles were. Only his sister still made use of their town house in Moscow and the Rubliov palace in St. Petersburg.

"You aren't going to like this, darling."

Constantin didn't glance at the woman who had spoken. Anna Veriovka stood only several feet away at the next window, watching the same scene in front of the house. Anna was one of those rare women who never seemed to age. To look at her with her dark brown hair always perfectly coiffed and her even darker brown eyes, the fine bone structure that was going to make her an eternal beauty, no one could guess she had seen thirty-five years.

Right now it was her tone, rather than her words, that made Constantin brace his hands on the window ledge and stare more intently at the oncoming horses.

Deep in his gut, he knew what he would see. It wouldn't be the first time, or, he feared, the last. But for a moment all he could see was that dust cloud, nearly reaching the house now, and in its midst the vague shape of six thoroughbreds crowding one another on the narrow road. Fur hats, long coats flapping, sleek legs stretching for the finish line at the nearby village, and the large white wolfhound racing along beside the road, barking, urging the animals to a little more speed. And wherever that dog was . . .

"Alex will win," Anna said in a smug voice.

"Of course Alex will win," Constantin grumbled, watching the lead rider crawl up on the saddle, squat there, slowly rise to standing, then toss off a fur cap, laughing, with the other riders following suit.

His eyes were squeezed shut as he added, "She always wins—and I wish you wouldn't call her that. It only encourages her to act the hoyden."

His longtime mistress merely clucked her tongue, but after a few more moments he felt her breasts press against his back and her arms circle his waist. "You can look now, darling. She didn't break her neck."

"Thank God," he whispered, and then the anger came, for the scare he'd just had was no less severe than it always was. "I'm going to beat her this time, I swear I am."

Anna chuckled. "So you always say, but you never do. Besides, the Razin boys wouldn't let you."

"Then I'll get their father to do it. Ermak will do anything I ask of him."

"Except hurt a hair on that sweet child's head. He adores Alex as much as you do."

Constantin sighed as he turned around to do some hugging of his own. "Anna, my love, that 'sweet child' is twenty-five years old, too old for the foolishness we just witnessed. You know it as well as I do. She should be married and nursing babies. Her two sisters had no difficulty in that respect. Lydia has given me five granddaughters. Elizaveta had three before she was widowed. Why has it been so impossible to get my youngest daughter married?"

Anna thought it prudent not to mention Alexandra's outrageous frankness that had caused such a stir and had made Czar Nicholas unofficially ban her from St. Petersburg. If Anna reminded Constantin of that, she was afraid she would laugh, which she did every time she recalled that scene at the Romanovsky dinner, when Princess Olga had lamented to the twenty or so guests sitting near her that, however much she tried, she couldn't keep from gaining weight that season.

Alexandra, hearing her, had suggested quite helpfully and with complete sincerity, "Why, ma'am, if you would just stop stuffing your mouth

4

with blinis and sour cream, you might lose a pound or two."

Since the princess had been stuffing her mouth with those very things at that very moment, it wasn't surprising that a good many of the guests had suddenly begun coughing into their napkins or looking beneath the table for something they had supposedly dropped, just to hide their snickers. Anna, who had been there as Alexandra's chaperone, had thought it hilarious herself, but Olga Romanovsky hadn't; she'd gone straight to the royal ear the next day with her complaint, likely asking for outright execution. Anna thought it fortunate for Alexandra that the Czar had merely politely suggested that Constantin take his daughter back to the country, where her wayward tongue would do no more than offend the peasants.

Unfortunately, Alexandra hadn't learned from her mistake. Her outspokenness had not been curbed the next season in Moscow, or later in Kharkov, and certainly not closer to home, in Kiev. She had managed, single-handedly, to make herself a social pariah. And Anna suspected, more than once, that she had not done it all in ignorance or by accident. After all, Alexandra was a fairly intelligent girl, and she *had* confessed after that first disastrous season in St. Petersburg that she was in love with the Honorable Christopher Leighton, whom she had met there, and she meant to marry him and no one else. How better to wait for the lagging Englishman than to ensure that no other young man would be asking for her hand in the meantime. Which was what had happened, regardless of whether Alexandra had intended it.

As for Constantin's question, Anna decided to remind him about the man who had stolen his daughter's heart all those years ago. "You don't think she could *still* be waiting for that English diplomat, do you?"

Constantin snorted. "After seven long years? Don't be absurd."

"But he left the country only three years ago," she pointed out.

"And Alexandra hasn't mentioned his name again, since I refused to let her follow him to England at the time," he replied.

"Isn't that when she told you she wasn't going to marry anyone, ever?"

Constantin flushed, recalling the argument he'd had with his lovely daughter, which had been one of their worst. "She didn't mean it. She was just angry."

Anna lifted a brow. "Are you trying to convince me of that, or yourself? Or maybe it's slipped your notice that Alex ignores every young man you bring home for her to meet, and she hasn't traveled any farther than Kiev in the past three years, and she made that trip only to shop. Even then, she managed to come up with one excuse after another to remain cooped up in your hotel suite."

It was actually a relief to Constantin to hear Anna voice his own suspicions, a relief and an easing of the guilt he'd been living with this past week. True, Alexandra's excuses were always logical and sounded sincere, but they were still

6

excuses. And when she had come up with one of them last week in order to refuse to travel with him to Vasilkov to visit her sister and nieces, he had come to the same conclusions Anna had just drawn, and got morose, thinking about his youngest daughter wasting her life pining for that damned foreigner. Unfortunately, he had also got quite drunk and done something he never would have if he had been sober.

Anna felt the change in his big body, which was no longer relaxed against hers, saw the flush climbing his cheeks, and noted how his deep midnight-blue eyes refused to meet hers. Anna knew him extremely well. Their spouses had died within a year of each other. The four of them had been close friends before that. She and Constantin had continued that friendship, and eight years ago, they had become even closer. She loved him dearly, though she refused to give up her widowed independence to marry him. Nor was it necessary to wed him when she lived in his home as his housekeeper and hostess, and as companion-chaperone to his youngest daughter whenever that duty was required, which was rarely these days.

Right now shame was fairly oozing from him, and she demanded as baldly as Alexandra would have, "Constantin Rubliov, what have you done?"

He moved out of her embrace without answering, walking straight to the mahogany cabinet where numerous crystal decanters were always kept full of his favorite spirits. Anna came up beside him while he filled one of the larger glasses to the brim with vodka. Immediately he lifted it to his lips.

"It's that bad?" she asked gently. At his barely perceptible nod, she said, "Maybe you should pour me one of those."

"No," he replied, setting the glass down, but keeping his hand around it. Half the contents was gone. "You'll likely throw it in my face, then the glass at my head, then come after me with the decanter."

His family might be prone to that sort of tempestuous reaction, but she wasn't. But she was definitely getting worried now. "Tell me."

He still wouldn't look at her. "I have found Alexandra a husband."

That gave her pause, because it was nothing she hadn't heard before. He had been trying to do just that for the past seven years. So wherein lay the shame he was presently exhibiting?

"A husband?" she said carefully. "But Alex will only refuse him, as she has all your other suggestions." He was slowly shaking his head. "She can't refuse him? How is that—?" She didn't finish, and laughed instead. "Don't tell me you think you can insist at this late date. Come now, darling, you know that does no good with this particular daughter of yours. She's more stubborn than you are, if you haven't noticed. You would end up raising the roof with your shouts, then give in to her as you always do."

Again he was shaking his head, and looking even more unhappy about it. And he still wouldn't meet her eyes. His color was also still high. He was a man genuinely wallowing in guilt.

Fearful now, she repeated her question. "What *have* you done?"

His head dropped so low on his chest, she could barely hear the words: "Given my daughter no choice."

She waved her hand dismissively at that answer. "There are always choices—"

"Not when I have involved family honor, which is the one thing she won't ignore—at least she's going to think it is involved."

"What does that mean?"

"That I sacrificed my own honor, my integrity, my principles, ethics, honesty—"

"What have you done?"

Anna never raised her voice. She was the epitome of all that was gracious and demure. Even when she was angry she would make her point quietly, and cause her antagonist to feel like an ogre in the process. That she was shouting now brought Constantin's eyes to her, not in surprise but in dread. He could well lose her when she learned how low he had sunk in his desire to give his youngest daughter the same happiness and fulfillment her sisters had found.

He looked so miserable, so utterly guilt-ridden and despondent, that Anna gave a little cry and threw her arms around his neck. "It can't be as terrible as you're letting on," she whispered by his ear, which was no easy feat since he towered over her by a foot. "Tell me."

"I have arranged for a betrothal."

"A betrothal?"

His response was anticlimactic, to say the least.

9

She relaxed against him, leaning back just enough so she could see his face.

"Thank God," she said with feeling, "I was beginning to think you had killed someone."

His expression didn't change; he looked just as miserable, although he was finally looking at her. "I believe I would feel the same if I had killed someone," he admitted.

Anna's eyes flared. She could have hit him at that moment, something she would never in her life have considered doing—until now. "Dammit, Constantin, get to the heart of it before you drive me mad!"

He flinched because she was yelling again. Yelling from Alexandra he could take; he even expected it, and could give it back with equal fervor every time, but he couldn't bear it from his little Anna. Yet he deserved it, and her scorn as well.

He finally said, "I sent a letter to Countess Maria Petroff."

The name brought a thoughtful frown to Anna's face. "Why does that name sound familiar to me?"

"Because you have heard me speak so often of Simeon Petroff."

"Ah, your good friend who died—what was it, thirteen or fourteen years ago?"

"Fourteen."

When he said no more, she frowned again, this time in annoyance. Obviously she was going to have to drag the facts out of him bit by bit.

"Maria would be Simeon's wife, or rather, his

widow. What has she to do with Alex's betrothal? And when did you arrange this?"

"Last week."

She had hoped, for the sake of her mounting exasperation, that he would have answered more than one of her direct questions. "But you were here last week," she pointed out. "And we have had no visitors—"

"The betrothal is with Simeon's son. I reminded Maria of it, and suggested that it was high time she send her son to collect his bride— but not in those words. I was quite diplomatic about it, though the essence was the same."

Anna was incredulous, more than incredulous, having never heard a word of this before. "*Why* did you never mention this betrothal? I assume it must be long-standing, at the very least made before Simeon's death. And why have we been pushing eligible men at Alex all these years, with the hope that one might interest her, when she is already bound in contract to this—he would be Cardinian, wouldn't he?"

Again he answered only her last question. "Yes."

She offered a smile. "So why the long face, darling? This match must delight you." And then she paused, drawing her own conclusion. "Don't tell me you actually forgot about it until last week."

"No, it wasn't forgotten." Constantin turned to drain his glass and then poured in more vodka before he added, "It wasn't even conceived."

Anna gasped. "What are you saying?"

He wouldn't meet her eyes again, and he had

11

to take yet another swallow of his drink before he said, "What I wrote to the count ess was mostly lies, with only a few truths thrown in. Simeon and I did discuss a betrothal of our children back when Alexandra was born. At least that is true. We discussed it at length. We both thought it was a splendid idea. But we never made it official. There were years to do so, after all. Alexandra was not even a year old yet; Simeon's boy was only six. So—so now you know what I've done."

Anna let out a sigh. It wasn't nearly as bad as she had thought, and could be corrected with another letter that could be dispatched immediately.

But just to be sure she understood the entire matter, she said, "You made claim to a betrothal that was never settled, and you did so because your friend is dead and can't dispute it. Is that what you've taken so long to tell me?"

"I was drunk at the time I did it. It was the night you stayed in the village to help with that birthing. When it occurred to me, it seemed like the perfect solution for Alexandra. In fact, I have not the slightest doubt that had Simeon lived, our children would have wed each other seven years ago."

"That may be so, but it didn't happen that way, and your wishing it were otherwise is not going to make it happen now. You must write Countess Petroff immediately with the truth, before she does send her son here."

"No."

"No?"

"It is still a perfect solution."

Anna's eyes narrowed on him. "So *that* is why you are feeling so guilty? You have no intention of correcting what you've done?"

"That will be my cross to bear," Constantin said with the stubbornness inherent in his family. "But think, Anna. What if they are ideally suited to each other? What if this one little lie—"

"*Little?*" she cut in.

"Harmless, then," he insisted, continuing. "What if it brings together two people who would never have met otherwise, and they are so taken with each other that they cannot help but fall in love?"

She shook her head. "You are dreaming. Or is it merely wishful thinking to absolve your guilt?"

"It's not impossible—"

"With *our* Alex?"

Her skeptical tone annoyed him. He, more than anyone, knew his daughter's faults.

Ignoring those faults, he stressed the one thing in Alexandra's favor. "She's beautiful."

"No one can deny that, darling, but has it gained her a long list of suitors? You know as well as I that she offends more than she charms, and men don't usually make a habit of courting embarrassment. It's a wonder that Englishman attended her as long as he did in St. Petersburg, and continued to correspond with her all these years. The English are sticklers for proper behavior, after all."

He didn't like reminders of the foreigner who had stolen his daughter's heart with no intention of nurturing it. Were the man still in Russia, Constantin would seriously consider shooting him. But that bounder was no longer at issue, and the saints be praised for that.

"Simeon was a tolerant man just like me. He admired frankness, scoffed at hypocrisy, and was certainly no snob. It isn't unrealistic to think that his son will have inherited his qualities."

"Didn't you also once tell me that your friend was a womanizer?"

Anna *would* have to remember that. "Simeon never confessed a great love for his wife," he explained. "Theirs was an arranged marriage."

Anna gave him a pointed look. "Which is exactly what you're trying to foist on his unsuspecting son—an arranged marriage. Do you honestly expect the son to be any more faithful than the father, or for Alex to stand for anything less than complete faithfulness, considering how possessive she is of what's hers?"

Constantin flushed bright red. "Dammit, Anna, it's not at all the same. What I expect, or rather hope for, is that these children will find love together. If Simeon had loved his wife even a little, he would have been faithful to her. I expect no less from his son."

"But therein lies the crux of the matter. *If.* You are putting all your hope on an 'if,' when you have never even met this young man. And for that matter, he's not all that young if he's about six years older than Alex. He would be thirty-one, more than likely already married—"

"He's not."

"How do you know?"

"Bohdan came through Cardinia on his way back from delivering the filly the Austrian duke requested. Bohdan knew I would appreciate word of the Petroffs."

She conceded that point with a shrug. "So he's not married, but you can't deny he's old enough to know his own mind and make his own decisions. What makes you think he will accept a betrothal to a woman he doesn't know just because his father might have arranged it? He's no longer a child who must do his father's bidding, even if his father were still alive. And another thing—won't the Petroffs wonder why they did not find a copy of this contract in Simeon's papers after he died?"

"Possibly, but I have a copy to show the young count when he arrives. He won't doubt his father's signature."

"You forged it?"

"It wasn't difficult, with a little practice. As for the count and Alex accepting the betrothal—" Constantin paused, then added almost bleakly, "It comes down to honor. Though I have misplaced mine, they will be trapped by it."

"What if your Cardinian has none?"

"He is Simeon's son," Constantin said, as if that were enough to explain his confidence.

Anna sighed. It was becoming quite obvious that nothing she said was going to make a difference. That damn Rubliov stubbornness. They all possessed it, but none so much as the father— and the youngest daughter. Once invoked, it was unshakable.

Even though Constantin was sick with guilt over what he'd done, he would cling tenaciously

15

to his reason for doing it. He wanted his daughter to find happiness.

Anna couldn't fault him for wanting what all parents wanted for their children, but happiness could be defined in a hundred different ways. After the eight years they had spent together, and the dozens of times she had turned down his proposals, he should have realized by now that marriage was not every woman's fondest desire.

She placed a hand gently on his arm, determined to try to make him understand that at least. "Perhaps you haven't noticed that Alex isn't exactly unhappy. She enjoys the freedom you allow her. She enjoys working with the horses, which a husband would never permit her to do. She has friends here. And she adores you—when you two are not fighting. Frankly, I think she even enjoys your arguments. Have you ever considered that Alex just wasn't meant to marry? Marriage would more than likely constrain her, might even stifle her—unless she can meet a man who doesn't give a damn for convention any more than she does, a rarity—"

"Or one who loves her enough to allow her certain freedoms," he cut in, "but also is capable of denying her those in which she risks her damn neck."

He sounded so exasperated with that statement, Anna almost laughed. "Is *that* one of your motives? You really think a husband will be able to control Alex's reckless nature even though you have failed?"

That got her a glower. "Perhaps not, but keeping her pregnant certainly will."

16

She couldn't argue with that. Motherhood would make a difference in Alexandra's life. At the very least it would keep her from racing her horses so energetically. And Alexandra was very good with children. Though she had never said so, she probably did want some of her own. And she had been willing to marry that Englishman, in fact had desired it greatly, so she was not opposed to marriage.

Anna sighed. If she wasn't careful, she would be applauding what Constantin had done.

"We have gotten away from the point," she said. "What you are doing is forcing Alex and Simeon's son into a marriage that neither one was expecting. It's likely that they will both protest it, but I am absolutely certain that Alex will. And what happens if they don't take to each other? If they are both against the marriage, they won't exactly meet under the best of terms. Alex could end up hating the man, which would hardly produce the happy life you envision for her."

"Purely suppositions, Anna."

"But more likely than those you anticipate."

"The truth will be clear when they meet," he replied stubbornly.

"And if I am right?"

"If it's obvious that they won't suit, then of course I will release them from the betrothal and compensate the count for his trouble in coming here."

"Well, thank God you're not going to be pigheaded about this to the very end."

He flinched at her sarcasm and retaliated by saying, "Actually, I'm feeling much better about

17

it, now that you've raised issues that hadn't occurred to me and I have successfully put them aside."

She was about to reply quite scathingly to that remark when the front door slammed, and a moment later, Alexandra appeared in the doorway. She didn't notice them yet, as she was busy slapping dust from her sleeves with her equally dusty fur cap, spreading a fine coating of it on the floor at her feet where her Borzoi was making a bigger cloud of it with his wagging tail. A single lock of ash-blond hair had escaped her coiffure and fell over her shoulder to her waist.

She looked like a Cossack, a *male* Cossack, in her baggy pants which were tucked into knee-high boots, her bright red sash tied around her narrow waist, her no-longer-white shirt with the fine blue embroidery down the front, and her knee-length coat with the wide skirt. This was her customary dress for riding and working with the horses. Her bedraggled and filthy appearance was nothing new to her family.

"Much, *much* better," Constantin said in a soft whisper that only Anna could hear, a reiteration of what he had said moments before. "And fortunate it is that a man with a new wife will lay down the laws early in their marriage and see that they are obeyed."

Anna's nostrils flared wide as she gritted her teeth. But because of Alexandra's present, she couldn't address that statement in the manner that it so richly deserved, so she picked up Constantin's second glass of vodka, which still had enough liquid in it for her purpose, and

18

without the slightest hesitation tipped it over his head.

Witnessing only the dunking and her father's sputtering, Alexandra laughed delightedly. "Anna? *You* have given in to temper? But then, I *told* you I would be a bad influence on you eventually, didn't I?"

"Indeed, darling—and you know where to find the bucket and mop, don't you?"

Glancing down at the trail of dust she had tracked into the hall, Alexandra was still grinning when she asked, "Before or after Bojik and I bathe?"

With visions of the disaster that the Russian wolfhound was going to leave in the bathhouse, Anna said, "I don't believe it matters."

Alexandra flashed one of the smiles that could so easily turn grown men into mush if she only knew how to utilize it, and marched off toward the kitchen, Bojik following at her heels as usual. It had been unnecessary to mention the mop and bucket. The girl always cleaned up after herself— and her overlarge pet. They might have a dozen servants on hand to wait on her, but she rarely made use of them.

"Anna?"

The word came softly for all that it was a growl—as if she could forget the undoubtedly furious man standing behind her reeking of vodka. She cringed inwardly at what she'd done. Never, ever, had she stooped to such a low level of behavior. It simply wasn't in her nature.

"Shall I pour you another glass?" she offered without looking around.

She heard a snort. "Will I get to drink it?"

After a moment's thought, Anna said, "Probably not," and marched out of the room herself.

2

Stefan Barony, the reigning King of Cardinia, had to laugh. He had found exactly what he had expected to find in the Gypsy camp—his cousin lying beneath a tree with a lovely young woman clinging to him. Actually, there were three women clinging to him, which was not expected, but not surprising either. Vasili had one tucked under each arm, and a third woman sat behind him, offering her ample breasts as a pillow for his golden head.

The camp was at its most boisterous at night, naked children wrestling at the feet of their dancing mothers, singing and storytelling at each campfire, pilfered fowl and rabbits steaming in cauldrons. This particular tribe specialized in horse trading. Other bands might offer repair services and blacksmithing, and still others strictly provided entertainment with their Carpathian bear trainers, snake charmers, fine musicians, and dancers.

Most of the tribes that passed through Cardinia, however, were cattle breeders who traveled with their large herds of water buffalo or regular cattle. But all the tribes offered their women for a price, and had their old ones who could heal with their herbs what town doctors had given up on, and of course they had their fortune-tellers and charm-sellers.

"Didn't I tell you we'd find him here?" said Lazar, who was on Stefan's right. "He still craves the wildness."

On Stefan's left, Serge snorted before giving his own opinion. "It's an abundance of women that he craves, and the Gypsies never fail to supply that."

Stefan couldn't argue with that statement, since he'd spent a fair amount of time in Gypsy camps himself. At least he had when he had been only the Crown Prince of Cardinia with few responsibilities, rather than the king. Now, there was simply something not quite dignified about a king cavorting with Gypsy wenches and dancing by firelight. Not that he wanted to any longer. The only cavorting he did these days was with his queen. But the sight of the camp brought back fond memories.

"I suppose you two will want to remain here with Vasili," Stefan said to his friends in a humorous tone. For all their derogatory remarks, they both held equally fond memories of Gypsy camps.

"You mean we aren't dragging him back to the city?" Lazar asked.

"My aunt merely requested that I locate Vasili, not deliver him. As long as he makes an appearance sometime tonight, that will suit her well enough."

Serge was grinning now. "It's a good thing old Max won't let just the three of us protect you anymore, or we would be forced to escort *you* back to the city."

Old Max was Maximilian Daneff, Cardinia's

prime minister, who was like a second father to Stefan. And Max took his duties quite seriously, including insisting that a full complement of soldiers accompany Stefan whenever he left the palace.

Those soldiers were waiting on the outskirts of the Gypsy camp so as not to cause alarm. But Stefan's appearance was still creating a stir, for the Gypsies recognized him. Although he hadn't been king the last time this tribe had passed through his country, its members would have found out immediately upon their arrival about any changes in government and whether they were still welcome. Such knowledge was pertinent to the Gypsies' continuing good health.

The *bulubasha* had been summoned and was waiting warily in front of his tent with a number of elders. But Stefan didn't care to be delayed by the time-consuming ritual of greetings and honor-bestowings which could last several hours, not when his Tanya, who was waiting for him back at the palace, had teased him with the promise that she *might* dance for him tonight.

He turned toward Serge and said, "Assure their leader that this is not an official visit, merely a family errand." And with a respectful nod to acknowledge the *bulubasha* and put the man at ease, he headed toward his cousin.

That single nod had put the whole camp at ease, and the singing and dancing resumed. More than a dozen women, young and old, immediately converged on Stefan. They would actually fight, to the death if necessary, for the opportunity to perform a service for him, any service, because his generosity was so well known and so prodigious that even a family of ten on whom it had been bestowed wouldn't have to work or steal for a year.

Stefan was only vaguely aware that Lazar was keeping him from being bothered by tossing out handfuls of coins and waving the women off. What held his fascination was his cousin Vasili's valiant effort to divide his attention among three women. And Stefan was close to laughing outright because as far as he could tell, Vasili was actually managing it, kissing first one eager wench, then another, while his hands roamed over all three. But the women weren't competing with one another as one might expect; they had probably already been assured that Vasili would see to each of them before the night was over, if not all three of them at the same time, which seemed to be the case at the moment.

Each of those women probably had a husband somewhere in the camp, but Vasili wasn't in danger of getting a knife in his back before he departed. Giving their bodies to men for payment was business and an accepted practice for the women—as long as those men weren't Gypsies. Yet let one of those women look at another Gypsy male with allure in her eyes, and her husband was more than likely to kill her. But Gypsies lived and died by their own peculiar rules, which were enforced by each tribe's *bulubasha*.

Vasili was so involved in his lovemaking that he hadn't even noticed the earlier quieting of the camp or the resumption of noise. He didn't hear his friends' approaching horses either, so Stefan

24

and Lazar just sat there for a while, mere feet away, enjoying the performance. Stefan was still fascinated, since he had never watched his cousin work his sensual magic before, at least not to this degree. He'd always been busy with some wench of his own whenever he and these three closest friends of his had pursued their pleasures together.

But Vasili was so far advanced in his endeavors—clothes were being rapidly discarded—that it was quite possible he had forgotten that he usually did this sort of thing with a little more privacy. Or perhaps he'd reached the point where it didn't matter to him one way or the other.

Only one of the women had noticed that they had an audience, and she didn't seem to care, as she was too busy caressing the wide male chest that another of the women had just bared. Of course, Vasili did tend to have that kind of effect on women. He made them forget morals, modesty, and the strictures of a lifetime. Wherever he went, whatever he was doing, women clamored to meet him, and, upon meeting him, clamored to get into his bed. Whereas other men had to work long and hard at seduction, Vasili merely had to walk into a room and crook a finger. Actually, he had to do nothing at all but be there, and women were drawn to him.

His handsomeness had always been the lure, and his friends benefited from his effect on women, so they hardly begrudged him his good fortune or his exceptional good looks. And although it might appear otherwise at the moment, Vasili didn't devote his life to the pursuit of sexual gratification—at least not the greater part of it.

He was well honed in the military arts—all four of them were—and he had been given numerous official duties upon Stefan's coronation. But the duty he took most seriously was being a member of the royal guard, Stefan's personal guard, and Vasili wouldn't be here tonight if he'd known Stefan was going to leave the palace. That Stefan wouldn't be here if Vasili weren't was a moot point. Vasili always made sure he wouldn't be needed before he pursued his own interests.

At the moment, there were three young women in differing stages of need who were about to be satisfied. For the sake of future peace—Lazar wouldn't be able to resist ribbing Vasili about his sudden lack of modesty, which would lead to blows before the two of them would laugh together over it—Stefan cleared his throat.

It didn't work. It still didn't work when he tried again.

So Lazar remarked quite loudly, "The Gypsies would be rich if they had thought to sell tickets."

And Serge had ridden up by then to add, "It doesn't look like Vasili would mind, and this sure as hell beats the new play that opened last week at the Grand."

Vasili had rolled over and now glared up at them, his groan caused not by embarrassment, but by being interrupted. "How the devil did you find me?"

"You told Fatima where you were going,"

Stefan explained, then added with a glance at the women, who made no effort to correct their varying states of undress and were still curled all around Vasili, "She doesn't mind?"

"Fatima doesn't own me any more than I own her. I gave her her freedom. What more can I do?"

"Find her a husband."

"She cries every time I suggest it."

Vasili sounded so disgusted, all three men laughed, not the least bit sympathetic. The concubine had been a gift to Vasili from the Turkish Grand Vezir, and she was a lovely, sensual creature trained in every aspect of pleasing a man. Vasili might have freed her, but they doubted that he made the offer to find her a husband very often.

Vasili didn't mind their humor, but in his present physical condition, which wasn't subsiding with more than one pair of naked breasts pressed against him, he still minded like hell their sudden appearance. "Just what are you doing here, Stefan, and why wasn't I informed that you intended to leave the palace tonight?"

Stefan grinned at him. "If you had bothered to receive your mother's messenger these past three days, instead of having him informed that you weren't home when you were, she wouldn't have found it necessary to come to me to demand to know where I had sent you. How did you avoid her at the palace, by the way?"

Vasili ran an agitated hand through his golden mane. "It wasn't easy. I suppose you told her you hadn't sent me anywhere."

"No, I merely said I would locate you and send you along to her posthaste. Why are you avoiding her, cousin?"

"Because anytime she sends me an 'official' summons, as this one was, it's almost guaranteed I won't like whatever it is she has to say. Either she's going to harp at me about getting married—it's been three months since the last time, so she's due—or she's going to blast me about my latest affair."

"Which affair?" Stefan asked curiously.

"Whichever one she's found out about."

Since Vasili had not one mistress but three at present in the city—not including Fatima, who was installed in his own house, or the other women who constantly threw themselves at him—the fact that he was spreading himself around among the Gypsies had to be wondered at. Vasili liked variety as well as any man, at least any man not in love, as Stefan was, but he already had more variety than any man could want.

"Why *don't* you send me somewhere?" Vasili suddenly suggested.

Stefan laughed. "When Aunt Maria managed to get me to assure her that I would deliver you personally if necessary? You'll have to take the harping or blasting this time, my friend. Next time give me prior warning, and I'll send you off to Austria or France for a few months, though I don't see what good it will do, since she'll still be here on your return. Have you thought about doing what she wants?"

"You mean get married?" Vasili snorted.

"Don't be ridiculous. I couldn't be satisfied with just one woman."

"Who says you have to be?"

Vasili gave Stefan a sour look. "Your queen probably would. She's got old-fashioned ideas about faithfulness, if you haven't noticed. Jesus, if I married, I wouldn't put it past Tanya to make it a royal command that my bed is off limits to any woman but my countess."

Serge and Lazar were laughing before he had finished speaking. Stefan wasn't quite amused and asked his cousin, "Has Tanya said something to you?"

"Merely that I ought to devote as much time to finding the right woman as I do to pursuing all the wrong ones. For some reason, she's got it into her head that I'm not happy. Can you imagine that? When I couldn't be happier."

"But she's a woman in love," Lazar remarked. "Women in love like to see *everyone* in love."

"Either that, or my mother's been complaining to her about me, as she does to anyone who'll listen," Vasili said. "It's a damn curse, being an only child, and having a mother worried about the continuation of the line."

"Try having a royal father worried about it," Stefan said dryly.

They all laughed, but it had been no laughing matter last year when Stefan had been sent to America to collect his princess bride. He'd been furious about it and had dreaded his marriage. But fortunately, he'd been smitten by the royal heiress, and even more fortunate, she had come to love him as well.

"I have the answer," Vasili said suddenly. "Why don't you order my mother to remarry, Stefan? That ought to give her something else to think about besides grandchildren."

Stefan shook his head, though he was grinning. "I'm too fond of my aunt to order her to do anything she doesn't want to do, and well you know it. Now, what are you doing here by yourself? You usually drag Lazar and Serge along with you—for this sort of entertainment."

Vasili finally smiled. "Actually, I hadn't planned on this sort of entertainment. I came here to purchase a new horse. Dinicu had sent his boy to tell me he had a fine stallion to sell."

Lazar perked up at that, for his passion for fancy horseflesh was as keen as Vasili's. "Did you buy it?"

"It wasn't so fine after all."

"Ah." Lazar nodded. "So you are compensating yourself for a wasted trip?"

"Certainly. You are welcome, of course, to join me, and Serge as well—but not you, Stefan."

"As if I would accept." Stefan grinned.

"I'm not taking any chances," Vasili assured him. "I'm staying on the queen's good side these days, now that she's deigned to forgive me."

Stefan quirked a brow and teased, "Are you sure she has? She still calls you a peacock, you know."

"Yes," Vasili replied rather smugly. "But she says it fondly now, and leaves off the 'jackassed' that use to go with it."

Stefan chuckled. His wife had never been one to mince words, and being the Queen of Cardinia and under almost constant attendance certainly didn't help to curb her tongue. But his court was becoming used to her Americanized ways, and her utter lack of diplomacy.

Thinking about his wife reminded him that she was waiting for him—and what she had *seemed* to promise. "We are forgetting about your mother."

"I was trying to," Vasili grumbled, and as his arms slipped around the two closest Gypsy wenches, he added, "Have a heart, cousin. Tell her you couldn't find me."

"I won't go that far, but I'll give you two hours to present yourself at your old home. Lazar and Serge will make sure that you're not one minute late. In the meantime, enjoy, my friends."

Lazar and Serge were already dismounting with eager anticipation. But as Stefan left them to ride out of camp alone, Vasili leapt up and shouted for him to wait. When he yanked his shirt out from under a nicely shaped hip, the women started protesting, loudly, and Lazar, realizing that Vasili was letting duty come before pleasure, as always, did some protesting of his own.

"Don't be ridiculous, Vasili. He's got twenty men waiting for him."

"Not good enough," was all Vasili said as he found his coat and tossed it over his shoulders.

Serge rolled his eyes. It wouldn't do any good to point out that Stefan would feel insulted that Vasili didn't think he could take care of himself for the short trip back to the palace. Stefan *would* feel insulted, but he'd be amused, too, that Vasili

31

would leave such accommodating wenches when he didn't have to.

Serge sighed and started to remount, but Vasili stopped him. "He needs only one of us. You two go ahead and enjoy. The ladies are already warmed up."

"Yes, but you did the warming."

"So thank me. I'm no longer in the mood, anyway, thinking about that appointment with my mother and having to endure one of her lectures. If you insist on coming along, I'll insist you endure it with me."

"In that case, we'll see you tomorrow."

3

Vasili's mother wasn't wearing the correct expression when she joined him in her parlor later that night. At least her expression wasn't the one he'd come to associate with her lectures. In fact, her expression was so pleased and happy, he had to wonder if he'd mistaken the reason for her summons.

Long experience assured him that good news would have brought her to him, and he wouldn't have even considered turning her away at his door as he had her messenger. After all, he did love her, and did try to please her when it was reasonably possible to do so.

It was only for the scoldings and the lectures, when she anticipated arguments from him, that she wanted him in her own territory, which was here in the house he had grown up in. It didn't matter that he'd moved out of the family home some twelve years ago, first into the palace to be closer at hand for Stefan's impromptu outings, then into his own town house after he had taken the grand European tour. His mother still felt that this house, and her own parlor in particular, somehow enhanced her authority. The hell of it was, it did.

The evening was young enough that he had caught the countess before she left for whichever party she was attending tonight. That was exactly what he had counted on, so he could get this over with and enjoy the rest of the night himself. He hoped her party was an important one for which she wouldn't want to arrive late, thereby keeping this meeting short. Her clothes were no indication, nor the amount of jewels she was wearing, for she never attended any social engagement without being decked out in grand style.

Maria Petroff was a handsome woman in her later years, perhaps more handsome now than she had been in her youth, for no one had ever considered her a beauty. Her thrusting chin and patrician nose, which weren't exactly feminine, endowed her with a close resemblance to her brother Sandor, the late king, and she'd never been far from robust and stocky of build, which now could kindly be termed matronly.

It had always been a source of bewilderment to her, as well as fierce pride, that she had produced a son like Vasili. But then he took after his father in his looks. All that he had from her were the Barony eyes, eyes so light a brown that strong emotion turned them golden.

On Cardinia's young King Stefan, with his raven-black hair and dark complexion, people called them devil's eyes. But on Vasili, with his golden hair and skin tone, they were merely beautiful, a complement to the fine bone structure that made him so very handsome.

"You look disgraceful," was the first thing Vasili's mother said to him.

Since he hadn't bothered to go home and change before making his appearance, his shirt and jacket were both understandably wrinkled.

His hair was also a mess, after so many hands had tested its softness tonight, but on Vasili, anything less than impeccable only gave him a rakish look that women found incredibly sensual.

But his mother's remark made him instantly nervous, for she'd been smiling when she'd said it. Something was definitely not right here.

His eyes narrowed suspiciously now, he demanded, "What are you gloating about, Mother?"

She actually laughed. "What a distasteful word, and something I would never do, of course." And with another smile: "Why don't you pour us a drink?"

He returned her smile, deciding to go along with her for the moment. "An excellent idea," he said, but as he headed for the sideboard where a variety of spirits were kept on hand for guests, he added under his breath, "Obviously I'm going to need it."

"I'll have some of that fine Russian vodka I keep stocked just for you," she said before he began to pour exactly that for himself.

The request arrested his hand and made him frown. "You don't like vodka," he reminded her.

"True," she replied with a shrug. "But it seems . . . appropriate tonight."

She was smiling again. He brought her a small amount of the potent liquor, but he went back to get the bottle for himself and took it with him to the chair opposite the sofa she had settled on. He had filled his glass twice, draining it both times, before he felt fortified enough to say, "All right, Mother, let's have it. What are you so disgustingly thrilled about?"

"You're going to have to leave within the week for a trip to Russia."

"And *that* delights you?"

She nodded, her smile positively glowing now. "Indeed it does, since you will be collecting your bride while you're there."

Vasili went very still, and the only thing he could think to say to that alarming statement was, "I'm not Stefan, Mother. He had to go and collect a bride. I don't happen to have one, thank God."

"You do now."

He shot out of his chair and came to stand over her, the very image of bristling male chagrin. He couldn't remember when he had ever been this annoyed with his mother. Interfering in his life was unacceptable. She knew that and had always respected it. Lectures and sermons she was allowed, worry and concern she was permitted, but something like this? What the devil had made her think she could get away with it?

"Whatever you have done, Mother, you can just undo. Whatever embarrassment you'll have to suffer for it, you'll suffer on your own. I don't even want to hear another word about it."

Incredibly, she was still smiling, and she didn't keep him in suspense as to why. "You might have to hear one or two more words about it, dearest—"

"Mother—" he tried to cut in warningly.

"—since I haven't done anything, so I have nothing to undo."

36

"That's absurd. Of course you—"

"No, *not* me. The fact that you have a bride waiting for you is entirely your father's doing."

With that piece of the puzzle supplied, Vasili began to relax. It wasn't like his mother to indulge in a practical joke, but he supposed there was a first time for everything.

"And how was he supposed to have arranged this marriage? From the grave?"

She drew in her breath sharply. "That was uncalled-for, Vasili."

"So is this joke of yours," he retorted.

"A joke? You insult me even to think that I would joke about something like this."

"But it's been fourteen years—"

"I know exactly how long it's been since your father died." Her tone was clipped, her displeasure with him still strong. "But according to the letter I received, your betrothal was made fifteen years ago. That would have been the last time your father was in Russia."

"You expect me to believe he did something like this without telling you about it—or me?"

"I don't know why he never mentioned it, but he most definitely did arrange it. I can only assume he felt there was ample time to apprise us of it. After all, you were so young back then—"

"I would have been sixteen, hardly in the cradle," he snapped.

As if he hadn't interrupted, she continued. "But he died the next year."

Vasili's eyes were glowing by now. This was sounding too serious by half for him to merely feel annoyed. "It's a lie," he stated emphatically.

"There is no conceivable reason why he would do such a thing."

Her smile was back, giving him clear warning that he wasn't going to like her answer. "There is one. Your betrothed is the daughter of your father's very dear friend, Baron Rubliov. Even you can remember how often Simeon spoke of the baron, how highly he thought of him. Several months out of every year your father went to Russia to visit him."

Vasili did remember, and remembered resenting the time his father had spent away from home. Of course, when he and his friends had had their grand tour, it had included Russia and the Imperial Court, and he had learned firsthand what his father would have found so appealing about Russia. The ladies there, at least the aristocrats, were incredibly bold in their promiscuity. They didn't even wait for marriage to take lovers, virginity apparently not being as highly prized there as it was in the rest of the world.

"I, for one, can imagine your father signing this betrothal contract," the countess went on. "After all, there was no one here in Cardinia whom he liked half as much as he did Constantin Rubliov. He would have been delighted to have his family joined to Rubliov's."

That word "betrothal" was making Vasili see red, and starting to make him panic. "But Rubliov waits fifteen years to bring it to our attention?"

Maria shrugged. "From the tone of his letter, I would say he didn't think he was telling us anything we didn't already know."

"But why wait fifteen years, or—what is the girl, just barely out of the schoolroom? Was he just waiting until she grew up?"

"He doesn't mention her age, but it doesn't sound as if she's *that* young, for he does mention that she was in no hurry to marry, which is why he hadn't written about the betrothal before now. He also says that he was waiting for you to write, but since you haven't . . ."

"Let me see that damn letter."

She didn't have to leave the room to retrieve it. Obviously she had expected the demand, and now pulled the letter out of a pocket in her skirt. Vasili tore it open to peruse the fine French scrawl. He had been hoping it had been written in Russian. His mother could have misinterpreted Russian, because even though they both spoke it fluently, neither of them could read or write it very well. But just about everyone in the Cardinian court could read and write French, and the letter left nothing for misinterpretation. For all its diplomacy, it was a demand for him to honor a betrothal contract that had promised he would marry one Alexandra Rubliov.

Vasili crumpled the letter in his fist and threw it across the room. It bounced off a vase of flowers and rolled to the floor. He felt an urge to grind it into the carpeting with the heel of his boot. Instead he went to the bottle of vodka he'd left by his chair and tilted it to his lips, uncaring that his mother would find such swilling the height of crudeness. Her *tsk*ing proved it, but that didn't stop him from draining half the bottle before he turned to acknowledge her disapproval with a mocking bow.

Casually now, as if he weren't seething inside, he said, "Answer his letter, Mother. You can tell him that I've already married. Or tell him I've died. I don't care what you tell him, as long as you make sure he understands I can't marry his daughter."

Her back straightened. Her lips pursed for battle. "You most certainly can."

"But I won't."

Before the bottle could reach his lips again, she said, "But you will."

"No!"

He shouted it, surprising them both. He never raised his voice to her, no matter how irritated he was; at least he never had before. But now he was feeling anger, gut-churning fury, and it stemmed from the sensation of having a trapdoor slam shut on him.

Softer, though no less emphatically, he added, "When I am ready to marry, I will, but it will be my decision, and my choice."

He would have liked that to be the end of it. It should have been the end of it. He even started to leave the room, taking the bottle of vodka with him. He didn't get very far before his mother's words struck his back like shards of glass, lacerating, drawing blood.

"Even you, disreputable scamp that you are, won't dishonor your father's name."

4

Tanya lifted her veil slightly, just enough so that her tongue could tease the flat male nipple she had exposed on her husband's chest. He groaned and reached for her, but she made a warning sound and his hands returned to their death grip on the back of the chaise longue he was lying on.

Not being able to touch his wife was driving Stefan crazy, especially with her straddling his loins and having no such restriction placed on her. But they'd made a deal. She would dance for him as long as he swore to control his response this time. He'd sworn, and she'd already danced, but now he was having the devil's own time keeping his word, and his sweet little witch had decided to do some teasing while she had the chance.

The night they'd first met, in a tavern in Mississippi, she'd danced the provocative harem dance, at least her version of it, for a roomful of avid river rats. He'd thought he could buy her for a few coins and had tried to do so. He hadn't known at the time, and neither had she, that she was the missing princess he'd been sent to find and bring home, the bride he'd been betrothed to from the very day she was born.

Tanya had danced just for him once before at his request, not long after they were married. Her sensual, though not very revealing, outfit for the

41

dance had been left behind in America, so she'd worn one of her silky negligees instead. Stefan's response had been unexpected, his desire so inflamed that their lovemaking, while incredibly satisfying, had been rather bruising as well.

But Tanya hadn't complained that time. She had actually laughed afterward, delighted that she could drive him so wild. His mistresses used to complain if he happened to leave the slightest bruise on them, but his Tanya's passion was always equal to his. And the very fact that she had created a new dancing outfit, one designed to bring out the savage in a man of Stefan's lusty proclivities, proved that she enjoyed provoking him.

The promise she had insisted on, however, had nothing to do with her own preference and everything to do with her new condition, which only recently had been confirmed. To the delight of the entire kingdom, his queen was already carrying the royal heir, and taking everything the court physicians told her as gospel. And for Stefan that meant no more losing control, instead having to make promises he could barely keep.

"You know I'm going to get even with you for this." He tried to sound casual, but there was nothing casual about what he was feeling.

Tanya raised her head and he could make out a grin beneath the sheer material of her veil, whose color nearly matched her pale green eyes. "How?"

"I know a merchant who sells fine silken cords," he told her.

"You would tie me down and do this to me?"

There was some very clear interest in her tone that wouldn't be there if she didn't trust him implicitly.

"I'm thinking about it," he replied in a half growl, half groan.

Her grin was positively impish. "When you make up your mind, let me know."

Her head dipped again and she scooted back so that her tongue could trail down the center of his chest toward his navel. He sucked in a breath. His loins lifted involuntarily, nearly unseating her.

"Tanya—I can't—bear any more," he gasped out.

She took pity on him instantly. "Then you don't have to," she said sweetly.

She sat up to toss off the double veils that had concealed her lower face and long black hair. The top of her two-piece outfit defied description in its transparency and secrets. He wanted to rip it off her. He wanted to kiss her right through it. But the promise he'd made prevented him from doing either. He was completely at her mercy. Fortunately, that didn't worry him in the least.

With a smile that promised that ecstasy would soon be his, Tanya reached for the cord on his lounging pants. But her fingers stilled when she heard the commotion outside their door, first raised voices, then the sounds of scuffling, then a very clear thud.

"What the—?" Stefan began, but his unfinished question was answered by the door opening and his cousin storming into the room.

Tanya gave a strangled shriek and rolled off

43

Stefan and the lounge, to crouch on the floor, concealing herself there while she snatched her robe from the end of the chaise where she had discarded it before the dance. She yanked it on, glaring over Stefan's belly at the intruder.

Vasili didn't notice, as he hadn't yet located them in the room. The royal bedchamber was so large, he was still crossing it and saying in no particular direction, "Stefan, I'm sorry to disturb you at this hour, but I have a problem that has me so furious, I fear I will murder someone if I can't find a solution."

"You didn't start with my guard, did you?"

Vasili turned toward the sound of that dry voice. "What? No, of course not. I merely knocked him out. Damned fool refused to let me pass."

"Perhaps because I didn't wish to be disturbed, and for a reason."

Tanya rejoined Stefan on the chaise as he sat up, his arm immediately coming around her to pull her close. Their state of semiundress made clear what that "reason" was.

But Vasili acknowledged it with a mere "Sorry, but this simply couldn't wait, Stefan. It's worse than a nightmare. It's so insane you won't believe it. I still can't believe it myself."

"Is he drunk, do you think?" Tanya whispered in Stefan's ear.

"Shh," he told her. To Vasili, he said, "I assume you've seen your mother?"

"Oh, yes, but had I even the slightest warning about what she was going to reveal to me—with absolute relish, I might add—I would be halfway to the border by now, vanished, never to be seen again. Did she tell *you?* So help me, Stefan, if you knew and didn't warn me—"

"You know better than that."

Vasili did, and for the third time he said, "I'm sorry. My reasoning has gone to hell, which is where my life will be going if something drastic doesn't happen to change what has befallen me."

"It would be nice if you would tell me what we're talking about."

Vasili was momentarily startled. "Didn't I?" Before Stefan could answer, he continued. "I have just learned that my father signed a betrothal contract fifteen years ago with my name on it. A *betrothal* contract! My mother didn't even know. Only the girl and her father have known all these years, and only now, when she is apparently ready to get married, do they bother to write and tell us."

"Who is she?"

"Is that all you have to say?" Vasili fairly shouted in his agitation. "Who the hell cares who she is, when I have no wish to marry her!"

"You knew you would have to get married eventually," Stefan said reasonably.

"Not for another ten years at least, and that is hardly the point. Suddenly I have a betrothed I've never laid eyes on, and don't remind me that you faced the same appalling circumstance, because you grew up knowing about your betrothal, whereas I grew up assuming the decision would be mine."

"Considering how splendidly my own

betrothal has worked out, you can't expect me to dredge up much sympathy for you, cousin."

"The hell I can't," Vasili snapped. "Kindly remember how you felt *before* you met your lovely wife."

With a squeeze for said wife to assure her that that had been then and not now, Stefan said, "Point taken."

"And heirs to the crown rarely have a choice about who they marry," Vasili continued heatedly, "but I'm merely a king's cousin. No one besides me has the slightest interest in who I marry, and I know damn well I would never have chosen a Russian."

"She's Russian?" Stefan said in surprise.

"A Russian baroness, and you know how damn promiscuous those ladies are. This one has probably already had a dozen lovers, and I wouldn't be the least surprised if I'm suddenly being summoned to marry her because she's found herself with child."

"Then hope that is the case, and wait to marry her until you bring her here," Stefan suggested. "By then you will know if she is pregnant, which will give you legitimate grounds to break the betrothal."

Vasili's relief didn't last long enough for him to complete the smile he had started. "I can't depend on that and end up committed if it isn't so. I would prefer not to go to Russia at all, which is why I'm here. You have been faced with this dilemma yourself, Stefan. What ideas did you come up with to get out of your betrothal?"

"You expect me to answer that *now?*"

Vasili looked at Tanya for the first time. "Would you mind—?"

"Not on your life."

He gave her a sour look, which she ignored. She wondered what he would do if she laughed, which was what she felt like doing: she was not the least bit sympathetic to his problem. But Stefan wouldn't appreciate her amusement at his cousin's expense, so she just listened to them discuss a few options that they both concluded weren't really options. And she watched Vasili become more and more upset.

She thought her husband was exceptionally handsome, but not like Vasili. No one was as mesmerizingly handsome as Vasili. But she'd never seen him looking so harried, or so angry. And she'd never seen his eyes glow just as brightly as Stefan's could, as they were now. He was pacing—*prowling* would be a better way to describe how he was moving—like a trapped tawny lion, golden and furious.

It was fascinating to watch six feet of masculine grace suddenly reveal this volatile, nearly savage side of his otherwise stoical nature. Of the four men who had grown up together and were such close friends, Vasili was the one who attacked verbally and with deadly accuracy, rather than with brute strength. But obviously he was as capable of violence as the rest of them.

Tanya had once been told that he was the man she would have to marry, because Stefan had wanted her to come along with them to Cardinia without any fuss, and he'd thought she, like every other woman, would prefer Vasili. But Vasili had insulted her from the first, thinking her a tavern whore, and she had despised him for that, and for his utter contempt. Besides, even with his scars and his "devil's eyes," Stefan had been the one she had been attracted to from the first night they had met, not the too handsome, golden Adonis.

"What are you going to do?" Stefan finally asked his cousin.

"I don't know."

"Yes, you do," Stefan said quietly.

"Yes, I do." Vasili sighed. "But there won't be a wedding, not if I can help it. One of them, either the girl or her father, will call this ridiculous thing off, even if I have to show them what I'm really like."

"What you're really like?" Tanya nearly choked on that one. "You mean, what you *can* be like when you don't want people to like you."

Since she spoke from experience, he had to concede her the point. "If you say so, Your Majesty."

It was Tanya's turn to give him a sour look. Stefan bit back a chuckle and said, "Go home, Vasili. A good night's sleep is bound to make your situation look less disastrous. After all, even if you have to marry the girl, you don't have to—"

"The hell he doesn't," Tanya cut in indignantly.

"I *told* you she'd make fidelity a royal command," Vasili growled and stomped out of the room.

Tanya barely waited for the door to close before

48

she said, "Oh, God, I love it. The peacock is finally going to get his feathers pulled."

"I thought you had forgiven Vasili for the way he behaved toward you on your trip to Cardinia."

"I have," she assured her husband. "I understand he was only trying to keep me from falling in love with him. But he should have figured out right away that that wasn't going to happen, instead of being such an utter ass nearly the entire trip. But he's still a peacock, and I can't tell you how much I've hoped that *some* woman would bring him down a peg or two, though I wish it were one he was interested in. Vasili's problem is that women don't tell him no. They don't wait to get to know him, they fall instantly for that face of his, and imagine what that's done to him. It's no wonder he's so insufferably arrogant. He can't get through a day that some woman isn't trying to seduce him."

Stefan laughed at her look of disgust. "You would be surprised, Tanya mine, how annoying Vasili finds that circumstance."

She snorted. "Oh, sure he does, about as much as I don't like being pregnant."

Since she was absolutely thrilled about her pregnancy and everyone knew it, she'd just dismissed his remark. "But it's true," he insisted, his sherry-gold eyes glinting with laughter. "There is, after all, only so much one man can do in one day."

There was no way she could restrain her sarcasm now. "Well, that explains it. He gets annoyed when he can't accommodate every woman who asks. I can't tell you how sorry I feel for him. I'm probably the only woman he's ever met who actually, *seriously,* disliked him, but that doesn't count, since that's just what he was striving for in my case. But I honestly think it would do him a world of good to meet a woman who ignores him. Unfortunately, I doubt we'll ever see it happen."

"And you say you've forgiven him?"

She sighed. "I'm sorry, Stefan. I suppose I do still have trouble separating the Vasili I met from the Vasili I know now. I know he's usually charming. I know he can be terribly sweet at times. And, of course, I know how fiercely loyal he is to you, and I love him for that. But the arrogance and condescension, the derision and scorn—that didn't come from nowhere. He has all those traits, though I will allow, not in the abundance I first thought."

"I'll go along with the arrogance, but that's all," he replied loyally.

She started to argue, but his raised brow stopped her. Vasili was, after all, not just his only cousin, but as close to him as any dearly loved brother could be.

"Oh, very well," she conceded. "But he's dreaming if he thinks he can get this Russian girl to cry off from marrying him, and you know it. She's going to fall instantly in love with him, and no matter how nasty he tries to be, it won't make any difference in the end. He'll break her heart, but she'll still want him for her own." And then Tanya sighed. "I pity that poor girl, I really do."

5

Two months later, the girl Tanya had pitied was still blissfully unaware that she had a betrothed, or that his arrival was imminent.

Anna was with Constantin when Bohdan brought the news that the Cardinian was only a few hours away. The baron had stationed a number of men along the roads leading to his estate for just that purpose, so he wouldn't be caught unawares, and because, despite Anna's pleading to do otherwise, he was waiting until nearly the last minute to apprise his daughter of the upcoming nuptials.

"He has certainly dragged his feet about getting here," Constantin felt compelled to grumble. "The countess's letter informing me that he was coming arrived more than a month ago. He should have been right behind it."

"And what does that tell you?" Anna asked, receiving no more than a scowl for an answer. "Exactly. It says he doesn't want to get married."

Constantin was nervous, extremely nervous, not only because Count Petroff was finally about to arrive, but because he had yet to inform Alexandra that she had a betrothed.

Anna read his thoughts correctly. "When are you going to tell her, *after* he's arrived here?"

"You don't think that might help, letting her meet him without knowing who he is?"

"Are you mad? *He'll* mention the betrothal and she'll laugh in his face, and that will start things off wonderfully, won't it?"

His scowl grew darker. Anna had done nothing but nag him about his decision since he'd first told her about it. Perversely, the more she inflamed his guilt on the subject, the more stubborn he turned.

Now, when he made no move to summon Alexandra to finally break the news to her, Anna sighed in exasperation. "At least give her time to change, or do you want him to meet her when she's in her britches?"

She was right, that wouldn't do at all, and he hadn't even thought of it. Alexandra would need at least an hour to wash the stink of the stable off her and to make herself pretty, and there was no telling how long their argument was going to last before then. Not once did he consider the possibility that there wouldn't be an argument. He knew his daughter too well.

Immediately he left the dining room, where he and Anna had been sharing a late breakfast. He sent a servant straight out to the stable, then retreated to his study to wait.

Anna poked her head around the door, and despite the odds they had been at over this subject, she gave him a fond smile and said, "Good luck, darling."

Some of the tension eased out of him. He was a very fortunate man when it came right down to it. He had three healthy children, a brood of grandchildren—and Anna.

"Now that we may have this house to ourselves," he said, "will you marry me?"

Her smile widened just a bit. "No."

He chuckled as she went off to another part of the house. One of these days she was going to surprise him and give him the answer he wanted. In the meantime, it was certainly no hardship being a lover rather than a husband.

A few minutes later, Alexandra marched into the study with her usual brisk energy. "This isn't going to take long, is it? I have to exercise Prince Micha." She was referring to one of her own stallions, one of her "babies," as she called all the offspring from her own personal stock.

"You might want to let one of the Razins exercise him today."

She lifted a finely arched brow. "It's going to take that long?"

"Quite possibly."

She removed her hat, sticking it in the pocket of her coat, and plopped into the chair across from his desk with a sigh. "All right, what have I done now?"

"What you *could* do is show me that you know how to sit like a lady rather than a—"

"It's so bad you're going to prevaricate?"

Her feigned look of surprise brought his brows together. Whenever Alexandra would rather be doing something else, she made sure people knew they were wasting her time. He decided to take a leaf from her book and get to the heart of the matter.

"You haven't done anything, Alexandra, but what you will be doing is getting married, possibly in the next few days. Your betrothed will be here in less than two hours, and I would appreciate it if you would be on your best—"

"You can stop right there, Papa. Whatever you have promised this man to marry me, you can go ahead and give it to him before you send him back where he came from. My mind hasn't changed since the last time we had this discussion."

She hadn't raised her voice and didn't even look the least bit annoyed with him. Of course, she hadn't yet grasped the full meaning of what he'd said.

He did not make a habit of lying to his daughter. He couldn't remember the last time he had done so. That he was going to now made the color rise in his cheeks. Fortunately, she mistook it for his usual high temper.

"This has nothing to do with our last discussion on the subject of marriage," he told her. "This has to do with a betrothal contract that Simeon Petroff and I signed fifteen years ago, before he died. And it is a binding contract, Alexandra. It promises that you will wed Simeon's son, Count Vasili Petroff."

She came to her feet and leaned over his desk, her color now as high as his, but there was no mistaking that hers was from temper. "Tell me you're lying!" At the hesitant shake of his head, she emitted a shriek of rage. "You are, I know you are! You can't tell me I've had a betrothed for more than half my life and you never bothered to mention it before now. It defies reason. You would have thrown this man in my face when I told you I was going to wait for Christopher's proposal. You wouldn't have let me go on waiting *seven* years if I were promised to another. And what about all those other men you hoped I would take an interest in?"

"If you will calm down for a moment, I can explain."

She didn't sit down, didn't calm down, but she held her tongue, which wasn't easy when all she wanted to do was scream. Constantin was aware of that fact, but he had had ample time to come up with a reasonable explanation for his so-called "silence" all these years.

"I can't deny I wanted you to marry Simeon's son, just as he wanted it. He was my closest friend, as you know. And you were so young then, so—biddable. There was no way to know that you would grow to be so willful and assertive, argumentative, obstinate—"

"I get the point, Papa," she practically growled.

He grunted before continuing. "I realized when you had your first season that you would balk at having a husband chosen for you. So with your happiness in mind, rather than my honor, I decided to give you time to choose for yourself—and hoped Count Petroff would turn out to be dishonorable and marry someone else, thereby breaking the betrothal."

"And what if I *had* married someone else?"

He was well prepared for that question. "First, you need to know that young Vasili never wrote to me, which caused me to wonder if Simeon had gotten around to telling his family about the betrothal before he died. It was a slim possibility that he hadn't, but one I was beginning to count on back then, especially when you showed such interest in that Englishman."

"Count on? You despised Christopher!"

"But if he would have made you happy—"

"Never mind that," she cut in impatiently. "If your friend's family never knew—"

"I didn't say that," he cut back in, "only that it was possible they might not know. But in either case, if you *had* accepted someone's proposal, I would have had to write Vasili Petroff to inform him of it, and I was fully prepared to *beg* him to relinquish his claim on you."

When Constantin had rehearsed this conversation in his mind, he had decided the word "beg" was brilliant, designed to let her know that he had been completely on her side in this before she became unreasonable in her refusal to marry. But her expression said she couldn't have cared less.

"So when did he write to you?" she demanded.

He had been dreading that question, had hoped she wouldn't have thought of it. Now all her rage would come squarely down on his head, because he couldn't lie about this when she was likely to get the truth from Count Petroff. "He didn't."

"*You* did?!"

"You have given me no choice," he said defensively. "You're twenty-five years old and still without a husband. If you had made the slightest effort to change that fact—"

"I don't *need* a husband!"

"Every woman needs a husband!"

"Who says so?"

"God in His wisdom—"

"You mean Constantin Rubliov in his!"

They were down to arguments they'd had before, ground he found much more familiar. "You need a husband to give you children."

"I don't want children!"

The lie was so blatantly obvious, he had to say so, though his voice gentled to a near whisper. "You know that isn't true, Alex."

Alexandra was close to tears in her fury—at least she told herself that her anger was responsible for her upset emotions and *not* the fact that she was childless and so far beyond a marriageable age that it was laughable. At times like this, she actually hated the man she'd sworn to wait for. Although Christopher still wrote to her frequently since he'd left Russia three years ago, not one of his letters had contained the marriage proposal she longed for.

She had nearly reached the point of finally giving up on Christopher, though she hadn't told her father so. Obviously she should have. Perversely, what her father had done had just changed her mind. But even if she weren't in love with someone else, she wouldn't accept a complete stranger for a husband. Betrothals were archaic. That her father had arranged one for her wasn't merely intolerable, it was outrageous.

She tried to moderate her tone and was only slightly successful. "When that man arrives, do the begging you would have done and get rid of him. You can give him Sultan's Pride for his trouble in coming here."

She'd managed to shock him. "You would *give* away your prize stud?"

"Do you begin to see that I don't want a stranger for a husband?" she countered, though the words were almost sticking in her throat. She'd raised Sultan's Pride from a colt and loved him passionately.

"He won't *be* a stranger once you meet him. For God's sake, Alexandra, Simeon's son is first cousin to King Stefan of Cardinia. Do you realize what a prime catch he is?"

"Is that supposed to matter to me?"

He came to his feet, facing her angrily across the desk. "Yes, and it most certainly matters to me. Besides, you are deliberately ignoring the fact that a betrothal is as binding as a marriage. This one was arranged in good faith, with the best of intentions, and duly sworn to by Simeon and me. And, my girl, after all these years, Vasili Petroff is still unwed. *You* are still unwed. So we can no longer in good conscience delay the nuptials."

"You could at least ask him to tear up that damn contract!" she cried.

"You could at least give the man a chance. He is coming here to marry you, thereby honoring his father's word. How can you do any less?"

"Honor," she choked. "You would make this a matter of honor?"

Constantin hesitated. He'd known she would be angry, but now she looked as if she were about to cry, and he couldn't stand to see her cry. It was that damn Englishman, he thought furiously. She was still hopeful that he would marry her. Such misplaced loyalty. But it was a father's duty

58

to protect his daughter from her own foolishness. However, he would end the betrothal, even if he had to confess the truth to do it, if there was no chance that Petroff could make her happy. But he wasn't going to end it before that could be ascertained.

"It already is a matter of honor. I gave my word when I signed the betrothal contract."

Her fingers curled into fists, and she slammed both against his desk before she turned her back on him. For good measure, she kicked the chair she had vacated, toppling it over.

"There's no call to wreck my study," her father said stiffly.

"You're wrecking my life," she replied bitterly.

"What life? All you care about is the horses. You spend nearly your every waking moment in the stables. Half the time I think that you forget you're a woman."

That comment brought forth the tears that she'd been fighting to hold back. But she vowed her father wouldn't see them. He'd betrayed her. It didn't matter that he'd done it fifteen years ago—*with the best of intentions.* And what he scorned, her so-called lack of femininity, was what allowed him to win. How many women cared about honor? But *she* did, and he knew she did.

"Very well, I won't refuse to marry your precious Cardinian." She was halfway to the door when she added, for her benefit alone, *But I promise you he will refuse to marry me.*

"Then you'll make yourself presentable? At least change your clothes."

"Oh, no. If he wants to marry me, he can see me as I am, not as I rarely am."

Red-faced, Constantin shouted for her to come back, but she marched out of the room and slammed out of the house. He slumped back in his chair, wondering if he'd won, and worried because she hadn't argued as much as he'd expected. Alexandra was not to be trusted when she gave in easily.

6

Alexandra rode past the village, past the town, beyond the fields to the grazing meadows, where she finally gave Prince Mischa his lead. One of the Razin boys was behind her as always, but she hadn't noticed which one had followed her, nor did she look back now.

It was probably Konrad, who at the age of thirty was the oldest and the most responsible of the three brothers. Timofee and Stenka, the twins, only scolded her whenever she went off on her own without telling them, but Konrad would give her hell and make her feel it.

She had grown up with the Razin boys and spent as much time in their home as she did in her own. They were like the brothers she never had, they were her friends, and sometimes they were pains in the neck. Their only sister, Nina, who was supposed to be her maid, was really her dearest friend. She was a year younger than Alexandra, but even she had married, though her husband had died two years ago.

Marriage.

The chill autumn wind had dried Alex's tears, a foolishness she so rarely gave in to, but her urge now wasn't to cry any more, but to keep on riding and never return home. Konrad, of course, wouldn't let her. Even when he found out what her father had done, he wouldn't let her take the cowardly route. He'd be angry, just as angry as she was, but Cossacks didn't run from battles, and he'd view this betrothal as a battle. She would, too, once she stopped hurting and feeling so betrayed.

Marriage.

Damn Christopher Leighton, why had he noticed her at her first ball in St. Petersburg? Why had he courted her so diligently and claimed he loved her? He was an assistant to the English ambassador, so worldly, so sophisticated, so handsome. She'd gotten her head turned royally.

She loved him—she *must* love him to wait seven years, which even she knew was a ridiculous amount of time to remain loyal to a man who had yet to propose marriage to her, and whose image she couldn't even recall clearly anymore, it had been so long since she'd last seen him. But his letters were always so full of passion and his depth of feeling for her, even the last one, which she had recently received.

Always he wrote of his love and how much he missed her. And since he had returned to England, he had been assuring her that he was trying to get his diplomatic posting switched back to Russia so he could be near her again. But in all his letters, not once had he ever mentioned marriage. And for all her boldness, she had never been able to write the few words that would have elicited from him a reply that would have either strengthened her hope or ended it. She simply couldn't bring herself to ask him outright if he intended to marry her.

She should have, she realized now. She also

should have followed him to England when she'd wanted to, instead of giving in to her father's refusal. If she could just see Christopher once more . . .

Alexandra made up her mind then and there. She would go to England as soon as she got rid of the Cardinian and the matter of honor was satisfied. After all, she had a sizable amount of money saved up from the sale of her horses. All she had to do was figure out a way to leave the country so that her father wouldn't immediately try to stop her. With so many routes to England, once she was on one of them, he'd have the devil's own time finding her.

With that decision made, some of the tightness left her chest and she pulled up on the reins, allowing Konrad to catch up to her. But it was Stenka Razin who drew up beside her and glared at her because of the mad ride he'd had trying to keep up with her.

"You were trying to kill us both, right? Or just the horses?"

"I was trying to outrun a few demons, if you must know," she replied.

"Any I know?"

"My father, for one."

"Ah, another fight with your papa," he said with a knowing grin.

Of the three Razin brothers, Stenka was the one who didn't have a serious bone in his body. He loved life and found pleasure, and more often than not humor, in just about every aspect of it. Whenever Alexandra was angry, or hurt, or just plain moody, he always managed to make her laugh. She was afraid he wasn't going to manage it this time if he tried.

His brother Timofee was only slightly less carefree. The twins were so alike it was uncanny, and not just in their identical features. They were twenty-seven, had the black hair and blue eyes that ran in their family, and wanted the exact same things, including women, which was why they constantly competed with each other—and fought. It didn't take much to set those two off, and it wasn't unusual for one or the other to sport a black eye or a split lip from their tussles.

"I don't know why you let these arguments with your papa upset you, since you always win," Stenka remarked.

"I didn't win," she mumbled.

"You didn't win?"

His deliberately incredulous look didn't bring the grin he was looking for. "I didn't win!"

"I suppose there is a first time for everything." He sighed. "So what didn't you win?"

"He has betrothed me to a Cardinian."

There was nothing feigned about his new incredulous look. "He wouldn't do that to you."

"He did it fifteen years ago."

"Ah, when you were still a baby," he said, as if that explained it.

"A ten-year-old baby?"

He waved his hand dismissively. "So what are you going to do?"

"Honesty would be the best strategy, I think," she said matter-of-factly. "I'll simply tell this Cardinian count that I don't want to marry him."

Stenka gave her an assessing look that ran from

her fur-topped head to her booted feet and, in his opinion, passed over a great many assets in between. "He could be as homely as hell, take one look at you, and think he's died and gone to heaven. Your honesty won't matter in that case."

Alexandra groaned over that possibility. "You aren't helping, Stenka."

"Was I supposed to?"

"It would be appreciated."

"Well, then," he said cheerfully, "Timofee and I could ambush him, beat him up, and warn him off."

"Except he's probably arriving even as we speak," she predicted, then added, just in case he'd mistaken her response to his suggestion as permission, "and we're not going to beat up a king's cousin—except as a last resort."

He whistled softly. "A *king's* cousin? So why don't you marry him?"

Her midnight-blue eyes took on a deep purple hue when she glared, which she was doing now. "Because I happen to love Christopher."

"Him!" Stenka said with such derision that she nearly winced. They all knew about her Englishman and they'd been happy for her—until the years had started to pass with no ring forthcoming for her finger. "That no-good laggard!"

"I don't want to hear it."

"You're sure?"

"Yes."

"But it would do me a world of good to get it off my chest."

His expression was so earnest, she couldn't

help chuckling. He grinned, having finally gotten the result he was after.

"So let's go and meet your betrothed," he suggested. "You never know, you might like him." When she just snorted, he added, "It's not impossible."

"But it wouldn't matter."

He didn't have to ask why, and that was the hell of it, Stenka thought, feeling disgust now. Their Alex was too damn loyal, even when her loyalty was misplaced. And her papa had the right idea. Stenka's own father, Ermak, had heard the baron repeat it more than once, and every one of the Razins seconded the opinion. Someone should have shot that Englishman a long time ago.

7

Alexandra had taken a leisurely ride home, so by the time she and Stenka approached the house, it was long past the "less than two hours" that her father had predicted for her betrothed's arrival. Count Vasili Petroff should have been settled in her home, either in his room or already in conference with her father. In either case, she wouldn't be likely to bump into him if she entered from the back of the house as she had planned. She had decided to let her father assess him first, then demand from him an *honest* opinion before she met the man herself.

That had been her plan, and a good one, she had thought—there was always the possibility that her father wouldn't be able to tolerate the man and would send him packing, so she wouldn't have to deal with him at all—but it didn't take into account that her betrothed might not be in any hurry to arrive. Seeing the eight men who were now dismounting in front of her house proved that.

Alex wasn't thrown off kilter, however, by having to abandon one plan for another. After all, there was a lot to be said for confrontations, and interesting things could be learned when you took someone by surprise. All in all, it might be better if she did meet him first, before her father had a chance to warn him about some of her

67

more "outrageous" habits, as he termed them. Seeing was believing, and she was never at her best in her work clothes. Whom, after all, did she have to impress in the stables?

She hadn't expected the Cardinian to arrive with a full entourage, though. There were eight men, but a dozen horses, the riderless ones bogged down with baggage. Obviously her betrothed didn't travel lightly, which told her right there that he was probably one of those spoiled and pampered aristocrats, the kind who would be appalled at the idea of sleeping outdoors and always had to have servants on hand to see to his simplest needs.

Alexandra had never in her life asked someone to do something for her that she wasn't able and willing to do herself, and, in fact, she preferred doing for herself. Nina might make sure her clothes were always neat and clean, but that was about the extent of the maid's duties that Alexandra allowed her friend to perform.

Alexandra and Stenka rode up behind the visitors without being noticed. The Cardinians had been inconsiderate in not taking their horses around to the stables. Two of the house servants had come out to take charge of the animals, but they weren't having much luck. Several of the horses were thoroughbreds, not as fine as those the Rubliovs bred, and not as well trained either. In fact, they were causing quite a disturbance among the more placid animals.

One was a stallion at which Prince Mischa snorted and tossed his proud head, but a soft word from Alexandra and he stilled, allowing her to dismount and ignore him, sure that he wouldn't embarrass her with any male theatrics. Her eyes had already settled on the man she assumed to be her betrothed, his fine clothes giving him away. She hadn't expected him to be so handsome. Dark brown hair, baby-blue eyes, and grooves in his cheeks that promised dimples when he smiled. She was further surprised to find his expression so open, making him seem accessible—even likable.

Right now, he was about the only one of his group who had heard her arrival and who had turned in her direction. But his eyes never reached Alexandra. They lit on Prince Mischa and went no further.

It was a reaction Alexandra was quite used to, expected even, and understandably filled her with no small amount of pride. But then her two stallions, Prince Mischa and his sire, Sultan's Pride, were both pure white thoroughbreds, with luxurious long manes and tails, deep blue eyes, and none of the usual patches of pink skin showing through their dense, smooth coats.

Their offspring were in constant demand and commanded ridiculously high prices, but Alexandra never sold her "babies" to anyone who wasn't a connoisseur of fine horseflesh. If the prospective buyers weren't going to pamper them the way she did, then they weren't going to own them.

Her betrothed, apparently, was just such a connoisseur. Figuratively, he was practically drooling over her horse. She was amused. She was relieved. Though it was going to kill her to

69

do it, she just might be able to buy him off with Prince Mischa. Of course, she would offer one of her mares or geldings first. All of her breeding stock and their offspring were of superior quality. But from the looks of the man, he was already in love with Prince Mischa.

Alexandra dismounted, and just to be sure she hadn't made a mistake in identifying her betrothed, she demanded, loud enough for the entire group to hear her, "Which one of you is Vasili Petroff?"

Vasili turned from his examination of the large country house and eyed the—female? He wasn't quite sure until his gaze dropped to a prime pair of breasts that actually widened the opening of the old woolen coat she was wearing. It was a shame the britches were so baggy, but the skin-hugging boots revealed nicely shaped calves.

He was attracted, no doubt about it. Breasts like those always did the trick for him. But there was more, for she had quite lovely features, too, flawless skin that still retained a summer tan, which attested to her peasant origins—no lady would expose herself to that much sun—with high cheekbones presently pinkened by the wind and a slim, straight nose that seemed too fine, almost aristocratic.

Her mouth was luscious, full, provocative, nearly as tempting as those breasts. The stubborn lift of her small chin was disconcerting, but could be ignored. What he could see of her hair beneath the fur hat that covered her head was almost lighter than her tanned skin. The nicely curved brows were darker, though, a light brown, and

70

the long, thick lashes that surrounded almond-shaped eyes were darker still, making for a very arresting, exotic combination.

Perhaps his short stay here wouldn't be completely unpleasant after all, Vasili decided, and he was grinning by the time he said, "That would be me, sweetheart. And who might you be?"

Alexandra's eyes left the dark-haired man, who had barely spared her a glance at her question, and swung to the one who had just spoken. So she *had* made a mistake . . .

The thought deserted her, along with every other one in her head. Her eyes grew enormous. Her mouth dropped open. She forgot about breathing. And her stomach felt as if it were trying to drop to her feet.

Time passed without her noticing it, until finally she was drawing in a starved breath just before she turned blue. She turned bright crimson instead. Her cheeks had to be giving off smoke. And his grin widened at her reaction to him. Was it shock? Was that what had just made a fool of her? And still was, for she still couldn't seem to find her tongue. It must be shock, but then no one had ever warned her that men could look like this one.

He was golden all over, hair of molten gold that curled softly over his temples and ears, tawny-gold skin, honey-gold eyes. He was absolutely beautiful, but it was a masculine beauty, with features perfectly symmetrical: lean cheeks, a straight, aquiline nose, thick, slashing brows, strong chin, and well-shaped lips that were entirely too sensual. The combination was mesmerizing.

But somehow Alexandra managed to pull her stunned senses together. *He* was Vasili Petroff? She was supposed to marry *him?* God, what a joke. Marry a man more beautiful than she was? Not in this century, she wouldn't.

Now that her mind was working again, she recalled her plan and she marched over to him, belatedly noting that he was tall, a good six feet tall. And his knee-length, fur-edged coat that was wrapped and belted around a lean waist showed a military physique that she found a bit disconcerting. Her father was taller and much stockier, but the whipcord strength of the man who stood before her was somehow more intimidating.

But Alexandra was not one to show her fear to anyone if she could help it, and she wasn't actually afraid of the man. He wasn't her husband, after all, merely her betrothed—and soon he wouldn't even be that.

"I'm sorry I stood there like a half-wit, Count Petroff," she told him matter-of-factly, "but I was a bit—surprised. After all, it's not ever day that I see a man who's prettier than I am."

She vaguely heard some chuckles from the men standing behind him and from the blue-eyed man she had first thought was her betrothed. She was quite disappointed that he wasn't Count Petroff, for it would have been far easier to deal with him. She gave him a brief, wistful glance that he must have misinterpreted—he was finally looking her way long enough to see it—for it wiped the humorous expression from his face.

Returning her attention to the golden Adonis, she noted his heightened color. It was amazing how she always managed to produce that effect in men once she opened her mouth—at least in men who didn't know her. She hadn't intended to shock him with her frankness, but she was unaccountably pleased that she'd managed it anyway. And having gotten rid of his grin at least, she felt more in control.

Remembering his question, she was about to introduce herself when, between one thought and the next, she also recalled what he'd called her. "Sweetheart?" Without knowing who she was? She almost laughed then, as she realized that the man had been flirting with her, or rather, with an unknown female, and on the doorstep of his betrothed's house. And *that* told her more about his character than she was likely to learn from any conversation with him.

She didn't laugh, but she couldn't quite keep the corners of her mouth from turning up. This really was a stroke of luck for her. She couldn't wait to tell her father about this paragon of honor and virtue he'd hoped to saddle her with.

She considered toying with him for a moment, just to see how far he could bury himself before she revealed who she was. It was actually very tempting, not that she really knew how to toy with a man. But she wasn't going to resort to trickery when honesty would serve just as well.

She was still grinning slightly, however, when she said, "Let me introduce myself, Count. I'm Alex Rubliov."

"Alex—as in Alexandra?"

"Yes."

The moment he had her answer, his whole demeanor changed. His honey-gold eyes traveled down her long length, but this time they were filled with utter contempt, with a heavy dose of disgust thrown in. And Alexandra couldn't have been more pleased.

To prove it, she gave him a dazzling smile that, unbeknownst to her, made him catch his breath. "It's rather obvious that neither of us is what the other expected, but don't despair. As it happens, I don't want to marry you."

Since she'd just taken the words right out of Vasili's mouth, so to speak, he was rendered nearly speechless. "You don't?"

"Not even a little," she reassured him. "But I *am* sorry you had to waste your time in coming here. You must insist that my father make it up to you when you break our betrothal. And if I don't see you again before you leave, well, it's been—interesting meeting you."

With that, she swung around and appeared to leap into the saddle of the white stallion, she mounted him so fluidly. Horse and rider then trotted off around the corner of the house, a brute of a Cossack following behind them.

It wasn't often that Vasili Petroff was dumbfounded, particularly by a woman. This one didn't look back once in his direction. She'd said her little speech, then seemed to have summarily dismissed him from her mind. But women didn't *do* that to him.

Lazar came to stand next to Vasili and also stared in the direction in which Alexandra

74

Rubliov had vanished. Without glancing at him, Vasili said, "If you laugh, I'm going to put my fist in your mouth."

Lazar didn't laugh, but he was certainly grinning. "You think that would stop me?"

The two friends had been known to tear into each other with very little provocation. Stefan had sent Lazar along with Vasili to keep him out of trouble. But he had jokingly admonished that they not kill each other before they returned to Cardinia. And the six guards, who accompanied the two friends at Stefan's insistence, were to see to that, as well as to protect their backs on the bandit-infested mountain passes.

"It would make it difficult for you to continue," Vasili promised.

"True—but what are you growling about? You should be delighted. Now you won't have to show her what a bastard you can be. She's told you exactly what you wanted to hear, and without any effort on your part."

"Exactly?" Vasili said with irritation. "You must not have been listening carefully, Lazar. The little peasant doesn't want to marry me, but she expects *me* to break the betrothal. As much as I'd love to, you know I can't do that."

"Yes, but look how much closer you are to achieving your goal, thanks to her unexpected revelation. You've already won half the battle without firing a single shot. How hard can it be to get her to break the betrothal, once you explain that you can't? She's on your side, my friend. She doesn't want you."

Having said that, Lazar finally couldn't resist

laughing. It really was incredibly funny, and Vasili's glower was funnier still. Who would have thought that the one woman who actually had an opportunity to marry Vasili, or at least assumed she did, wouldn't want to, when hundreds of others would have killed to be in her position?

"By the way," Lazar added, just to rub it in, "I don't think she was the least bit impressed by that splendid display of contempt you treated her to. I can't say that I blame her, but then I saw the way you were looking at her before you knew who she was." He had to pause for another laugh. "Jesus, I can't wait to tell Stefan and Serge about this. They simply aren't going to believe it."

8

"Come, sit down, Vasili—you will permit me to call you so?"

Constantin didn't wait for an answer, resuming his seat behind his desk. His study was what one might expect from a man of his years, sedate, and lacking all flamboyance. It reminded Vasili of his father's study, before Maria had turned it into a sewing room after his death.

"Though we have never met, I feel as if I have known you all your life," Constantin was explaining. "But then, you were all your father ever talked about. He was so proud of you and your accomplishments. He wanted to show you off, you know, to take you with him on his travels and hunting trips, but he felt your schooling was more important, particularly since you shared the royal tutors with the crown prince. He was proud of that, too, since he never had such advantages himself, having no connection with the royal family until he married your mother. But I do know he intended to bring you with him to Russia after you turned eighteen. I remember when he . . ."

Constantin continued reminiscing for more than an hour. Vasili was required to make few comments in reply, merely to listen, and he did that avidly, hearing things about his father he'd never known. Long before the baron had finished speaking, the resentment Vasili had harbored against the man for most of his life was beginning to lessen, and by the time Constantin finished with "I still miss him, you know," it was gone completely.

Ridiculously, Vasili felt close to tears, damn close. He hadn't cried since he was a small child, and the urge he felt now was all but choking him. He missed his father, too, and until now he hadn't realized how much. Once his anger over his father's untimely death had passed, he'd felt a good deal of regret, in particular that he'd never had the opportunity to be friends with Simeon, the way Stefan had become friends with his own father, Sandor, after he'd reached his manhood.

This was certainly not the way Vasili had anticipated his interview with the baron to go. Of course, nothing was going the way he had anticipated, especially his first encounter with his betrothed.

Her remark that *she* wasn't what he had expected was an understatement. He had pictured a pampered and frivolous aristocratic woman whom he could easily intimidate. But he couldn't imagine intimidating the audacious wench he'd just met. She spoke her mind with brazen disregard for decorum. She dressed like a peasant, a *male* peasant at that. And she rode a horse astride, as if she had been born in a saddle. There didn't seem to be a shy bone in her body. And why the hell didn't she want to marry him?

Vasili wasn't sure how he felt about that, but he wasn't relieved, as Lazar thought he'd be. He had been rejected. *Rejected.* It was a unique experience for him—well, not quite.

Tanya had also rejected him out of hand when she'd been told he was the king she would have to marry. "I wouldn't marry your king if you paid me," was the way she had put it. Of course, she hadn't believed that she was Princess Tatiana Janacek, or that she had been betrothed at birth to the present King of Cardinia. It wouldn't have made a difference if she had believed it, though, since she had scorned Vasili at the time, just as he had scorned her.

But even then he hadn't felt rejected. Nor had he felt whatever it was that had him so irritated now. And his inability to identify exactly what was bothering him only added to his irritation. He was careful, however, to conceal his feelings from the baron.

Originally he had intended to present himself to Constantin Rubliov as a completely undesirable son-in-law. He had assumed, based on his experience with women, that his betrothed would be pleased to have him, and so would be the more difficult of the two Rubliovs to dissuade from this marriage, whereas her father could be easily outraged. But after listening to the baron speak so highly and with genuine affection about his father, he knew he couldn't do it—at least not in the more obvious ways he had planned.

He'd already lied about why he had been delayed in arriving, blaming it on an illness in his party, when in fact he had deliberately wasted time, staying over in each town for days, once for a full week—because of a pretty little redhead—

instead of just for the night. The delay was to allow the cold of the approaching winter to hinder travel. If for some reason he had to take Alexandra Rubliov back to Cardinia with him, he wanted the weather to give her an added incentive to turn back. He was, of course, going to give her a great many reasons to end this ridiculous betrothal, but he would utilize anything extra that might aid his cause, including the weather.

But now the rest of his campaign, at least where the baron was concerned, had to be set aside. He wasn't going to disgrace his father in this man's eyes by behaving like an utterly detestable son.

But he didn't have to be perfect either. Perhaps he could disappoint him by not having—or pretending not to have—certain qualities or attitudes the man was hoping to find in him. He just had to figure out what they might be.

"About your daughter, sir?"

"Yes, I was watching from the drawing room when you met her."

And Constantin couldn't have been more pleased when he'd witnessed firsthand Alexandra's reaction to the young count. It was all he could do to contain his relief now, it was so great. Somehow he managed.

"I regret that she wasn't at her best," he continued. "But you see, she spends most of each day working with the horses, and so she dresses for convenience, rather than—"

"*Working* with horses?" Vasili's surprise was genuine, giving him no time to ascertain whether he should approve or disapprove. His tone said it all, and turned Constantin defensive.

"This is a horse-breeding farm, after all," he explained. "And Alexandra was the only one of my three daughters who showed any interest at all in the horses. I probably shouldn't have encouraged her, but I did, and once I did, there was no turning back."

Vasili was relieved to see that he had taken the correct tone, at least for his purposes. The father obviously allowed the girl her unusual occupation, and Vasili would not be out of line in expressing disapproval of that. The baron's quick defense told him the older man had probably anticipated that he would disapprove.

And just so there would be no mistaking that he was scandalized, albeit mildly, Vasili said, "You actually *permit* this?"

As if I could stop her, Constantin thought but refrained from replying. He would just as soon Vasili not find out how willful and stubborn his betrothed could be, at least until after the wedding.

"I saw no harm in this, and she is highly skilled with the animals," he replied. "She doctors them, trains them, breeds them—"

"I beg your pardon?"

Color rose in Constantin's cheeks, and he became defensive again. "Now see here. Alexandra is not some pampered, ignorant city girl who never gets her hands dirty. She was raised here in the country—"

Constantin stopped, for Vasili's expression was eloquent. *Well, that explains it,* he might as well have said aloud, and in the driest tones.

The baron's sigh was just as eloquent, the

81

sound of a father at his wit's end. "I will concede that my daughter's activities need to be channeled in a new direction. And as with any new bride, a husband and children should see to that nicely."

Vasili groaned inwardly, wondering now if his attitude wasn't just what the baron had been hoping for. He said carefully, "You do realize that I live in the capital city, near the palace. With the court functions she will be expected to attend, her life will be quite different from what she is accustomed to."

"The change will do her good, though I warn you, she won't give up her daily riding."

That was such a moot point, Vasili said indifferently, "Most noblewomen ride for pleasure."

"What about racing?"

"Preposterous. No lady races—she races?"

"Occasionally."

"Not anymore," Vasili said stiffly.

"Splendid."

Vasili slumped a bit in his chair. He was supposed to be hitting on the things that would *not* please the baron, not turn out to be the ideal solution to the man's apparent problems with an *un*natural daughter.

Trying for a desperate about-face, Vasili said, "I do, of course, own several country estates not too distant from the capital. I suppose she could be allowed to pursue her . . . hobby there."

Constantin smiled. "Alexandra will be delighted to hear that."

Vasili gritted his teeth, giving up. His last hope, with the baron at least, was that the man might be lying about this betrothal. It was a slim hope, but Vasili was feeling desperate again.

"I would like to see a copy of the betrothal contract, sir. Apparently my father's copy was misplaced or lost, since it was never found."

"Certainly."

Vasili flushed slightly, seeing that the contract had been lying there on the desk between them. Constantin handed it over, obviously having anticipated the request, and it didn't take long for Vasili to peruse the brief document—and find his father's signature on it. So much for slim hopes.

"Might I ask why you waited so long to write?" Vasili asked as he handed the contract back. "Your daughter is quite beyond the age when most girls marry."

"That was selfishness on my part, wanting to keep her with me for a bit longer," Constantin said. "And she was content with her life here."

"I don't doubt it. Are you aware that she doesn't want to marry me?"

"She *told* you that?"

"She did."

Constantin thought frantically for a moment before he waved his hand dismissively. "Nervousness, and the thought of change. It happens to many brides—and grooms."

"Usually such feelings are kept to oneself," Vasili replied in a near grumble.

Constantin chuckled. "Ah, you've discovered my daughter's propensity for frankness. I'll admit it can be disconcerting at times, but refreshing at others. Alexandra will never waste your time getting to the point, you can be sure of that. But you needn't take her remark to heart. It's not you she doesn't want to marry, but anyone. As I said, she would have been perfectly happy going on as she has been—indefinitely. But she *will* marry you. I have her word on that."

That was *not* what Vasili was hoping to hear. "With all due respect, sir, are you sure you want to force your daughter to marry a man she doesn't want?"

"Come now, doesn't want?" Constantin smiled in such a knowing way that Vasili nearly blushed. "I saw what happened when she first beheld you, and I assure you, no man has ever rendered her speechless before." *Not even that damn Englishman.*

Vasili *was* blushing now—unaccountably, because it wasn't as if he weren't used to rendering women speechless. "She claims I surprised her."

"No doubt you did."

"It was mutual."

"No doubt it was. My youngest daughter is nothing if not unique," Constantin said with a good deal of fatherly pride. "I also have no doubt that a man of your years and experience will have little difficulty in winning her affections—and easing her fears."

Not if Vasili could help it. And he was getting nowhere with the baron. The man had accepted him wholeheartedly, would apparently use any excuse to continue to do so. Vasili knew he needed to concentrate his efforts on Alexandra, and there was no time to spare.

He assured the baron, "I will make every effort where your daughter is concerned." It wasn't exactly a lie, just a statement that was open to different interpretations. He stood up to end the interview. "Because of my delay in arriving, I'm afraid we'll have to leave very soon, preferably tomorrow, before the weather makes traveling too dangerous."

He'd managed to surprise the older man. "But arrangements aren't finished for the wedding."

Vasili feigned a look of remorse. "I'm sorry, but did I forget to mention that my cousin insists the wedding take place in Cardinia, in the palace? It was the queen's suggestion, and Stefan does love to give her anything she desires."

Constantin had no comment for that and could think of nothing but the dilemma this unexpected development was going to cause. "But I've made no provisions to travel at this time."

"You can always wait until spring next year and bring her to Cardinia then," Vasili was quick to suggest.

Too quick, Constantin noted, which was why he said, "No, it isn't necessary for me to witness her wedding. With the betrothal, you are almost as good as married. I'll wait and visit when she has her first child."

Jesus, the man already had him married and soon to be a father, Vasili thought with dread. "But surely she'll be disappointed?"

As angry as she was with Constantin? He barely kept from snorting. "Not at all. If anything, she'll be glad to be out from under my authority."

And instead be under mine, Vasili realized, the

thought intriguing him—until the consequences reared up to horrify him. Seducing the little wench was no longer a possibility, in fact, it was absolutely forbidden. But it would be easier to get her to break the betrothal if her father wasn't there to see how utterly despicable he intended to be—if he couldn't get her to cry off before tomorrow.

9

Constantin sat back behind his desk and waited, almost positive that Alexandra would join him as soon as she saw that he was alone. It took less than two minutes for her to arrive. She must have been watching for the count to leave the study. She would try to avoid Vasili. Constantin wouldn't be that lucky.

She still hadn't changed out of her work clothes and looked anything but a lady. After what Vasili had told him she had said to him, Constantin was afraid the oversight was deliberate. It would be her way of protesting, and he knew from experience that she could be quite stubborn about it. He almost wished he could make the trip with them, just to watch her rough edges being softened by a man who, by the look of him, was no doubt an expert where women were concerned.

Come to think of it, the change in events could be quite beneficial, he concluded. Had plans gone apace, the pair would have been wed in less than a week, which was not very much time for them to get to know each other. But traveling to Cardinia first, which could take close to a month, depending on how encumbered they were, would give Vasili the opportunity to court Alexandra and win her over completely before they were actually married.

Knowing his daughter, Constantin had a

feeling she wouldn't be very appreciative of that possibility, not yet anyway. And, as expected, she got right to the point of her visit.

"When is he leaving?" she demanded.

"You are both leaving tomorrow."

"Both? Then he didn't cry off?"

"What made you think he would? What you told him? You disappoint me, Alexandra. I thought honor meant more to you than—"

"Enough!" she snapped. "I merely tried to end this farce by telling him the truth. But if he wants a woman who wants nothing to do with him—I should have known it would make no difference."

When she said no more, he asked hesitantly, "But you will marry him?"

"I won't be the one to cry off," she replied with all the bitterness she was feeling.

"But you think he will?"

"Once he gets to know me—"

"Dammit, Alex, I know you are attracted to the man. I saw that myself."

She gave a shrug that was supposed to indicate her indifference, but her tone was vehement. "I can't deny he comes in a very pretty package, so pretty he's more than likely as vain as a peacock, but with the personality of a worm—a lecherous worm."

"You have some reason for phrasing that remark just so?" he asked sternly.

"Merely that he flirted with me—*before* he knew I was his betrothed."

"And you have so much experience with men that you know the difference between flirting and being friendly?"

88

Alexandra snorted. "Friendliness doesn't call for endearments like 'sweetheart.' "

Instead of the fatherly outrage she had counted on, he smiled. "I am delighted to hear that he was attracted to you, even dressed as you are. And since we have also established that you are equally attracted to him—"

"We didn't establish that," she cut in hotly.

But Constantin ignored her to finish, "—you could at least try to like him."

She made him wait a long, tense moment before she said, "Very well, I'll try."

Constantin blinked in surprise. "You will?"

It had been such a bald-faced lie, she couldn't repeat it, so she asked instead, "What was that you said about leaving tomorrow?"

"An unexpected development, I'm afraid. I had assumed you would be wed here, within a matter of days, but apparently you're going to have a grand ceremony at the royal palace in Cardinia—at their king's insistence."

"Well, isn't it fortunate that I can manage to pack in so little time."

She said it so dryly, her opinion of the situation was obvious, at least to her father. After all, women were known to take days, weeks even, to prepare for a journey. And although Alexandra usually traveled lightly, even she began packing several days before a scheduled trip.

"You're wrong, Alex. He's not trying to inconvenience you. It's merely the time of year. His delay in getting here makes it imperative that you travel quickly now, to avoid the harsh snowstorms in the mountains."

Her brows suddenly rose with interest. "I happen to like snow. You mean he doesn't?"

The fact that she grinned as she said it made Constantin groan. "You wouldn't intentionally delay the journey, would you?"

"To postpone the wedding?" Her grin got wider. "What do you think? Besides, it's only fair that he finds out what life with me will be like."

"Alexandra, I insist that you behave on this—"

"You've already gotten the only promise you'll get from me, Papa, and you were lucky to get it."

His face was turning red as he became upset. "You said you would try to like him."

"Oh, I will, and I'll have *lots* of time to do so before the wedding. Not tonight, however, so you'll have to entertain our guest this evening by yourself. I have *so* much packing to do, after all, that I'm quite certain I'll need a wagon for all my trunks."

"You'll pack lightly, dammit, just as you always do. I won't have you caught in one of those storms in the mountains because of your stubbornness. I'll send the bulk of your things as soon—"

"Make that two wagons," she tossed out as she headed for the door.

"Alex!"

She closed the door quietly behind her. She would have preferred to slam it, to throw things, to scream, but there was no point when she had already lost the battle, at least with her father. She still felt hurt and betrayed, and doubted she'd ever forgive him for that. And to think she had awakened this morning to an ordinary day. Now her whole world had been turned upside down, and it wasn't going to be easy to right it.

But she would. It might have been a jolt to hear that the wedding was still on, when she had thought she had settled the matter to her satisfaction, but she was not defeated yet where the Cardinian was concerned. The anger still simmering inside her was no longer just for her father. She was now infuriated with that pretty-faced popinjay. How did he dare to still want her after what she had told him? And how did he dare to drag his feet in getting here, so that she had to be rushed in leaving?

Her hands were clenched as she marched up the stairs, and still tightly fisted as she pounded on the door to the guest room she assumed the count had been put in. Vaguely she noted that three of the upstairs maids were loitering at the end of the corridor, but she gave it no thought, unaware that her betrothed was like a flame to moths in the way he drew females to him. Since she would rather be doing anything except having to deal with him again, it wasn't surprising that she failed to make the connection.

She'd picked the right room, though. Abruptly Vasili Petroff stood before her, half dressed, his coat and boots removed, his white shirt open, the wrinkled tails pulled out of his pants, a wide stretch of chest and belly showing. Her eyes got ensnared, could move no farther than his chest, which was sparsely sprinkled with hair so light it was barely noticeable. He really was golden all over, like a tawny lion, and like a lion, he was a predator, and very, very dangerous. She knew this instinctively.

"Just the little wench I wanted to see."

His tone was utterly condescending and contemptuous of her. It wasn't difficult to guess why. She was still wearing her work clothes, minus her hat and coat. She hadn't even bothered to repair her hair after returning from her ride. The tight coiffure she had started with that morning was now quite straggly, and without her hat to stuff the loose ends into, she had a number of errant, silky strands streaming down her back and shoulders. The people who knew her were used to seeing her this way, she tended to pay so little attention to her appearance. Guests were not.

When she looked up at his face, she was startled to see that he was smiling. And what a smile. Her stomach seemed to turn over, which was such a funny feeling, she was appalled by the urge to giggle. She *never* giggled. She was never at a loss for words either, but for the second time that day, words deserted her.

Incredibly, in the space of a few hours, her memory didn't do him justice. He was so beautiful, she found it hard to look at him with any calm, much less coherent thoughts. For God's sake, was she going to have to mentally pull herself together every time she saw the man?

Getting yanked into the room and hearing the door close behind her brought her back to her senses real quick. With some contempt of her own, she cocked her brow and said, "Is this where you try to seduce me?"

His eyes had been inspecting every inch of her, yet it still disconcerted her to hear him ignore her question and remark with considerable surprise, "Jesus, you look like you're fresh out of bed."

On top of his condescension, that observation was more than she could easily tolerate, and recalled to her every bit of the anger she was feeling—for him. "It will be a wonder if I find my bed tonight at all. Thanks to your inconsideration, I'll be packing all night."

He stopped looking at her as if he'd like to see her back in bed, his in particular, and said with an indifferent shrug, "To answer your question, this is where I tell you that I'm on your side. I have no wish to marry, either, so if you'll just inform your father that you won't have me, I'll be able to leave here tomorrow without you, and you needn't lose any sleep tonight packing."

"You expect *me* to break the betrothal?"

"Certainly," he said, his tone patronizing. "Women are known to be notoriously fickle."

"I wouldn't know. But in this case, there is a little matter of honor and sworn oaths that happens to mean something to me, much as I wish it didn't. So you'll have to be the fickle one and do the crying off, and I would appreciate it if you got around to it before you waste my time with a trip to Cardinia."

"Impossible," he replied, his exasperation beginning to show. "Just tell your father that you don't want me. How difficult can that be for you?"

"I've already told him that, you dolt, clearly without result. But I've also given my word that

I would marry you—if you don't cry off." And then she sighed. Getting into a shouting match with him was not going to help. She forced herself to use a reasonable tone. "Look, as long as we're being honest with each other, Count Petroff, you and I agreed that neither one of us wants to marry the other, why don't you use the most obvious excuse and simply tell my father that I wouldn't make a suitable wife for you?"

"An excellent idea, except it would be a lie. As a baroness, you are, unfortunately, quite suitable. That I don't want to marry you, or any woman for that matter, is no reason to go against my father's wishes—at least, that is what my mother assures me."

She gave him a look of disgust. "You let your *mother* dictate your life?"

She'd managed to get to him with that. He flushed, snarling, "You let your father dictate yours!"

"My father is one of the two parties who arranged this ridiculous marriage. I couldn't face him again if I failed to keep his word. But your father is deceased."

"All the more reason I can't get out of this damned trap. My father is not available to be argued out of it, but yours is. So change your mind, wench—or do you need to hear how it will be if we marry? I promise you that you will never be anything to me but a nuisance, though one that I will endeavor to ignore. To please my mother, I'll have an heir from you, and then you will be free to pursue your own amusements, as I intend to do. My life won't change one bit, but yours most certainly will. Does that sound acceptable to you?"

Alexandra had to grit her teeth for a moment before she could manage a smile. "Certainly, as long as you don't mind embarrassing public scenes."

"I beg your pardon?"

"Be warned. If you force me to marry you, you will be mine, and I don't share what's mine. And you won't be able to ignore me, I promise you that." And then she threw his words back at him. "Does that sound acceptable to you?"

He took a step toward her so that his height would intimidate her, but she didn't budge an inch. "I don't like threats, wench."

"Who's threatening? You told me how it's going to be, and I merely told you how I'll react. I'd sleep on it if I were you, Petroff. It's liable to be the last night of untroubled sleep you'll get."

10

Alexandra managed to close Vasili's door quietly, just as she had closed her father's door, but she couldn't quite manage to do the same with her own, which was just down the corridor. She was so angry she could spit and chew nails. How did that man dare to threaten her with a loveless marriage, with mistresses—she hadn't misunderstood his *amusements*—and with babies? Babies! He was tempting her and didn't even know it, the cad, the arrogant swine! to mention the one thing she *did* want. But not from him. From anyone but him.

Her room wasn't empty. Her loud entrance startled both Nina, who'd been bending over a valise on the bed, and Bojik, who gave a short growl before he realized who it was and charged Alexandra with a demonstration of apology.

She had locked him in her room that afternoon out of habit, because they would be having guests in the house, and he didn't get along well with guests he didn't know. She shouldn't have. She should have let him run loose to do what he did best to unsuspecting strangers. A chunk missing from the popinjay's backside might have made that interview she'd just suffered through end more to her liking.

The thought calmed her somewhat. She hadn't realized she could be vindictive—at least in her

96

thoughts. Too bad she'd never use an animal as a weapon other than for defense, because it had been a really satisfying thought, imagining that Cardinian howling with pain.

After assuring the large wolfhound that she wasn't angry about the way he had first greeted her, she glanced over at Nina, the valise, and the pile of clothes strewn across her bed. "So you've heard?"

"Everyone has heard," Nina said neutrally. "What we don't know is what you're going to do. So I started packing in case you decide to marry the man, but I can just as quickly put all this away."

Nina didn't betray by the slightest expression which answer she'd like to hear, even if she *was* strongly opinionated and had already decided which answer Alexandra ought to make. Loyally, she'd support whatever Alexandra decided to do, though it was likely that there would be some arguments first if Nina thought Alexandra had made the wrong decision. Alexandra loved her for that.

Socially they weren't equals, and they were the exact opposite in looks. Nina's black hair was a riot of curls, and her light blue eyes were huge, giving her an owlish appearance that could be disconcerting when she was serious. Otherwise, she was a sweet dumpling with her slight chubbiness, her short stature, her dimples, and her bawdy sense of humor. And they were the dearest of friends.

Alexandra sat on the edge of the bed and fingered a pale mauve ball gown, recalling the one time she'd worn it. She'd received her first kiss that night—from Christopher, and it had been everything she'd ever imagined a kiss to be.

She held up the skirt of the old gown and asked Nina, "What were you packing this for?"

"You'll need something to get married in," the girl said pragmatically.

Alexandra prayed it wouldn't get to that point, and if it did, she'd insist on having a grand wedding gown made in order to buy herself more time. Perhaps something in black.

"You can forget about the valise," she said decisively. "I want trunks, and lots of them. Have someone dig out whatever is in the attic, and then beg, borrow, or steal some more from town. I want enough to fill at least two wagons."

Nina no longer contained her opinion. Her grin was self-explanatory. "So you're actually going to marry a king's cousin?"

Alexandra ignored her friend's delight. "No. I gave my word I would, but that doesn't mean it's going to happen—not if I can help it. My betrothed thinks he can't break the betrothal—I know I can't—and arguing with him about it isn't going to get me anywhere. So I'll just have to show him that I'll make him a terrible wife."

"But you'd make him an excellent wife," Nina contradicted loyally.

"Not him I wouldn't. But even if it were so, he's never going to know it, and he certainly isn't going to think it by the time I'm done with him."

Nina sat down beside her and asked hesitantly, "Why don't you marry him instead?"

"And betray Christopher?"

"Christopher ought to be betrayed," Nina muttered.

Alexandra sighed, not prepared to argue with her friend about the love of her life—again. None of the Razins had anything good to say about Christopher anymore—*especially* not Nina—and she was tired of taking his side when she had nothing to show to support her loyalty.

"Even if I weren't in love with someone else, I wouldn't marry that arrogant Cardinian. And before you build up to a really good protest, you might as well know he doesn't want to marry me either."

Nina was incredulous, not to mention indignant. "He said that?"

"He did. But he still plans to sacrifice himself *and* me, even though his father isn't alive to be disgraced by his breaking the betrothal. And would you like to hear what *he* has planned for our marriage? To get a child from me and then to ignore me. He threw it in my face that he's got mistresses and will continue to keep them. Of course, he'll be magnanimous and allow me some lovers."

"He said *that?*"

"He did."

Nina bristled. "Well, you aren't going to marry him. I won't let you. And neither will your papa, once you tell him about this."

To that, Alexandra snorted. "That's what you think. I told him that the man flirted with me before he knew who I was, and he was *delighted*. Petroff proves himself to be a damned libertine, and all my papa sees in that is that he was *attracted*

99

to me. So Papa's not going to believe the rest of this, not when he knows I don't want this marriage. He'll think I've made it up and probably be too embarrassed to confront Petroff about it. Even if Papa did mention it, I'd wager even money that the arrogant coxcomb would take the coward's route and deny it. After all, they've had their little meeting and seem to be getting along wonderfully. If the man didn't admit his true feelings when he had the chance, he won't now. Only *I* was privileged to be informed of them."

Nina stared broodingly at the floor for a moment before she replied, "It sounds as if you will have an . . . aristocratic marriage."

Alexandra dropped back on the bed, laughing. Nina turned to scowl at her.

"It's not funny," the younger girl said.

"I know." But Alexandra was still grinning. "I wasn't blind at all those balls and parties I attended in the cities, in St. Petersburg especially. More than half the married people I met were having affairs. And, appallingly, the women discuss it, either by gossiping about someone else or by bragging about their own conquests. What the Cardinian suggested *is* standard practice in his circles, I would imagine. I just don't believe he thought I was aware of it, since he was trying to shock me into breaking the betrothal, not to propose to me a normal marriage."

"But you don't want that kind of marriage. You're too possessive to tolerate—"

"I am not."

"I know you, Alex. You'd take a horsewhip to a husband who wasn't faithful to you."

"I would not," Alexandra protested vehemently.

She was aware that she'd said something quite different to Vasili. But that had been for effect. She certainly hadn't meant it.

She added for good measure, "I couldn't care less who that man sleeps with before or after the—never mind, there isn't going to be any wedding anyway. I told you, I have no intention of marrying him."

" 'If you can help it' were your exact words, and just how do you intend to do that?"

Alexandra dropped an arm over her eyes before she sighed. "I don't know. Delaying this journey with the wagons was as far ahead as I've thought."

"That might annoy him, but it won't make him refuse to marry you," Nina pointed out.

"I know, so help me think. What would make a man refuse a marriage he's already agreed to?"

"Repugnance," Nina suggested.

"Shame," Alexandra added.

"Disgust—"

"Wait, I can handle that one," Alex said excitedly as she sat up.

"Good, because you couldn't have managed repugnance, no matter how hard you tried. And I can't see you managing to disgust him either, for that matter."

"I already have." Alexandra grinned. "As toplofty and disdainful as he is, he took exception to the way I'm dressed, found me quite disgusting, or so his expression said. And you can be sure he didn't like my frankness one bit either. So that's it, Nina."

101

"What is? You're still betrothed to him, so how did that work?"

"It hasn't yet, but then, he's only met me, he hasn't met the *new* me."

"Ah, a little pretense." Nina nodded. "Is that what you have in mind?"

"No, a *lot* of pretense," Alexandra said, warming to the idea. "He must already consider me a provincial, but I'll be the worst provincial he's ever encountered. I'll be coarse and vulgar, ill-mannered, an utter embarrassment to him. He'll be horrified at the very thought of introducing me to his family and friends. And he'll quickly conclude that even his father would have broken the betrothal if he could have seen how I turned out."

"This sounds like fun." Nina grinned.

"Then you'll come along with me?"

"You thought you could leave me behind?"

Alexandra laughed and hugged her friend. "It shouldn't take more than a week for him to send me back, so we won't be gone that long. I'm still going to cart along everything I own, though."

"You still think you'll need the delay the wagons will cause?"

"I hope he'll come to his senses in only a week, but I'm not leaving anything to chance. If I do need more time to convince him he'd be a fool to marry me, then I'll have it. But don't worry about the packing. Just stuff everything in the trunks when they get here. I'll send him a bill for whatever is ruined because there was no time to pack properly, as soon as this betrothal is over."

"That will be throwing salt on an open wound," Nina predicted.

"I'm counting on it."

Nina left to start gathering the trunks, but Alexandra had only a few moments alone to reflect on what she had decided to do. Anna arrived, and the feelings of hurt and betrayal that Alexandra had been trying to ignore returned with a vengeance.

"Your father tells me you won't be joining us for dinner," Anna began.

"I'll be too busy packing."

Anna couldn't miss the bitterness in her tone. "I'm sorry, Alex. I know you're against this marriage right now, but you must admit your father picked an exceedingly handsome man for you."

An exceedingly handsome, *rotten* man, whom she wasn't going to discuss. "So you *did* know about the betrothal?" Alexandra said instead, as if it weren't a foregone conclusion, considering how close Anna was to the baron.

Anna winced. "Yes, and your father listened to everything I had to say about it, which was a great deal. He just wouldn't agree with my opinion."

"You could have warned me, Anna."

"I'm your friend, darling, but you know my first loyalty is to your father."

Alexandra did know it, and she had never resented Anna's relationship with her father. She even hoped that Anna would give in one day and marry him, which she knew was his hope as well. And she should have known that Anna wouldn't have approved of something as archaic as a betrothal, that she would have been on her side.

"I believe your father was afraid you would run away if you knew beforehand," Anna continued.

If Alexandra had known and hadn't run away, she would be wishing right now that she had, instead of wishing she'd been given that option. But she relaxed her tone and even offered Anna a smile. It certainly wasn't the older woman's fault that any of this had come about.

"Don't worry about it. I've already accepted what I must do," Alexandra said truthfully, since she wasn't referring to getting married. "So take care of my papa."

"You know I will."

"You might also prepare him for my return."

Anna was startled by that remark, but after a moment she laughed. "Now, why don't I think that you are referring to a visit?"

All of the bitterness Alexandra had been feeling returned abruptly, and with an aching heart she promised, "If I *do* have to visit, Papa won't be forgiven."

"Oh, Alex." Anna sighed. "He only wants what's best for you."

"Then it's too bad we couldn't agree on what that is, isn't it?"

Anna shook her head sadly. "If you change your mind about dinner—"

"I won't."

But Alexandra did; at least she decided to make an appearance when it occurred to her that a little rudeness and a vulgar display or two, made in the presence of both the Cardinian and her father, would give Vasili the perfect excuse to protest this marriage. Of course, she'd do nothing too outrageous, nothing she hadn't done before, so her father couldn't claim her behavior was out of the ordinary just for their benefit, even though it would be. And it would also give her father the opportunity to see how Vasili disdained her and that whatever attraction Constantin had deluded himself into thinking Vasili had felt when he'd first seen her certainly wouldn't withstand such disgust and contempt.

She couldn't have asked for better timing. The lavish dinner that her father had planned in order to impress the Cardinian was well under way, the main course just having been served. Anna had donned her finest gown; Constantin looked grand himself in his formal evening wear. And Count Petroff—she was going to have to keep her eyes off him. One brief glance at that superb body, at that beautiful face, and she nearly forgot what she was doing there.

He was impeccably groomed, of course. She had expected nothing less from the fastidious popinjay. So was his companion, the one with the friendly blue eyes, who happened to be the first to notice her in the doorway. He didn't appear shocked, merely surprised, that she hadn't changed for dinner and was still in her work clothes, her hair even more straggly than before since she had purposely pulled loose a few more locks. But then, she wasn't there to have dinner.

"Don't mind me. I've just come for a bite to eat, since I don't have time for dinner tonight."

She hoped *someone* was embarrassed over that

remark, though she didn't look to find out. She strolled forward and snatched an already buttered slice of hot bread from the blue-eyed Cardinian's plate. That she hadn't been introduced to him made it all the worse, but she figured he was the only one there who wouldn't say anything about her behavior.

A glance down at him showed him more on the shocked side now than surprised. She merely flashed him a smile in exchange for the food, then glanced across the table. Anna had a hand over her mouth. Well, it wouldn't do to laugh out loud, which she surely was trying to avoid. Constantin's cheeks had gone red, and not just with embarrassment. Alexandra and her father would really have had a roof-raising argument over this latest unrefined display of hers—if she were around for it. But she wouldn't be around for any more fights with him . . .

"Alexandra—" Constantin managed in a choked voice.

She gave him an innocent, inquiring look, which assured him that she was hoping for a display of temper, eager for it, and quite willing to match it. Realizing that, he didn't oblige and had to swallow his rancor and hope that she wouldn't further embarrass him.

She would have, except her newest plan backfired on her at that point. Count Petroff, instead of taking advantage of this golden opportunity she was offering him, had risen from the table and was now standing behind her.

"I am delighted you decided to join us, Baroness, however briefly. It allows me to correct an oversight. Will you give me your hand, please?"

She turned to face him, suspicious. Give him her hand? If he thought he was going to slap her hand for pilfering that slice of bread, as if she were some naughty child, she promised herself she'd give him back much worse. But when she hesitantly offered her free hand, he ignored it and took up the one grasping the buttery roll. With two fingers and an inscrutable expression that was surely hiding his disgust, he took the bread from her and set it aside; then, before she could snatch her hand back, he was slipping a ring on her finger.

It didn't go on easily, probably wouldn't have gone on at all if her fingers weren't coated with butter. She stared at the ring for a moment, bemused to find it so lovely. It was an enormous sparkling diamond surrounded by a twinkling array of sapphires, emeralds, and rubies.

"Now that I've seen to my duty, you can run along and finish your packing," Vasili said. "I realize it is an imposition, for which I apologize, but we really must leave tomorrow. I do hope you will get *some* sleep tonight, though, so do hurry with the chore."

His apology rang as false as his hope that she would be able to get some sleep—at least to her ears. To the others, he probably sounded sincere. And she was even more furious with the man now, for his duplicity, for pretending in front of her father, when she knew his true feelings. That she had come down here to do some pretending of her own was a moot point. She'd obviously wasted her time.

She picked up the slice of bread again simply because she was hungry, and left.

11

Vasili was up at dawn the next morning, not because he'd planned to leave at such an ungodly hour, but because he'd spent such a restless night, managing to get only a few hours of sleep off and on, and had been quite awake when the sun finally approached the horizon. He couldn't remember the last time he had spent such a hellish night.

Alexandra's remark that he should sleep on what she'd told him, that *it's liable to be the last night of untroubled sleep you'll get,* was partly responsible. What the hell had she meant by that? What she'd told him was designed to make him lose sleep, yet she'd predicted he'd have worse nights.

The other reason for his sleeplessness was, surprisingly, Alexandra herself. Vasili had rarely ever been around a woman who was in such a tousled state of appearance as she'd been in, unless he'd been romping in bed with her. And that damn red sash of hers that cinched in her waist so tightly showed just how shapely she really was. And white linen had never looked so good as it did draping and contouring those large, heavenly breasts of hers.

He'd been aroused. And despite the heated words they'd had in his room, and the exasperating subject matter, he'd still been aroused when she'd left him. Then damned if it hadn't happened again when she'd briefly joined them in the dining room, looking just as tousled.

He should have done something about it, sought out one of those giggling maids who had kept bothering him yesterday with the pretense of asking if he needed anything. Any one of them would have been willing to accommodate him. They'd made that perfectly clear. But he had already decided to be on his best behavior for Constantin Rubliov's benefit, and that excluded bedding one of the servants when his betrothed slept just doors away.

Fortunately, the baron wouldn't be making the return trip with him, so Vasili's very correct behavior would end as soon as he and his men parted from Rubliov's company. And there had been that girl—he'd forgotten her name already—who had shared his bed at the posting inn the other night. They'd be staying there again tonight, and he'd most certainly make use of her charms again, *and* make sure that Alexandra knew it. The sooner she took offense and demanded that he return her to her father, the sooner he would rid himself of the feeling of being trapped.

Since Vasili was already up and wide awake, he decided they might as well get an early start, and he left his room to rouse the others in his party. He sincerely hoped that Alexandra had been kept up all night packing as she'd predicted. Forcing a lady to rise sooner than she'd intended usually resulted in said lady's being in a sour mood, and his own mood was sour enough to want company.

He was disappointed, however, in his hope to further inconvenience his betrothed. Finding the household already astir at that hour, he sent one of the maids to wake Alexandra, and was informed that "Alex" was already outside, most likely at her stable. He was surprised enough at hearing a servant refer to the lady of the house so informally that the maid's calling the stable *hers* barely registered with him.

As it happened, his own mood worsened because Alexandra had gotten a head start on him, and he rushed a grumbling Lazar down to breakfast with the baron, only to find that his betrothed wasn't going to be joining them for the meal—again. Perversely, he took his time after drawing that conclusion, wasting a good hour unnecessarily, until Lazar was clearing his throat repeatedly and rolling his eyebrows toward the door, all of which Vasili ignored.

When he did finally leave the dining room, the same three maids who had been such a nuisance yesterday converged on him, one carrying his hat, one his coat, and the third his gloves. His own servant, Boris, whom Vasili had brought along for himself and Lazar, stood behind the women, shrugging his shoulders as if to say he'd been helpless in the face of their combined determination.

Fortunately, it was a situation Vasili found so normal, he barely noticed, accepting the articles of clothing and the maids' assistance in donning them, ignoring the hands that lingered. But that was how Alexandra found him when she came through the front door to discover what was keeping the Cardinians. The three women surrounding Vasili were touching him as if some shared intimacy gave them the right to do so.

Which happened to be the exact conclusion Alexandra came to, and quite possibly why she remarked with such blatant sarcasm, "I could have sworn someone told me you were in a hurry to return to Cardinia, Petroff. Of course, I should have known a man of your proclivities couldn't get his arse out of bed at a decent hour."

Without giving him a chance to answer, she was back out the door before he had even thought of one. The three maids had scattered at the first sound of her voice. Lazar was making noises into the palm of his hand. The baron, however, stood in the doorway to the dining room and looked truly pained in his embarrassment—but no more than he'd been last night when he had apologized for his daughter's behavior.

"She—ah—she—"

Vasili took pity on the man. Someone ought to, considering he had a daughter like that. "No need for explanations, sir. As you said, she requires . . . careful handling."

And he was looking forward to it now, damned if he wasn't. Ridicule him, would she? He'd have that little wench in tears before the end of the day. After all, contempt was a skill, and could become a weapon in the right hands, and his was developed to perfection for use whenever he needed it.

Alexandra was mounted on her white stallion when Vasili and his men reached the stable yard, or rather, one of the stable yards. Having declined a tour of the estate yesterday, Vasili hadn't realized that the Rubliovs maintained not one but five large stables, which were spread out from the house to the nearby village.

He still wasn't curious about the Rubliov estate. Now he was interested only in the object of his present rancor. Again she was wearing a shirt and those unorthodox britches, albeit clean ones, and with a blue sash today, and a much finer coat, this one trimmed in black fur to match the hat that completely concealed her hair.

He was still simmering over her latest effrontery, yet he found himself annoyed about her clothing for an unexpected reason—because he'd actually been looking forward to seeing her properly gowned. Even if she had worn a riding habit, it would have been a feminine riding habit. He had anticipated seeing her dressed in feminine attire because he had been told the britches were her work clothes. And since she wouldn't be working on the trip, she shouldn't be wearing them. Yet there she sat in her male finery, looking impatient—and vibrantly beautiful in the early morning light.

He looked at her left hand and noticed she wasn't wearing the ring. Why wasn't he surprised? No doubt she'd wait for the right moment to throw it in his face.

It took him several moments to notice the wagons, but when he did, his eyes narrowed suspiciously. Whatever was in them was piled high under canvas covers. They looked extremely cumbersome, and certainly too heavy for the mere four horses hitched to each of them.

113

He didn't question his betrothed, who was watching him silently. He moved straight to the wagon beds to examine their contents. One was filled with at least a dozen trunks. The other held a few more trunks along with a great deal of tack, saddles and the like, and a *great* many sacks of grain. Did she think he wasn't going to feed her?

Alexandra led her mount over to him, stopping right behind him. She was still silent, watching him closely, waiting for the exact moment when he realized what she was up to. It didn't take all that long.

He turned, looked up at her and said simply, unequivocally, "No."

She didn't even try to mistake his meaning, merely lifted a slim brow as she told him, "We aren't married yet, Petroff. You don't *really* think you can dictate to me until we are, do you?"

He didn't lose his temper and his expression didn't reveal how her words goaded him. Instead he raised a brow back at her—he did it so much better than she—and countered, "You don't really think I can't, do you?"

She gave him a tight little smile. "I can see you're going to try. But in this case, you're wasting your time. This isn't a brief visit you're dragging me to, but a new life. I'm not about to leave my belongings behind. If you thought I would, you were deluding yourself."

"No one is suggesting you do anything of the kind," he replied.

"Then there is nothing more to say."

"On the contrary. I will grant you fifteen minutes to gather whatever essentials you will need for the trip, which, by the way, does *not* include sacks of grain, and then—"

She interrupted him with an explanation. "The grain is top-grade and is for my babies. I don't trust the fodder offered at posting houses."

Since those few words made not the least bit of sense to him in relation to the subject, and actually confounded him, he was lucky to get out, "Babies?"

But she didn't have to answer him. At that moment three pure white thoroughbreds were being led by a groom out of the stable. Behind them came three more with another groom, and another three after that, and . . . When Vasili stopped counting, there were sixteen of the magnificent animals filling the stable yard.

"Yours?" he asked flatly.

"Every one of them," she replied, unmistakable pride in her voice.

"Your father is foolishly generous," he couldn't resist pointing out.

"My father gifted me with Sultan's Pride on my sixteenth birthday." She lovingly patted the animal she sat so he'd know just who Sultan's Pride was. "The rest of my babies I purchased myself, traded for, and bred."

A hell of an accomplishment, if he cared to admit it. He didn't. All he saw was that she expected to transport them over the mountains, with winter approaching, with bandits around every corner who would sell their own mothers for just one of those animals.

"This is ridiculous," he said. "Your *babies,* as

well as your belongings, can follow us if you insist, but we aren't going to be held back by them."

She smiled, telling him she'd hoped he'd say something like that. "You're welcome to go on without me. I certainly don't need your escort. Of course, if I get lost along the way and end up in another country instead of Cardinia, I'm sure I won't mind."

Vasili couldn't believe they were having a standoff. As much as he would like to go on without her at that point, he couldn't convince her to end the betrothal if they weren't traveling together, so they had to travel together. But her refusal to obey him was unacceptable. The betrothal gave him complete authority over her, which she obviously hadn't realized yet. But until they left her father's authority, which took precedence over his, he couldn't enforce his will as he would like—yet. Her father . . .

Suddenly he smiled. "Your father won't find that suggestion acceptable, wench, and you know it. So I believe I'll let him explain to you the merits of following my suggestion instead."

"How typical," she sneered. "The little boy doesn't get his way, so he runs to Papa, mine in this case. But by all means, waste some more of the time you're so concerned about by enlisting his aid—or trying to. You'll find, however, that he already knows he's gotten all the cooperation from me that he's going to get. Or were you under the mistaken impression that I'm an obedient daughter?"

He was angry enough to yank her off her horse and shake her. She knew it and didn't appear the least bit concerned, probably because of the large wolfhound that was suddenly there between them. The stallion she sat didn't move a muscle, apparently acquainted with the beast. She was obviously even better acquainted, because she ordered, "Sit, Bojik," and the dog immediately complied.

Vasili nearly growled, "Something else you think to bring along?"

"Certainly. My pet goes wherever I go."

"Anything else I should know about?"

He was being sarcastic, but she answered, "Just my maid and my men."

"Your men?"

She nodded toward the stable. He looked in that direction to find the entrance now filled with three mounted Cossacks, large brutes by the look of them, craggy-faced, each heavily armed and each looking back at him with—he wasn't quite sure. The men were so ugly, it was hard to read their expressions accurately, to discern hostility from amusement and amusement from mere curiosity.

"They will see to my safety on the journey," Alexandra informed him.

Stiffly, he looked back at her. "I believe that is my responsibility."

She actually laughed. "Don't be absurd. You travel with your own guards because you obviously can't see to your own safety, much less anyone else's." And then she added, with the contempt that *he* should have been utilizing, "But that's quite understandable, Petroff. It's been my experience that you court dandies are pretty much useless for anything other than gossip and whoring."

He was crimson-cheeked by the time she had finished, and so furious he barely got out, "Is that *firsthand* experience?"

Color bloomed in her cheeks now, and with a heated glare she retreated, trotting off with those three brutes flanking her, the oversized Russian wolfhound racing ahead of them, the wagons following, and five grooms leading the herd of prized stock.

Vasili stood there staring after them, seriously thinking about heading out in the opposite direction himself.

12

It was a long first day on the road, exceedingly so. The stallion in Vasili's party turned out to be his and was a high-strung animal that refused to keep to the sedate pace of the wagons, at least during the morning. Vasili was continuously forced to ride ahead of the group and back, though Alexandra was sure a few of those rides were merely to demonstrate his impatience with the slow progress they were making.

Her two stallions were much better behaved. They yearned for some brisk exercise themselves, but when denied, they didn't make a fuss about it. Even when Vasili drew abreast of her in the early afternoon, to inform her that they wouldn't be stopping for lunch or even to rest, Sultan's Pride ignored the big roan he was riding, while Vasili had to fight to keep his horse from nipping at hers.

As for their not stopping, Vasili had delivered the news smugly, and Alexandra received it with a good deal of amusement, which she managed to keep to herself. She had been informed that they needed that extra time to reach the first posting house. They should have arrived by early evening. As it was now, even without the stop for lunch, they wouldn't arrive until late that night.

It wasn't difficult for Alexandra to figure out that Vasili thought he was getting even with her for the delay the wagons were causing them, but she had planned for just such a contingency. All of her people had packed food that didn't require cooking, but Vasili's group hadn't been given the same. His own empty belly wouldn't let him keep up that ploy for more than a day or two, she didn't doubt.

As far as Alexandra was concerned, she had won the first round hands down and was feeling pleased about that, which was fortunate, because she needed some positive feelings to counteract the tight knot of misery her leave-taking was causing. Her last glimpse of her father had been all too brief, but her memory of it was engraved in her mind.

She'd paused momentarily in front of the house, where he'd been standing on the porch, but only to give him one last opportunity to prevent her from leaving home. She hadn't even drawn close, had remained on the road, and when it was apparent that he wasn't going to say the words that she needed to hear, she said, "Good-bye, Papa," so softly that it was doubtful he'd heard. And that had been all she'd said, no hug, no kiss, no pleading for him to change his mind.

Her father had been hurt by her unforgiving attitude. She'd seen it in his face before she had ridden on, and it had brought such a tightness to her chest that she'd thought she would suffocate from it. But her own hurt had forbidden her to soften and bid him a proper good-bye.

And her own hurt was making her decide that she would never see him again after today. She'd get the count to end the damn betrothal in order to satisfy her honor, but she wouldn't go back home. She'd go to England instead. That was what she should have done three years ago.

Alexandra was tired by the time they finally reached the posting house. It was late at night, just as Vasili had predicted it would be, and although she was satisfied with the way the day had gone, she wasn't going to repeat the arduous pace tomorrow.

The wagons were supposed to delay the trip, not keep everyone in the saddle longer to make up for lost time. Besides, she didn't like her animals traveling in the dark, where unseen potholes might crop up to cause injury. If they couldn't reach the next posting house, town, or village before dark tomorrow, they would camp beside the road, with or without her betrothed's permission or presence.

She didn't wait for his presence now before entering the posting house. She'd been there before on a trip west to purchase one of her mares, so she knew the proprietor and took it upon herself to order the necessary number of rooms for the night. She'd be sharing hers with Nina. The men could divide the remaining four however they liked.

Since Vasili would be paying the bill, she would have ordered more rooms if they had been available. As it was, with twelve in her party, he had a lot more mouths to feed than he'd counted on, and she also took it upon herself to order food for everyone. She didn't go overboard there, because she couldn't see food going to waste. But how nice it would be if Vasili ran out of money before he got home.

She waited for the others in the common room. Nina was the first to join her there. The maid had ridden on one of the wagons because she was not as comfortable riding for long hours on horseback as Alexandra was. So they hadn't had a chance to talk all day, but Alexandra wasn't all that surprised by what was prominently on her friend's mind.

"You didn't tell me he's the most handsome man you've ever seen in your life," Nina said accusingly as she sat down at Alexandra's table.

Alexandra raised a brow. "How do you know I haven't seen better?"

"Because no man can be more handsome than that," Nina said with absolute conviction.

Alexandra had already drawn that conclusion for herself, so she didn't bother to argue about it. "Is that supposed to make some sort of difference?"

"It would to me."

Alexandra sighed. "Nina, the man is *too* handsome. If you haven't realized what significance that has, then I'll be pleased to tell you. It's already got you looking on him favorably again, when last I heard, you were on my side. And it got one, two, or all three of the housemaids to sleep with him last night, even though they knew he was my betrothed."

Nina gasped. "How do you know that?"

"Because I found all three of them crawling all over him this morning."

"Which doesn't mean he slept with them," Nina was quick to point out.

"No, but it proves he's irresistible to women, at least to most woman. It also proves that even if he's married, women will still be chasing him. Am I supposed to *live* with that? I don't think so."

Nina still wasn't convinced. "Chasing doesn't mean catching."

"But it does mean constant temptation coming his way," Alexandra replied. "And I don't intend to turn into a jealous shrew for any man."

Nina grinned. "You're saying you *could* love him if you gave it a try."

"I'm saying no such thing, and be quiet, your brothers are coming."

Stenka took the chair next to Alexandra and, like his sister, skipped a greeting in order to get straight to his own complaint. "It would have been simpler and less exhausting to beat him up and warn him off, Alex."

Timofee arrived to catch only the end of that comment. As he took his seat, he asked, "Are we going to beat the Cardinian up? We should have done it this morning, before I developed saddle sores."

And Konrad, the last to arrive, addressed only the portion he caught. "Saddle sores, Alex? You? Your arse should be tough as—"

"That's enough," Alexandra interrupted, and she looked at each of them separately as she said, "No, no, and no," in answer to their remarks. "I've already explained my plan to you, and you agreed it's a good one. We'll give it a chance

123

before I consider any other options. But beating him up isn't going to be one of them."

"A shame," Stenka said with a sigh.

She gave him a stern look before continuing. "Rest assured, we won't have another day like today. He's trying to keep us on *his* schedule, and even if we can manage it much easier than he can, I won't wait for him to give it up, not with my babies along. Speaking of which, have they been settled in for the night?"

"They're rigging up a separate corral for the mares, since they aren't equipped for so many horses here," Timofee told her. "It will do for one night."

They went on to discuss a few other matters pertinent to traveling, but were interrupted when Vasili finally made an appearance with his friend, Lazar Dimitrieff. That one had approached Alexandra earlier in the day to introduce himself. She hadn't been a bit surprised to find out that he'd purchased one of her father's whites and was riding him, a gelding she knew to be of easy temperament.

Ordinarily she would have discussed the merits of the animal with him, would have enjoyed doing so and at length, but she had decided not to be friendly to *anyone* in Vasili's group, and that included Count Dimitrieff, which was a shame, because he seemed quite likable, and they obviously had a love of fine horseflesh in common. It didn't take him long, though, to give up trying to instigate a conversation with her when she all but ignored him.

She had deigned to share a few words with him

only because he'd asked about Nina. "Who's the little cherub?" had been his exact question.

"My maid, Nina Razin."

"Related to those Cossacks?"

"Their only sister," she had told him.

Her reply had produced a drawn-out sigh. "And here I thought I just might enjoy the trip home."

She had wanted to laugh at his forlorn expression, it was so funny. Instead she had warned him, "You'll stay away from Nina—unless she wants to be bothered." And she had said no more.

She wondered now if he had informed Vasili of her rudeness. She certainly hoped so. She wanted him to know that her contempt wasn't reserved just for him, and that his friends and family weren't going to be immune from it.

Vasili gave her only a cursory glance upon his entrance. There was one seat left at her table, but she was sure he wouldn't take it. But then, as long as he could witness her table manners, which were going to be atrocious for his benefit, it didn't matter where he sat.

He stopped to speak to the proprietor for a few moments, probably finding out that there was nothing left for him to arrange, that she'd taken care of everything. She hoped that would annoy him, which was why she'd done it. Men did have a habit of liking to think they were in charge.

Watching him closely, she could discern no indication that he was hearing anything that might disturb him. Then there was a squeal across the room, made by one of the two serving girls, this one having just noticed him. And the girl apparently knew him, because the pleased noise was followed by her rushing across the room to him.

Alexandra's brows went up, then came abruptly together when she saw the smile Vasili bestowed on the girl, a smile so beautiful that Alexandra drew in her breath, and she wasn't even the recipient of it. The girl wasn't exceptionally pretty, but the way Vasili was looking at her, you'd have thought she was the loveliest creature he'd ever seen.

When she reached him, he leaned close to whisper something in her ear. She laughed and placed a hand intimately on his chest before answering him. His hand came to her derriere for a pat before she sauntered away to return to her work, though she cast more than one sultry glance back over her shoulder at him. Any half-wit could have figured out that they'd just made an assignation for later.

Alexandra left her table and caught up with the girl as she was about to leave the room for the kitchen. Without warning—Alexandra hadn't known what she was going to do when she started across the room—she grabbed a fistful of the girl's hair and jerked her around. The tray she was holding went flying from her fingers. If people had not been looking in their direction before, they were now.

"That's my betrothed you were thinking about bedding," Alexandra said, her voice actually quite casual for such a volatile subject. "Go anywhere near him again and I'll cut off your ears and make you eat them. Or perhaps you consider him worth the loss?"

"No, Baroness," the girl squeaked, her eyes wide and her complexion gone white.

Alexandra frowned. "You know me?"

"Y-yes, Baroness."

"So you know I mean what I say?"

"Yes!"

"Good. Then let us hope I don't have to speak to you again."

Alexandra returned to her table. She didn't glance at Vasili as she passed him. She was rather amazed at herself, not for what she'd said, but for having been able to cause a scene like that without feeling the least bit embarrassed. Proving to her betrothed that she was far below his social stratum was going to be much easier than she'd thought.

"Was he shocked?" she whispered to Stenka as she resumed her seat.

"I couldn't say," he answered honestly, his eyes twinkling. "I couldn't take my eyes off you and such a splendid display of jealousy."

"Don't be absurd," she said irritably. "I only did it for his benefit."

That got her a snort and a scoffing tone as he replied, "This is Stenka, Alex. I know just how possessive you can be. I was there, remember, when you took a horsewhip to that army lieutenant when he abused the horse you let him borrow. You never hesitated to light into Konrad with both fists whenever he made Nina cry with his teasing. You blistered my father's ears the last time he took a strap to me—let me know when you've heard enough."

That got *him* a scowl. "You and your family are different. So are my animals."

"We are yours, and what's yours is yours. Everyone who knows you knows that, Alex. And until one or the other of you breaks that betrothal, the Cardinian is also yours, so where is the difference?"

"The difference is, I don't want him to be mine." And then she looked at the rest of her friends. "Did at least one of you notice his reaction?"

"I did," Konrad admitted, a partial grin touching his lips. "And it wasn't shock he was experiencing. Anger was more like it."

Alexandra still didn't look for herself to see it, but she sat back, quite satisfied. "That will do just as well. I warned him what to expect. Now he knows I wasn't spouting empty threats."

"I'd say he's figured that out," Timofee put in with a chuckle. "It's going to be interesting to see what he does about it."

"What can he do?" she countered without concern. "We aren't married yet."

The three men just stared at her. Nina did the opposite and looked in another direction. Alexandra began to squirm in her seat.

"What?" she demanded.

"A betrothal isn't like your usual engagement, Alex," Konrad told her. "It's damn close to actually being married. Sworn oaths were made. Even you gave your word you'd marry him, and your father likely apprised him of it. That gives the man some definite authority where you're concerned, or didn't you know that?"

"What kind of authority?"

Konrad didn't mince words. "The same authority a husband would have."

"Nonsense. I already told him he couldn't dictate to me, and he didn't try to prove otherwise." She didn't bother to mention that he *had* insisted that he could, in fact, do just that.

"You were still at home when you said it, under your father's rule. Now you're not."

She really didn't like the sound of this. "It makes no difference where I was," she insisted. "He can rail at me and complain all he wants. I'm quite experienced by now at ignoring angry men."

"An angry father, yes, but not an angry betrothed," Konrad pointed out. "I hate to say it, Alex, but the two are not the same."

"All right, damn it," she practically growled. "Just what are you getting at?"

"What happens if he starts giving you some 'or elses' and backs them up?"

Her eyes narrowed at that, but her tone turned excessively dry. "You aren't by any chance suggesting that the man might try to beat me, are you?"

"Actually—yes."

"And you'd simply stand around and let him, I suppose? And Bojik wouldn't rip his throat out if he tried?"

"Bojik isn't going to be at your heels every moment of the day," Konrad informed her. "Most nights he'll be put in the stable, where he is now, since most inns won't allow him inside.

129

And we aren't going to be at your side constantly either. We might be able to make the Cardinian regret whatever he does to you, but that would be after the fact. And a king's cousin, regardless of the less-than-impressive title he carries, ranks higher than any of our princes, and you know how powerful they are. It wouldn't be all that difficult for him to get us tossed in jail. Hell, he could have us shot, and no one would do anything to him for it. *That's* the kind of authority he can wield."

Alexandra was simmering by now. "Is there a point to all of this?"

Konrad finally grinned at her, now that he'd ruined her mood. "Just don't get him *too* mad, Alex. Find out your limit and don't overstep it, even if you have to give in to his demands occasionally—and hope *he* hasn't realized how much power he has over you now."

It was too late to hope for that, she was almost certain. And if she had been naive in thinking her friends could protect her in any given situation, they were forgetting that she didn't do so bad at protecting herself. Give in, indeed. She'd start carrying a horsewhip first.

13

The food had been served, but it sat untouched in front of Vasili. Lazar, who was sharing his table, had no trouble making headway through the plain but filling meal. Vasili was making headway through a bottle of vodka instead.

He'd been angry all day after being unable to get Alexandra to leave those damn wagons behind, but what he was feeling now was a bit more on the explosive side. His anger had escalated when the meal arrived, the girl delivering it barely looking at him, hurrying away, terrified that she might draw his notice. The other wench—he still couldn't recall her name—had disappeared completely, nor did he expect to see her again. He recognized absolute fear when he saw it. At the moment, he'd like to see it on the face of his betrothed.

It was beyond belief what he'd witnessed, what the entire room had witnessed. Such barbarous behavior, such viciousness. She couldn't bring her complaint to him, could she? She couldn't make her threats in private, as any civilized person would have. She had to demonstrate for one and all what a little savage she was. And this was the woman his father had chosen for him to marry.

Vasili and Lazar had been friends long enough for Lazar to know what was on Vasili's mind without asking. But he just couldn't sympathize, and actually was quietly amused. Because of his incredible looks, Vasili *never* had trouble with women, at least not this kind. It would do him a world of good to find out what other men had to deal with from the fairer sex.

"You might as well forget it," Lazar offered, his tone neutral.

Those golden eyes, presently glowing, came to meet Lazar's blue ones. "Forget that my bed is going to be empty again tonight, when I had been looking forward to sharing it with that very accommodating wench? Or forget that my betrothed is a walking, breathing scandal?"

Lazar nearly choked as he tried to cut off the laughter that Vasili's last comment had prompted. "Forget both," he managed to suggest. "Your bed was filled to its usual capacity nearly the entire trip here, so a little abstinence on the way back isn't going to kill you."

Vasili wasn't so sure of that, considering the way he'd been feeling since last night, but he replied, "Certainly it won't, but you're overlooking the fact that my dalliance was for Alexandra's benefit more than for my own. It was supposed to enrage her enough to cry off, not to allow her to demonstrate an unexpected tendency toward violence."

"Or bluffing."

"I wish I could believe that, Lazar. I really did think exactly that when she first made the threat to do what she did tonight. But she's done just what she said she'd do if I attempted to entertain myself with another woman—cause an embarrassing public scene. Can you imagine her doing something like that at Stefan's court?"

Lazar grinned. "Stefan might find it amusing. I know Tanya would."

"And my mother would collapse from the shock. I have *got* to get rid of the little barbarian before we reach Cardinia. But tell me how I'm to do that when she has effectively taken away one of my better means of accomplishing it."

"But you do have other means," Lazar reminded him. "Which, by the way, you can't put to use when you're sitting across the room from her."

"If I were sitting next to her, I would have throttled her by now," Vasili replied. "I still may."

He was not exaggerating. While he still felt such a strong urge to wring her pretty neck, he had been avoiding even glancing in her direction. Yet thinking about it, he did just that. He didn't expect to be astonished, however, or momentarily to forget his anger.

Alexandra had a chicken leg in one hand that she was waving around as she spoke to her companions. There was a leaf of boiled cabbage in her other hand, a rather large leaf, that she managed to stuff into her mouth with her fingers. She was drinking the wine she had ordered straight from the bottle. Even the bread she ate she dipped into the butter instead of spreading it with a knife. In the five minutes that he stared, utterly amazed, she didn't once reach for the utensils that lay unused beside her plate.

It came to him then, with swift and thrilling

relief, that the answer to his dilemma was Alexandra herself. And it wouldn't even have occurred to him if he hadn't just mentioned his mother and the shock she was going to suffer if she had to witness a scene like the one he had viewed tonight. But that and this combined, and heaven knew what else, were going to so revolt his mother, there would be no question of a wedding. She would absolutely forbid it.

"Jesus, Lazar, I may not have to do another thing except take her home and let her dine with my mother. Look at her. She has the table manners of a pig."

"I'd already noticed, just forbore mentioning it," Lazar replied, humor in his tone. "I take it you're not excessively appalled?"

"Are you joking? I couldn't be more delighted. I'm not going to have to break off this betrothal, and neither is she. If my mother can spend just one day with her, and I'll make sure she does, *she* will refuse to let me marry her, and that'll be the end of it."

"Are you going to depend on that when Maria's fondest wish is to see you wed?"

Vasili frowned at that depressing reminder. "A good point. I will proceed as planned, yet I'm happy to say the urgency is gone. I no longer have any doubt that this matter will right itself."

"You had doubts?"

"I was close to terrified, if you must know," Vasili said with little exaggeration.

Lazar snorted. "I don't see why. If you had to take a wife, this one is at least easy on the eyes, full of surprises, which is not a bad thing, and you could always teach her some proper manners. She also glows with good health, which means she'd have no trouble supplying you with a great many heirs."

"*If* I was looking for a wife, everything you've said is true, I suppose. But you've left out a few important facts. Alexandra's attitude happens to really irritate me, I don't particularly like her, and I can name a dozen women who would suit me better *and* who wouldn't tell me they don't want to marry me."

Lazar couldn't resist chuckling. "Is that still twisting the screw?"

"Don't be absurd," Vasili replied and went on to insist, "Her reluctance was merely a surprise, and as it happens, a fortuitous one. I had been dreading the possibility of having to deal with her hurt feelings before she got angry enough to call this off."

Lazar nodded, as if he truly believed that. "Now you'll earn her eternal gratitude for proving to be so unacceptable to her that she has the excuse she needs to end it. I wouldn't be surprised if she laughs all the way home."

That remark had Vasili scowling, though he wasn't even aware he was doing it, and he still said, "I'm the one who will be eternally grateful that she's such a backwater provincial. Her father said she was unique, he just didn't specify how. Do you think those three Cossacks are her lovers?"

The question was so unexpected, Lazar choked, literally, his food going down the wrong way. It took him a full minute of coughing and throat-clearing before he was able to glare at Vasili and say with rancor, "Just because you think nothing of pleasuring three women at the same time doesn't mean your betrothed would consider trying the same."

Vasili had meant nothing of the kind and was amused that Lazar thought he had. "Oh, I don't know. Countess Eva managed four once—or so I've heard."

Lazar blinked. "Four? How?"

"One can only imagine. But that certainly wasn't what I meant about Alexandra. It takes a degree of sophistication to even think of such amusements, which we can unanimously agree she lacks. I meant individually, singly—how shall I put this?—one at a time."

Lazar was glaring again. "Save the sarcasm for the little lady, will you? With me it's liable to get you a bloody nose."

Vasili was in the habit of being provocative with his friends regardless of consequences, so he ignored Lazar's threat as he always did. However, he was too interested in the subject he had introduced to continue needling Lazar as he might have done otherwise.

"Let's get back to my question, shall we?" he said. "Those three Cossacks might be ugly as sin, but we know how insignificant looks are when there is a need. And it would supply one more reason why she doesn't want to marry, if she's got her own studs working for her."

"Dare I mention that 'if' is a supposition?"

"You can mention it, but I wouldn't buy it—and neither do you."

136

Lazar shrugged, inclined to agree after their tour of St. Petersburg. He didn't think the three burly men were that ugly, however, but that was a moot point. "What does it matter if she's slept with one of them or all?"

"It doesn't, except that if she's going to continue to curtail my amusements, and I have little doubt that she intends to do just that, I'm damned if I'll allow her any of her own on this trip."

"I suppose that's only fair." Then Lazar grinned, his humor restored. "Do you plan to threaten them the way she threatened the serving wench?"

"If I have to," Vasili growled.

And since Lazar had only been teasing, he groaned and said no more.

14

It wasn't easy to abandon twenty-five years of refined breeding. There were times when a little dirt was acceptable, when one's job was a dirty job. Then there were times when one had to remain spotlessly clean. Alexandra knew both times very well, but bringing the two together took constant concentration on her part. Her friends weren't helping in that respect.

Timofee kept looking as if he were going to burst into laughter at any moment. Stenka was teasing Alexandra by copying her actions. Konrad couldn't keep the disapproval from his expression, but fortunately, he wasn't sitting where Vasili could see him.

Somehow she managed just fine, and only had one near blunder when she started to reach for her napkin at the end of the messy meal. But she caught herself in time and licked her fingers instead, then wiped her sticky hands on her clothes, mentally grimacing as she did so. It was a nice touch, however. She might even wear the same clothes tomorrow, possibly even longer.

Actually, that wasn't a bad idea at all. By the end of the week, she ought to be reeking. The oh-so-impeccably groomed count from Cardinia would have to stand upwind of her if he wanted to have words with her. She could convince him that she found bathing unhealthy and never bathed more than once a month.

As for convincing, she was sure she'd done a splendid job of it with the meal. She had known to the second, without looking to confirm it, when Vasili had started watching her. It had been a disturbing sensation, to actually *feel* those honey-gold eyes on her. But he had to be disgusted, maybe even revolted. She knew she would have been if she'd been able to watch herself.

Perhaps she went a little too far when she left the common room with her friends, still not glancing in Vasili's direction, passing near his table yet pointedly ignoring him. Common courtesy demanded at least an acknowledgment of his presence, which she hadn't given him all evening. He was her betrothed, after all. But for the time being, common courtesy was on the list of prohibitions she had made for herself, and she had to be scrupulously consistent about adhering to it if she wanted her plan to work.

Yet she had to wonder, when he showed up at her door a while later, if that last bit of rudeness on her part hadn't goaded him to visit her.

She certainly hadn't expected his sudden appearance. She was already dressed for bed in one of her plain white cotton nightgowns. Nina had already brushed out her hair and was still mumbling under her breath about the bath she'd ordered that Alexandra had refused to make use of. Nina was presently brushing the dust from their clothes with a few extra grumbles about the food stains she'd been told to leave alone. She

139

didn't even hear the knock at the door, not that Alexandra expected her to answer it.

She answered it herself, by habit pulling on the dark blue velvet robe that had been laid out for her. Modest by nature, she was grateful for the robe when she saw who stood there. She even drew the garment closer to her throat and held it there with both hands, a reflexive defense against the potent masculinity that exuded from the man who was her betrothed.

He said nothing at first, his eyes moving slowly over her—they seemed lighter in color than she remembered—finally resting on her hair, which flowed over her shoulders in shining waves. Those few moments of silence unnerved her, and she was further unsettled when it seemed he had to force his eyes away from her to scan the room.

When he saw Nina, he said to her, "Your mistress and I require a few minutes of privacy."

Nina responded to his commanding tone with a quick nod and headed straight for the door. Alexandra bristled at his presumption *and* her friend's defection. The last thing she wanted was to be left alone with him, especially after all those gloomy predictions the Razins had made.

So her voice was a bit sharp when she said, "You don't have to leave, Nina."

No one paid her the least attention. Vasili stepped into the room, held the door for Nina's exit, and closed it behind her. Alexandra considered shouting before Nina got out of earshot, for her not to go far, but that smacked too much of cowardice.

Besides, whatever worry she felt was overridden by pure annoyance, which was unmistakable in her tone. "Couldn't this wait until tomorrow, Petroff?"

His eyes came back to her. Were they even brighter now? Impossible.

"No, it can't wait, not if I'm going to get any sleep," he replied as he took the step that narrowed the distance between them and forced her to tilt her head if she wanted to maintain eye contact with him. "You do want me to get some sleep, don't you, Alexandra?"

His tone sounded too ominous by half. "Are you actually assuming it matters to me one way or the other?"

"It should." His tone became even softer. "You see, I've just discovered I'm rather perverse and selfish in that respect. If my needs aren't seen to, why, then, I ask myself, should yours be?"

Alexandra hated to say it, but had to. "Are we talking about sleep?"

"Are we?" As he said it, he reached for a lock of her hair that rested on her shoulder, and rubbed it between his fingers. "So this is what it looks like," he added to himself. Spun moonbeams came to mind.

Vasili wasn't sure what he was doing. Anger had brought him here and it was still with him, but now it was more self-directed, and not the only emotion he had to deal with. That damn dinner. He'd never forget it, and how he'd gone from fury to satisfaction and back to fury again, ending up furious with himself rather than *her*.

He shouldn't have continued to watch Alexandra and her appalling eating habits. He should have taken his satisfaction and relief to bed with him, and the serving wench, too, despite the fact that he no longer found her appealing. But he hadn't left the common room soon enough. And so he'd witnessed the very sensual way Alexandra had licked her fingers, which had instantly stirred his senses to vibrant life.

He'd groaned then. He groaned again now, though silently, because he still didn't have his desire under control. It was intolerable that he could want her again when he despised every-thing about her: her manners, her morals, her apparent vicious tendencies.

He recalled those vicious tendencies and that embarrassing scene he had suffered through, and remarked none too pleasantly, "What a little savage you are, sweetheart."

Alexandra should have been pleased, delighted, even laughing over his derision, so she had no business blushing, yet that was what she was doing. And it got worse when he added with a deliberate sneer, "Tell me, do you bring that kind of passion to your bed?"

Stiffly, she replied, "You don't expect me to answer that, do you?"

"Maybe I expect to find out firsthand."

Had she been blushing before? She could swear she was giving off steam now.

"I wouldn't have thought you'd be in such a hurry to seal our fate."

He cocked a brow at her in a look that was designed to provoke by its very arrogance. "Is that remark supposed to be pertinent to anything?"

"You'd be forcing this marriage, which would

put an end to any mind-changing for either of us."

He actually laughed before he told her, "Don't be absurd, Alex. What's one more lover to you when you've already had so many?"

By his expression, she realized he wasn't merely trying to offend her this time. He really believed what he'd just said—which gave her a horribly contradictory feeling. She was glad, she truly was, that he could think such a thing about her, because it could aid her own plan. So why did she feel insulted?

She tried, desperately, to change the subject by picking one word out of what he'd just said. "Only my friends get to call me that," she stated, in reference to the "Alex" he'd used.

His smile was condescending, as if he were about to explain something to a simpleton. "But I'm more than a friend. I'm soon to be your husband, with all the rights that entails. Shall we have a demonstration of some of those rights?"

"The only demonstration you'll be giving is how to leave a room in a hurry. You can begin now."

His answer was to grab her shoulders and slowly pull her toward him. The unexpected move brought her hands away from her throat to brace flat against his chest so she could push. Her effort was useless. He didn't budge.

Only he noticed that her robe fell open. With her excessively modest nightgown it shouldn't have mattered, and it wouldn't have if she didn't have such large breasts that were no longer hidden beneath her arms. His eyes were drawn to the unbound pair instantly.

He drew her closer to him. Her braced arms were actually bending . . .

"What the hell do you think you're doing, Petroff?" she demanded, grateful not to hear the panic she was feeling in her voice.

He heard it, and ignored it. "I'm thinking I'm going to find out what you taste like."

"No!"

Her refusal wasn't too late, it was merely ignored. His strong arms were drawing her so close now that she was flush with his body, feeling more of it than she'd ever hoped to feel. And warm lips took care of any more protests she'd been about to make, at least temporarily. Shock took care of the rest.

Not once had she considered that this might be one of the dangers of this trip. How could she have, when she knew exactly how Vasili felt about marrying her, and he knew she felt exactly the same? Yet here she stood, wrapped in his arms, being kissed by him. The shock came from discovering immediately that Christopher hadn't taught her all there was to know about kissing, as she'd naively thought.

She'd been thrilled with Christopher's kisses because she loved him, but the truth was, he knew next to nothing about kissing compared with this man. This man consumed her senses and controlled every one of them, and not just with his mouth, but with his body. The hand he placed on her back kept her from retreating from the slow rub and press of his chest, which gave her the oddest feeling, as if her breasts were being caressed and kneaded by turns. The position of his other hand on the soft curve of her behind was even worse, lifting her as it did until the hard bulge of him was settled directly at the juncture of her legs. She was assailed on every sensual front, overwhelmed by sensations newly discovered, and all the while his tongue made a deep, erotic foray into her mouth to complete the destruction of her will.

Vasili was no less caught in the storm of his own creation. What had started as a means to coerce her into backing down from her threat of public scenes became something else entirely. The second he felt the weight of those luscious breasts against him, she became simply a very desirable woman. And Vasili never denied himself desirable women, especially when a bed was near at hand and the door firmly closed . . .

The door opened abruptly, slammed open, actually. Vasili and Alexandra separated just as abruptly, she in somewhat of a daze, he scowling at the intruder.

"Sorry," Nina offered for the noise, but the reason for it was apparent when they noted she had her hands full trying to restrain the huge wolfhound that was determined to charge Alexandra with a greeting. "He was whining and disturbing all the horses," she said by way of explanation for Bojik's presence.

It was a blatant lie and Alexandra knew it, so she forgave Nina for her earlier defection—until the girl added, albeit innocently, "He's not going to be happy until he's sleeping with you, Alex."

They all three blushed within seconds after that last statement, each of them thinking of a "he" other than Bojik—and that they were all thinking the same thing, and knew it, made it so much worse.

Alexandra went down on one knee to summon her pet, and the way he flew out of Nina's grip proved how little control she'd actually had of him. Alexandra hid her hot cheek against Bojik's neck as she said frostily, "Good night, Petroff. And in the future, if you wish to speak to me, you will do so in public, at a decent hour."

"Don't count on it—Alex."

After the door closed again, loudly, Nina remarked in a subdued tone, "You're lucky you didn't see his face when he said that."

Alexandra glanced up now, but still made a quick scan of the room to assure herself he was really gone, before she asked, "Why?"

"Because as expression go, his said he meant it."

15

If Vasili accomplished anything during his visit to Alexandra's room, it was ensuring that Alexandra shared his anticipated lack of sleep that night. She could not stop thinking about his kiss and the unexpected feelings it had produced in her, sensations she had never known she *could* feel. She also berated herself for standing there like a half-wit and letting him do that to her, regardless of the fact that she knew perfectly well she'd been too stunned to do anything but let him. Which wouldn't happen again, she promised herself. Not that there would be any more kissing with him at all, she also promised herself.

Mostly, though, she spent long hours trying to figure out why Vasili had kissed her at all, because she certainly didn't believe that it had had anything to do with keeping her awake, as he'd suggested, even if that was exactly what it had done. And what, heaven help her, would have happened if Nina hadn't come back when she had?

Alexandra would have liked to think she would have come to her senses and shouted for the Razin brothers, who were sleeping in the room next to hers. But she couldn't be sure of anything last night.

This morning, however, with a lack of sleep making her irritable, she was much more sure about what she would have done. She wouldn't have done any shouting, but would have slapped that profligate rake soundly for his effort, then warned him graphically what would happen if he ever tried it again. She had a new image to uphold, after all, and the new, ill-mannered, crude, outlandish Alexandra wouldn't tolerate being trifled with by that master seducer, even if he *did* think he had some rights where she was concerned.

Hadn't she proved just that the previous evening in the common room? She had pulled that public scene off beautifully, yet she wished she hadn't had an underlying fury goading her. His propositioning another woman, right in front of her, shouldn't have affected her. She'd been warned it would happen, and it merely confirmed that he was the despicable man she had already guessed him to be. But that, too, accounted for some tossing and turning last night.

Alexandra was the last to arrive at the stables for departure, which didn't help her disposition any. If that golden popinjay had gotten a good night's sleep after disturbing hers, she'd have a score to settle that had nothing to do with her plan to get rid of her betrothed.

The wagons had already been sent on their way and were far down the road, as were most of her horses. Stenka held Prince Mischa in readiness for her. Vasili, who was mounted on his roan stallion, was close enough to her horse that it was obvious he was waiting for her. To have more words? She'd be happy to oblige him.

The look he gave her could have been merely

inquiring, but she saw more in it than that—gloating smugness, to be exact. So the moment she mounted she turned to him and asked, "Why did you kiss me last night?"

Vasili said nothing for a moment, and not because he was waiting for Stenka to move out of hearing distance. He was gritting his teeth against his surprise. He *would* get used to her bluntness. The advantage it gave her by catching him off guard like this was intolerable.

Finally, tight-lipped, he gave her an answer. "The little wench I would have been kissing last night took fright and disappeared."

When he ended there, she was forced to draw her own conclusion. "Ah, I see. If you don't get your first choice, you settle for second? But I have a third option for you that you would be wise to consider. Keep your pants on, Petroff—at least until you break this betrothal."

She smiled as she said the last part. He smiled right back at her and leaned forward to reach for her neck. She knew exactly what he meant to do—draw her forward to kiss her again, to prove he wouldn't be dictated to. With a nudge and a yank from Alexandra, Prince Mischa reared up on his hind legs. Vasili was forced to control his roan, which shied away. Alexandra rode off before he had quite managed it.

She considered that round hers—for all of five minutes. That was how long it took Vasili to catch up with her and literally lift her off her horse and onto his. The action was too unexpected and not the least bit pleasant. By the time he was done situating her for his comfort, she was nestled

149

firmly between his thighs, his arms caging her sideways against his chest. And being that close to him, surrounded by him, recalled to her too many sensations of the previous night.

She pushed those feelings aside to glare up at him. "And what are you going to do now, Petroff—besides make an ass of yourself?"

"Goad me any further, sweetheart, and we'll ride off to locate some private place to find out."

She would as soon not, but didn't say so. Bojik was already barking at the roan's feet, making the stallion sidestep and dance nervously. All three Razin brothers rode up behind them to make their presence felt, Stenka having taken up Prince Micha's reins.

They wouldn't say anything, at least not yet. She didn't want them interfering anyway, and getting on Vasili's bad side. This was not an alarming situation, after all—except to her emotions.

"About my question?" she prompted.

His answer was a curt "Call off the dog."

She would have laughed, if she were in any other position. She lied instead. "Bojik won't listen as long as he thinks I'm in danger."

"You have the best-trained horses I've ever seen. You expect me to believe you wouldn't give the same discipline to your dog?"

He was playing unfairly, making a comment that she had to accept as a compliment. Her horses were her pride and joy. She couldn't help being pleased that he'd noticed how superbly they handled. Besides, she wasn't going to risk injury to a horse, even his, just because she'd like to get off his lap immediately. So she said Bojik's name in a tone the animal recognized and instantly heeded.

The barking stopped. The big stallion settled down soon after. And Vasili said, "Now you can do the same with your Cossacks."

One concession on her part was enough as far as she was concerned. "When they start barking, I will," she replied in a low grumble.

"I'm going to pretend I didn't hear that."

"And I'll pretend you haven't lost your mind," she shot back.

Suddenly she felt his chest rumbling with laughter. It hadn't been her intention to amuse him, anything but, yet what she was hearing was the sound of genuine humor. And it had him stopping his mount.

"It's about time," she said, but apparently she had said this too soon.

He wasn't putting her down, he was turning to address the Razins. "My betrothed and I are going to talk, to get to know each other better. Ride ahead. We don't need your escort for conversation."

They didn't ride ahead, of course. They stared at Vasili for a moment, then they stared at Alexandra, and she was close to growling, she was so infuriated. Vasili was going to force her to make this concession, too, or pit him against her men, which could have repercussions she didn't want to find out about. Did he *know* she would give in, or would he back down if she didn't? She wasn't going to risk it.

She gave the nod that allowed her friends to

151

depart without worry, but she did it so impercep-
tibly, she hoped Vasili hadn't noticed. And she
thought he might not have when he turned to
follow the Razins and the rest of their party,
though at a much more leisurely pace.

But as soon as they were beyond shouting
distance, he said, "A wise choice."

Since she had no desire to find out what he
meant by that, she ignored it and said instead,
"You don't want to get to *know* me, Petroff, any
more than I want to know you any better, so what
was the point of this?"

"To prove that you are subject to me, whether
you like it or not."

"Well, you certainly made your point, didn't
you?" she replied sourly. "But nothing has been
proved, since your authority requires my cooperation, and my cooperation is in no way
guaranteed."

His arms closed a little tighter around her and
his head bent forward until his lips were very near
to her ear. "Then perhaps I should extract a few
promises from you," he said in a voice she recognized as seductive because of what it made her
feel.

Her elbow to his belly worked to gain her some
breathing space, but only because he wasn't
expecting it. "No promises, Petroff. Not a single
one. And we've had enough point-proving *and*
talk, so put me down."

"When you say please, very, *very* nicely," he
said in a soft hiss.

She'd managed to make him angry, probably
with her elbow. But she was just as angry that

152

he'd made her panic enough to hit him. "Go to hell," was her curt reply, but it didn't get her put down.

He continued at a mere walk, still maintaining a far distance from the rest of their group. Her silence said he wasn't going to get the "please" he'd requested, so she wondered how long he would make them suffer this uncomfortable ride before joining the others. Could he be as stubborn as she was?

"I believe it was mentioned that you have sisters," he said suddenly, proving that he was curious about her, if only mildly. "Are they . . . like you?"

Curiosity? Or was he paving the way for more insults?

"They are nothing like me," she answered hesitantly. "I was never all that close to either of them. They had their interests, and I had mine."

"And your interest would be breeding horses."

She detected the censure, and replied defensively. "Just because I'm a woman doesn't mean—"

"I wasn't criticizing you," he cut in.

"Weren't you? I doubt that. But it certainly doesn't matter to me *what* you think."

Now his tone turned dry. "So I've gathered."

When he fell silent again, she decided she might as well catch up on some lost sleep. Her back was supported by his arm. She just had to lean her head against his chest . . .

"Usually when a woman is this close to me, I am compelled to touch her," Vasili remarked offhandedly. "Since most of the time you don't look like a woman in your ridiculous attire, except for those lovely breasts of yours, I can probably restrain myself—for a while."

Alexandra's eyes rounded incredulously. All thoughts of sleep were gone, all thoughts of escape prevalent. But she wasn't ready to say "Please" yet.

"That isn't funny, Petroff."

"Actually, it's something of a joke, and I don't find it amusing either, since it's on me."

She refused to ask for an explanation that she was sure she wouldn't like. "Put me down."

"Say please."

"Dammit, put me down!"

It looked like he was going to when he put both reins in the hand whose arm was supporting her. That left his other hand free, but instead of using it to lower her to the ground, he lifted her chin so that she was staring at him as his head began to lower.

"I did try," he said in a husky whisper.

She was mesmerized, for all of two breathless seconds. Then the fear of being lost to those same sensations she had experienced last night had her bursting out with "Please, please, please."

For a brief moment, he looked disappointed that she'd given in. And then he found satisfaction in winning. Another moment and she was on the ground, and had to suffer that smug smile looking down at her.

"There is a lesson to be learned here, sweetheart," he said with a heavy dose of arrogance. "It pays to give in sooner, because delay will cause nothing but unpleasantness."

154

Lesson, or warning? But she didn't have to wonder whether he had changed the subject and was talking about the betrothal now, rather than the "pleases" he'd just got.

"Then it's a lesson you should heed yourself, Petroff," she replied, and then called sharply, "Bojik!"

The wolfhound was at her side almost instantly, barking so loud and viciously that Vasili's stallion took fright this time and raced off at a breakneck speed, not down the road, but across a nearby field. Alexandra grinned as she watched Vasili try to bring the animal under control, and not very successfully. She might have to walk a while until one of the Razins noticed she was on foot and came back for her, but she didn't mind in the least.

She even laughed as she ruffled her dog's hair and started down the road. "He wants to make points, Bojik, but I don't think he's going to like ours, is he?"

16

A full week passed without any further incidents, possibly because Vasili and Alexandra took pains to avoid talking to each other. Both would have preferred to avoid seeing each other as well, but that was impossible to manage, though Vasili certainly gave it his best effort by continuing to ride far ahead of the party each day.

Twice they had camped out in the countryside, and although Alexandra had expected a fight about doing so from the fastidious popinjay, she didn't get one either time. Had she been privy to Vasili's true feelings, she'd have known how close she'd come to inciting one. But Vasili had come to understand in the short time he'd known her that her horses were of paramount importance to her and that she couldn't be budged on the issue of their safety. And truth be known, he didn't like traveling in the dark any more than she did. Had he objected, he would have done so out of sheer contrariness, which wasn't to say that an objection wasn't highly probable in his present state of mind.

He wasn't happy with the progress he was making. Lazar was right: he couldn't leave his fate entirely in his mother's hands. He *did* believe she would forbid the marriage once she saw how far from a lady Alexandra actually was, baroness or not. But there was a slim chance that she might think she could correct Alexandra's faults instead. And although Vasili viewed such an undertaking as an impossibility, he knew his opinion wouldn't be taken into account if his mother made up her mind to try.

Ignoring Alexandra had seemed another ideal solution to his dilemma when it had first occurred to him. Any other woman whom he was involved with wouldn't have stood for such lack of attention on his part. She would have shown him extremes of emotion in retaliation. But Alexandra was not any woman. And that she seemed happy that he was avoiding her annoyed *him* in the extreme. Perhaps he should have seduced her first and *then* ignored her. Damned woman, couldn't she even react properly? Did she have to be different in *every* way?

Even the rare few times they did happen to have words, and he turned on his contempt full blast, it seemed to just roll off her. Vasili was even beginning to suspect that she somehow found his derision amusing. It was nothing that he could put his finger on, no turning of the lips however slight, no crinkling of those pretty blue eyes. It was more an utterly bland look she gave him that was so devoid of expression that it *had* to be suspect.

The fact was, he was out of his element where his betrothed was concerned. He was too used to dealing with women in only one way, with practiced charm and seduction, neither of which was an option with Alexandra if he wanted her to despise him.

It had been a mistake to kiss her, and to nearly

kiss her again, even if it had been an attempt to make her back down from her threat of "public scenes." The mistake had been a serious one for him, because he would rather not have found out how perfectly her body fit to his. And he could definitely have done without discovering that the taste of her was like ambrosia, her hair like spun silk, her skin warm velvet. And to know the feel of those magnificent breasts crushed against him . . .

It had been an even worse mistake not to explore those breasts thoroughly when he'd had the chance, because now he dreamed of fondling them, licking them, biting them. He dreamed of hearing her moan with pleasure beneath him. He had no business dreaming of her at all.

"I can't tell whether they're trying to save you from the embarrassment of Alexandra's causing another scene," Lazar remarked offhandedly, "or if they're abetting her in keeping the wenches away from you."

They were seated in a private dining room tonight, at Vasili's request, yet it was only a small alcove that was open on one side to the common room, where the rest of their party was gathered. Vasili glanced out now to see what Lazar was talking about, and noticed that the Cossack twins, Stenka and Timofee, were both vying for the attentions of the cook's assistant. And the cook herself was being whispered to by the older brother, Konrad, on the other side of the room.

This was a small posting house that employed no serving wenches. Yet the only two women who worked on the premises were being engaged.

158

It had been happening all week. Whatever females were available, the Cossacks got to them first and monopolized their time. Vasili had been brooding too much to really notice or care.

"Whatever they're doing, you can be sure it's not to my benefit," Vasili grumbled in reply.

"Why don't you ride ahead tomorrow to the next town and get it out of your system?" Lazar suggested. "I might even join you."

"An excellent idea, except I don't trust Alexandra to show up in the next town if I do that."

And he wasn't about to let her camp in the countryside without his being there to protect her. He *did* have a duty to her, after all, whether he wanted it or not.

Vasili added in disgust, "Either that, or she *will* show up and tear the town apart until she finds whichever wench I bedded so she can cut her ears off."

Lazar burst out laughing. Vasili scowled, because it wasn't the least bit funny.

"Actually," Lazar said, "I've heard she does much better with a horsewhip than a knife."

"Who told you that?"

"One of her grooms. Something about a young lieutenant who abused one of her horses."

Vasili groaned. "So she really is prone to violence."

"Only in defense of what's hers." Lazar started laughing again before he got out, "And you, my friend, she considers hers."

Vasili gave that remark the silence it deserved,

but a while later, he wondered aloud, "Have you had any luck yourself, Lazar?"

As usual, Lazar had no difficulty following the drift of Vasili's thoughts, even when they weren't fully expressed. "I've been turned down twice due to association," Lazar admitted, since it was women they were still discussing. "Mind you, I'm not complaining. I'm having more fun watching you pulling hairs anyway."

"Don't think I haven't noticed," Vasili replied dryly. "For a friend, your good cheer warms my heart, it's so offensive."

Lazar grinned unrepentantly. "At least one of us is beginning to enjoy this trip."

Vasili waited a while before he asked, "And is my nemesis enjoying herself tonight?"

"Why don't you look for yourself?"

"Because it turns my stomach to watch her when she's eating," Vasili lied.

The truth was, the way Alexandra fed herself with her fingers, then licked them afterward, was too damn erotic for him to watch without becoming aroused every time. He'd stopped watching.

"Actually, those musicians who wandered in a few minutes ago have her full attention now."

Vasili's eyes immediately sought the musicians setting up in a corner of the room. He relaxed only after noting that all three of them were beyond their middle years, with nothing about them to interest a young woman other than the entertainment they could offer . . .

Vasili slumped in his chair, incredulous over what he'd just done. What the hell did he care whom Alexandra might be attracted to? He didn't care.

To prove it, he turned to Lazar and said, "Why don't you seduce her?"

"Why don't I *what?*"

"Not so loud, dammit," Vasili complained. "I wasn't joking."

"Yes, you were," Lazar replied emphatically.

"When it would give me legitimate grounds to take her back to her father, you know I'm not joking. I don't know why I didn't think of it sooner."

"But this is not one of your forget-the-next-day women you don't mind sharing, Vasili. We're talking about your betrothed, chosen by your father, approved by your mother—at least until she meets her—your soon-to-be wife."

"A fact I'm trying to change with a little cooperation from a *friend.*"

"That's dirty. Next you'll tell me you'd do the same thing for me."

"You know I would."

Lazar did know it. He also knew Vasili didn't have a jealous bone in his body, at least where women were concerned, so that wasn't what bothered him. It was that Alexandra wasn't like all those other women, even though Vasili was determined to give her no special distinction.

"It would never work, when she knows she can have you instead," Lazar pointed out. "She doesn't even look at me, and if she looks at me, she doesn't *see* me. I've never been quite so uniquely ignored by a woman before."

"You could at least try."

161

Lazar grimaced, but nodded. "When am I supposed to accomplish this miracle? Tonight?"

That question seemed to startle Vasili. It certainly brought a frown to his brow. "No—you don't want to ruin your chances by being too hasty. Take some time to consider your strategy first. Sleep on it."

Since Lazar wasn't looking forward to the rejection he anticipated, he said, "By all means."

The musicians had started playing a lively folk song by then. Three men got up from their table and began to dance one of the Russian dances traditionally reserved only for men.

The Cossack twins looked on disdainfully. Alexandra was apparently teasing them, because they suddenly got up and joined the dance, and Vasili had to admit they were definitely more exuberant, as well as adept at it.

He knew the dance himself, though it had been years since he'd tried it. It required strong thighs and excellent balance for the kicks and . . . He didn't believe it. Alexandra wouldn't dare . . .

She would. She was actually dancing with the men, and they didn't seem to mind. More of her own men joined in. The shouts were becoming deafening.

Beside him, Lazar said, "I'll be damned—she never ceases to amaze!"

Vasili wasn't listening. He was watching how those baggy pants of hers tightened with each squat and kick, how her breasts bounced when she leapt, how her face glowed with enjoyment.

He had to get a closer view. He didn't have to dance to do so, but that was what he did.

Later that night, in the bed they were sharing because of the shortage of rooms—a problem they were often encountering because of the size of their party—Lazar was still chuckling to himself over Vasili's unexpected participation in that dance. He had acquitted himself well, and Alexandra couldn't have helped but be impressed. It was probably the first agreeable interaction they'd had, and without a word spoken. Too bad they'd both been embarrassed when it was over.

Vasili wasn't sleeping yet either, but it wasn't the dance he was thinking about. He suddenly cleared his throat to say, "Forget I mentioned it."

Once again, Lazar knew exactly what was on his friend's mind, in this case the seduction of his betrothed. "It's already forgotten," Lazar assured him with a great deal of relief.

Vasili didn't let the subject drop there. "You weren't really considering it, were you?"

"I was merely humoring you."

"Good."

Somehow Lazar kept from laughing out loud, but damn, it wasn't easy.

17

Snow greeted them the next morning. The flurries didn't last long and didn't stick to the ground, but the temperature dropped considerably from what it had been the day before. And they weren't anywhere near the mountains yet, where it was going to be much, much colder.

Alexandra loved such weather, but she had too many things on her mind to enjoy it. Her plan wasn't working as swiftly as she had thought it would. Actually, it didn't seem to be working at all.

Not once had Vasili remarked on her disgusting eating habits. The twins had fought one night, and instead of stopping them with a word, as she usually did when she witnessed their tussles, she'd pretended to be fascinated and encouraged them. But Vasili hadn't commented on her bloodthirsty behavior. He hadn't noticed yet that she was beginning to stink, either, though Nina certainly had and frequently complained about it. He hadn't even been properly scandalized last night when she had danced a strictly male dance, and she wasn't going to think about how much fun she'd had, even with him joining in, *particularly* after he'd joined in.

The only thing Vasili had alluded to at all was her unique way of keeping him faithful. If she thought that was all it would take to make him break the betrothal, she could relax, but he hadn't been nearly angry enough the first time she'd used that ploy, proving that much more was needed to finally make him disgusted enough to sever their association. Not that she wasn't going to continue to curtail his sexual peccadillos, publicly and privately. Doing so privately wasn't as satisfying or as scandalous as making a public scene, but he had been careful not to proposition any more women in front of her. Because the embarrassment had been worse than his sexual frustration?

If that was the case, perhaps another "scene" was in order. Maybe a simple demonstration of temper this time, something completely unrelated to Vasili, to show him that even if he was on his best behavior, she could still be an embarrassment to him. The idea had some definite merit, and when she discussed it with the Razins that day, they agreed it couldn't hurt to give it a try.

Timofee volunteered to be the cause of her anger, but Stenka argued that he wanted the privilege, so she assured them it would be a pleasure to scorch both their ears. And the reason? She decided that one wasn't necessary and that if Vasili asked about it, she would merely tell him it was none of his business.

She would have preferred to stage the "scene" in a town, where it would be even more public, but when they didn't reach one before dark that night and ended up making camp again, she was too eager to see Vasili's reaction to postpone the demonstration. She still had to wait, however, because as usual, he was riding far in advance of the party and it would take a while for him to realize they weren't going to catch up with him.

But it took Vasili more than an hour after dark had fallen to return, long enough to make Alexandra begin to suspect that he had found himself a willing woman somewhere up ahead. So when he rode into camp and she immediately began cursing the twins at the top of her lungs, she really was as angry as she sounded.

Unfortunately, her knowledge of vulgarities was rather limited. And not having considered that lack beforehand, Alexandra was forced to pause in her diatribe to whisper to the twins, "I've run out of names to call you. Quickly, give me some more."

Timofee was too busy covering an unrepentant grin with his hands, but Stenka was happy to oblige, and Alexandra's eyes widened and her cheeks bloomed with color as she shouted the new names at him. But with her back to Vasili, he couldn't see her reaction, could merely hear her outrageousness, so she wasn't worried about his noticing her own embarrassment.

She was impatient to know his reaction, however, and couldn't resist another whisper to Stenka. "Is he properly scandalized yet?"

"I hate to say it, Alex, but he's laughing."

She was too surprised to answer for a moment, but then her shoulders dropped and she said in disgust, "Well, hell, what does it take to shock that man?"

Stenka could no longer hold back his own chuckles. "You could try dancing naked around the camp. That ought to get a reaction out of him, and the rest of us would, of course, look the other way."

"Of course you would," she replied dryly before tossing out a few more invectives for each of them, this time quite sincerely.

She marched off then, annoyed with them, annoyed with herself for somehow failing at her objective—again—and furious with Vasili for not reacting as he ought to. *Why* would he be amused to hear such terrible language coming out of her mouth? Didn't he realize that if she could do something like this here, she could as easily do it in a drawing room where his king might be present?

He sought her out among the horses, where she had gone to take advantage of the soothing effect they usually had on her. Usually. It wasn't working tonight. She continued to move among them, though, ignoring the presence she felt behind her, knowing instinctively who it was. And that was another thing that kept her from calming down. She didn't *like* it that she was able to sense Vasili, just as her mares could sense when one of the stallions came near.

He didn't wait for her to turn around and acknowledge him. "Perhaps you will tell me why you were so angry with your Cossacks."

"Why should I?"

"Because I ask."

She changed her mind about saying it was none of his business, for the horses gave her an adequate lie. She turned to give it to Vasili, but, as happened too frequently, she was disturbed

167

by his handsomeness. Anytime she was this close to him, she found it difficult to breathe, much less have a conversation.

But she finally got out, "They let Prince Mischa cover one of the mares today."

"So?"

"So they know I am to be present for every breeding," she explained, and that much was true.

"You actually watch?"

From his expression, she realized she had finally shocked him, and by something she *did* do, rather than what she'd been doing only for his benefit.

"Of course I watch. These are my babies, and I have better control over them than anyone else. I have to assure that the mares aren't hurt— exactly as any other conscientious breeder would do."

"But—"

"Yes?"

Her tone dared him to object because she was a woman, especially when she'd been doing her damnedest to appear and act *un*womanly for him. And he must have remembered just that, because he dropped that subject to address another.

"Where were you that you didn't witness it?"

She smiled at him. "Didn't you know? You aren't the only one who goes riding off alone—" She started to add, "in search of amusement," but he didn't give her a chance to.

"You did *what?*"

"Of course, when I ride," she continued, "I

don't stick to the road as you do. I find the countryside much more—exhilarating."

She managed the insinuation this time, but instead of pouncing on it, he said with complete confidence, "You're lying, Alex."

She ground her teeth before retorting, "Of course I am, but what made you think so?"

He was suddenly frowning. "What do you mean, 'Of course I am'? Do you make a habit of lying?"

"Certainly," she replied offhandedly. "It makes life so much more interesting, don't you think?"

"No, I don't," he said sternly. "Life is interesting enough without complicating— Never mind. You're a grown woman. Far be it from me to change any of your—habits."

His condescension infuriated her this time, and she'd much rather take out some real anger on him than pretend to be angry at her friends. And she did it with a smile.

"How positively magnanimous of you, Petroff. Don't expect me to be as generous, though. But then, we already know what habits of yours I'm changing, don't we?"

He didn't take the bait, but his smile was as false as hers. "Habits you *think* you're changing. But as for how I knew you were lying, it's because one of my men would have found me to tell me if you'd ridden off on your own, and another would have followed you."

"I'm being spied on? Well, then, I'll have to return the favor, won't I? And I'll start by finding out tomorrow what you were doing today."

169

His brows rose. "You mean at the farmhouse I discovered—"

"You philandering—!"

"Now, now, what *are* you accusing me of?" He was almost laughing, he was so pleased by what she was thinking. "As it happens, it was already getting dark when I found the place, so I didn't have time to dally. But as long as we're on the subject, let me remind you that your own behavior had better remain completely virtuous—at least until after you've borne me an heir. Then you can do whatever you like."

"Oh, I intend to do whatever I like, but I won't wait until I have your permission. You, on the other hand, have had your last tawdry liaison."

He was no longer pleased, but frankly incredulous. "In other words, you can, but I can't?"

"You men have had a monopoly on that sentiment for far too long. You should have known that *some*day a woman would turn the tables on you."

"But it isn't going to be you, sweetheart," he said with a cold, sharp edge to his tone. "You're fond of cutting off ears? I'll cut off a hell of a lot more than that from any man who puts his hands on you—at least until after—"

"Yes, yes, you've already said *that*," she snapped, out of patience. "What makes you think I can even bear children? Maybe I've already tried and failed."

She struck a nerve with that barb. "Then maybe we ought to find out beforehand."

"Don't even think it, Petroff, or *I'll* cut off more than ears."

They were glaring at each other nearly nose to nose. Stalemates were so *un*satisfying, but they each knew that they'd reached one.

And then Vasili's nose suddenly twitched and he leaned back to say, "Damn, what is that smell? I thought it was the horses, but it's coming from you."

Alexandra blinked, then stopped herself just in time from laughing. "Me?" She tried to sound indignant. "I don't smell any different than I always do."

He was really scowling now. "Woman, you did not stink when I met you."

She shrugged. "I had just had my monthly bath when you met me."

"Monthly?" he choked out.

She opened her eyes wide. "You think that's too often? I always thought so, but Papa insisted."

Vasili walked away in disgust.

Alexandra grinned from ear to ear.

18

Alexandra's embarrassment lasted for two days. She should have taken Vasili at his word, but no, she'd had to stop at that farmhouse he'd mentioned—and find out that the only inhabitants were an old couple and their two grandsons.

Whether he had dallied or not, it wouldn't have been with the old woman there unless he was *really* desperate, and apparently he wasn't, because he had been laughing when Alexandra had come back out to mount her horse. And he'd been smiling ever since, or so it seemed. That round had definitely been his, damn him.

But he had gone one better. When they'd stopped at an inn last night, he had sent a bath to her room with a message she couldn't ignore. *Use it or I will be pleased to assist you.* And the insufferable popinjay had sniffed her when she had come down to dine afterward.

But when an opportunity came for her to get even, she pounced on it, not realizing just how effective it would be.

The town they arrived at later that week had a small but elegant hotel, and as usual, it was an establishment that Vasili was already familiar with, since they were retracing the route he had taken to her home. She had at first worried that the hotel would have too many women on staff for her to keep track of them all, so she determined that she would have to keep track of Vasili instead.

But she found out that he had spent only one night at the hotel the last time he'd been there, even though the rest of his party had stayed much longer. This was where they had stopped for an entire week, and not because a member of his group had been ill. Vasili had lied to her father. He had caused her to pack and leave her home with less than a day's notice. Why?

The lady's name was Claudia Shevchenko, a young widowed countess, and Vasili had spent the entire week in her bed, or not far from it. Her home was down the street from the hotel, and he had met her the night of his arrival in town, when she had been at the hotel dining with friends.

The story had been easy enough to obtain because the two had created quite a scandal. It wasn't a large town, after all, and the widow was well known here—and supposedly pious; at least she used to be, before she had met one extremely handsome Cardinian who could seduce an angel if he cared to try. Or so the story went.

So Alexandra was surprised that Vasili didn't once try to leave the hotel the night they spent there, that he went to bed and actually stayed in it, according to the report she had from Timofee as soon as she left her room the next morning. What didn't surprise her was to find him absent when she joined everyone outside the hotel to leave.

It was Lazar, looking extremely uncomfortable,

who had apparently been chosen to tell her, "Vasili has already departed."

"Has he indeed. How long ago?"

"Ten minutes."

She didn't doubt that Lazar had a number of excuses ready to explain this change in routine if she cared to hear any of them. She didn't. She looked to Konrad for confirmation of the time that had passed since Vasili had left. At his affirmative nod, she simply smiled and rode out of town.

She decided she would give Vasili twenty minutes and no more. If he didn't show up to join them by then, she would return and find him, because she didn't believe for a second that he was on the road, merely riding ahead of them, as had become his habit.

Vasili was at that very moment knocking on the door of the redhead who had entertained him so well the first time he'd passed through this town. And as his luck was holding, she happened to be the one to open the door, instead of one of her servants—and slammed it abruptly in his face.

"Go away!" he heard her shout hysterically from the other side of that solid, and now locked, barrier. "I like my ears just as they are!"

For the briefest moment, he doubted his hearing. But then his fingers slowly curled into fists, his face suffused with heat, and a low growl rumbled from his chest.

And he reached Alexandra in much less than the twenty minutes she'd figured on.

She heard him galloping up behind her and

swung Sultan's Pride about to face him. They nearly collided. It was damn close.

"Over there," he said ominously. "Now! Or there will be hell to pay."

He'd pointed to a lone tree that was at least a quarter mile away, and he rode directly to it without waiting to see if she would follow. As angry as he appeared, she considered staying right where she was—but no, she was too hopeful that this was it, the end she had been working toward. Her friends weren't as optimistic. She had to order them to remain with the wagons.

On Sultan's Pride, she reached Vasili in no time at all. He had already dismounted and was pacing beneath the tree. He didn't give her a chance to dismount herself, but dragged her off her horse, then let go of her instantly to resume his pacing.

She'd never seen him like this, never imagined that a popinjay like him was capable of such fury. And there was no mistaking that he was furious.

Warily, she tried to put some distance between them, deciding she could wait to hear whatever he had to say. But as soon as she moved, he closed the distance in a flash and was towering over her, and his eyes—heaven help her—seemed aglow with an inner fire.

"I won't stand for it any longer," he said, and he was just short of shouting. "There will be no more threats from you, Alexandra. I will bed any woman I please, when I please, and if you cause one more to hide from me in terror, I'll bed you instead."

That wasn't what she had hoped to hear, but

it wasn't as bad as it could have been either. So she crossed her arms and replied calmly, "No, you won't. As long as you belong to me, you'll be faithful to me. I don't know why you keep making me repeat that. And you *won't* be bedding me until after we have a wedding. If you want your women back, Vasili, you know what you have to do."

"And you think I'll abide by that?" This time he was shouting, and quite loudly.

She knew it would be an insult to him if she continued calmly in the face of his fury, but that was what she did. "No one says you have to abide by it, Petroff. You'll just have to accept the consequences if you don't."

That started him pacing again. He was really quite fascinating like this, so volatile, even unpredictable. She ought to be frightened, but she wasn't. Nervous, yes, but that was all—until it occurred to her that they wouldn't be having this discussion if he hadn't gone to that woman. And he'd gone to her to bed her, *and* would have done so if Alexandra hadn't been told about her and sent along that little message. He was guilty by intent. What she felt about that didn't bear describing.

Suddenly he demanded, "How the hell did you find out about—about—?"

"Claudia?" she prompted.

"Yes, Claudia, or whatever her name is."

That he wasn't sure what the woman's name was should have appeased Alexandra somewhat, but it merely disgusted her all the more. The man obviously had so many women that he couldn't keep track of them. She'd already figured as much, but hated seeing proof of it.

But he wasn't going to know how disturbed she was, so she shrugged before answering. "You'd be amazed at the kind of information you can gain with a few coins placed in the right pockets."

"And you paid her a visit? When? You didn't leave the inn."

Apparently his spies hadn't gotten much sleep last night either. "I didn't bother seeing to it myself," she said, striving for a tone of indifference. "I sent someone with my message. It must have been delivered accurately."

"Oh, I don't doubt that," he sneered. "Your people are thorough."

"It's called loyalty."

"Are you implying that I have none?"

She gave him a tight little smile. "You said it, I didn't."

He bristled at that, too, though he sounded merely indignant. "I'll have you know my loyalty is beyond reproach, but reserved for only a select few."

She knew the answer, but still wanted confirmation. "And I'm not one of the few?"

"You said it, I didn't," he shot back at her with a nasty smile.

She could no longer keep her voice from rising. "Not even if I become your wife?"

"You'd better hope you come to your senses before then," he growled.

"You'd better hope you do, Petroff!"

Once again, they were standing nearly nose to

nose, she glaring up at him, he scowling down at her. Her bosom was heaving. He noticed, and there was no unusual odor to distract him this time.

Passion was a fickle emotion, easily redirected. Suddenly Vasili felt he would die if he couldn't kiss her. Suddenly Alexandra couldn't take her eyes off his sensual mouth.

And then, as if she'd willed it, she had the taste of him, fiery hot, wild. It was better than she remembered. He was crushing her against him and that was also better than she remembered.

Her fingers gripped his arms, pressing into his muscles, but not to push him away. A hand on her bottom lifted her, locked her to his heat, and she was melting, dissolving, mindlessly wanting something just beyond her reach and understanding.

She was arched to the point of breaking, Vasili was bent over her so far, as if he would take her to the ground by his lips alone. His wanting to make love to her so badly made him forget every golden rule of seduction that he had adhered to in the past.

This was no seduction where he controlled every move and nuance to a desired end. He had no control, was in the grip of pure emotion, the taste and scent of her filling his senses, the feel of her intoxicating him, driving him beyond what he knew as rational.

And then they *were* suddenly on the ground, neither of them the least bit aware of it. Vasili was driven toward a single goal; Alexandra was consumed only by the sensations clamoring inside her, the sheer pleasure derived from his touch, his weight now covering her, his hand sliding up her thigh, until . . .

Her moan was lost in the depth of his kiss, his hand now cupping her heat sending her so close to the edge—and he knew, and had never felt such keen satisfaction in a woman's yielding response before.

He would have taken her right there on the ground, and she would have let him. That was the horrifying realization that dawned on both of them when Sultan's Pride nudged them a few breathless moments later, and they both scrambled to their feet.

Alexandra was mortified by what Vasili had made her feel, again, and her reaction was to slap him this time, hard. She should have given it more thought first, because his reaction was to slap her back, not hard, but just enough to shock her that he would.

"Well, that certainly served no purpose," she remarked dryly.

Vasili was still trembling, wanting nothing more than to yank her back into his arms. How did she dare to stand there and appear totally unaffected by what had just passed between them? As for that slap, she shouldn't have caught him when he was so—not himself.

"Yell at me all you like, sweetheart, only the next time you want to get physical, you can be sure I won't hit back," he promised.

"You won't?"

He shook his head slowly. "No. I'll take you off in the bushes and make love to you instead."

She had to be crazy not to try to change this subject. "Why didn't you this time?"

"I believe in fair warning—when your choice in the matter will be taken from you."

"You'd do it even if I fight you?"

His smile was chilling. "Exactly."

"You know what that's called, don't you?" she said with biting scorn.

"When you've been given fair warning? I would call it an invitation."

It was his sexual frustration that had led him to make this alarming threat, she was sure. And she could think of no way to gain back the upper hand when his promised consequence far surpassed her own. But she wasn't worried about slapping him again. She could restrain herself from doing that—somehow. It was the kissing she had to keep from ever happening again, the kissing caused by his frustration, the kissing that she had succumbed to so completely.

She was going to have to concede or risk having his frustration get worse, risk having him start thinking about his rights again. Heaven help her, he might even try seduction on her if he got desperate enough, and she could still remember the special smile of his that he had turned on that tavern wench. She didn't want to find out if she could withstand its being turned on her.

But she *hated* giving in, and she did it now with ill grace, snapping, "Go, then! Go back to the last town and find yourself a whore. Spend the whole day with her. We'll wait for you in the next town."

Whether that was what Vasili wanted to hear,

he was damned if he was going to go with her *permission.*

"No, I don't think so," he said thoughtfully, his eyes dropping deliberately to her breasts. "I think I'll wait until you slap me again."

Alexandra gritted her teeth against the blush she felt rising, but it mounted her cheeks anyway. Slapping him again was just what she felt like doing. She had never known anyone who deserved it more.

Instead she threw caution to the wind and taunted him. "A wise decision, Petroff, one that won't benefit you, of course, but nonetheless wise—because I probably would have changed my mind as soon as you left. And think how embarrassing it would have been when I interrupted you and your whore—hopefully at a crucial moment."

"Did anyone ever tell you what a bitch you can be, sweetheart?" he asked in a deceptively lazy tone. The glow was back in his eyes.

She injected some sweetness into her own tone, just as false. "I do try."

She then turned abruptly toward her horse. Vasili reached out to stop her, though she didn't notice it. But whatever might have happened next didn't happen at all, because they were both distracted.

Alexandra first saw why Sultan's Pride had nudged them earlier. He'd wanted to get her attention because Vasili's stallion was encroaching too close and taking nips at his haunches. Then she saw something even worse, but something she should have expected.

The Razin brothers had started after her. And apparently Vasili's guards had ridden after them to prevent their interference, because the lot of them were halfway between the road and the tree, literally rolling on the ground as they pounded one another.

Vasili swore beneath his breath before he cast Alexandra a black look. "Now look what you've done," he growled accusingly.

"*Me?* Did you think my Cossacks would just sit there and do nothing when they saw you hit me?"

"I didn't hit you."

"Then what would you call it?" she demanded even as she mounted.

"A tap on the cheek to get your attention," he said, also mounting. "If I *had* hit you, you would have been knocked flat on your back—which isn't a bad idea, actually."

That was the last straw. "Consider yourself lucky that Bojik didn't follow me, or your men would be spending the rest of the morning burying you instead of attending to their black eyes. And get control of your damn horse!" She was shouting at him now, since they were both riding back to break up the fight, and she had easily taken the lead. "If he nips at mine again, I'm going to let Sultan's Pride have at him—and I hope you're on him at the time!"

"Alex?"

"*What?*"

"I'll consider any violence from you or at your instigation a slap."

She shut up.

19

"The hell of it is," Vasili was telling Lazar as they rode ahead of the party, "I had no desire to bed her. I merely wanted to prove to myself, *and* to my little barbarian, that I could."

Lazar nodded, not the least bit surprised. But then, Lazar understood Vasili better than most people did because he knew all of his quirks and foibles, all of his faults and virtues.

Vasili had met Claudia Shevchenko not long after they'd come down from crossing the Carpathians, when he was still boiling with resentment that he was even making this trip. He hadn't stayed with the lady a week because he couldn't resist her. He'd stayed to prove the betrothal wasn't going to change his self-indulgent lifestyle.

Like most men, Vasili enjoyed two kinds of women, the ones he was actually attracted to and those who were merely available for the taking. He had the latter in abundance because of his looks. These were mostly women who offered themselves without being asked. And Vasili accommodated most of them because he was, after all, used to overindulgence.

Countess Shevchenko fell into the latter group. She was pretty enough, but she was definitely on the skinny side, and Vasili preferred a more voluptuous, full-figured form—like Alexandra's.

Lazar said now, "Well, one thing did come out of that nonsense. You found out that the baroness knows how to use a horsewhip."

Lazar got a glare for that reminder. He would have been disappointed by any other reaction. Five days had passed since the incident that he wasn't likely to ever forget had occurred, and he'd been mentioning it at least once a day just to rile Vasili.

One of Alexandra's Cossacks had suffered a broken finger from *the fight,* which was how it was now being referred to by all of them. Jesus, it had been hilarious, not the broken finger, but the fight itself, and Lazar had sat back and enjoyed the entire spectacle. And it had only gotten better once Alexandra had discovered the Cossack's injury.

She had gone after Vasili's man with a horse-whip, and Vasili had been the only one daring enough—or annoyed enough—to get near her while she was wielding that vicious thing, to yank it out of her hands. She had been giving the guard, *and* Vasili, killing looks ever since.

After that display, it was easy to see that Alexandra loved the Razins like family. She treated them as if they were her brothers, defended them like brothers, insulted them like brothers. How Vasili could ever have gotten the notion that they had been her lovers was beyond Lazar, but his friend had not been acting like himself since he had met his "little barbarian."

Lazar wondered if Vasili knew how possessive he was beginning to sound whenever he mentioned Alexandra. For that matter, he wondered if Vasili was even aware of how often he glanced back throughout the day just to look at her.

He had stopped riding off by himself as often, too, and stopped completely when they reached the mountains. But then, the Carpathians weren't known to be friendly territory to travelers, weather-wise or otherwise, and especially if those travelers appeared to be carrying anything of value. They had managed to cross these mountains once without incident. Twice was more than they could hope for, particularly with the addition of two bulging wagons and a herd of prize thoroughbreds.

They were taking precautions, posting extra guards at night. But short of hiring more men from one of the mountain villages, which Vasili refused to do, given the odds were about half that they'd be hiring the thieves themselves, there was nothing else they could do.

Some things had changed, yes, but even with the additional danger in crossing the mountains, Vasili hadn't let up on his personal campaign. If anything, he seemed to be increasing his efforts to insult and ridicule Alexandra and to provoke her temper at every opportunity. The fact that they would reach Cardinia in another week or so, depending on the weather, was likely the reason. But who would have thought it would go on this long?

Lazar was actually finding the whole thing highly amusing, though he was quite possibly the only one who did. He'd been bored for a while when Vasili and Alexandra had been trying to avoid each other. But now they were having blowups at least once a day. And still neither one said the magic words that would end the betrothal. Instead they were both giving new meaning to the word "stubborn."

The weather was frigid, despite the sun's periodic appearances, but they hadn't yet encountered a snowstorm, which Vasili was hoping would send Alexandra running for home. And this was another example of Vasili's desperation. While Cardinia had its share of severe winters just like every other country in this area of the continent, Vasili rarely ventured far from a warm fire during this time of year. If anyone was going to suffer during the extreme cold of a snowstorm, it would be he, rather than Alexandra.

Of course, to give Vasili his due, he and Lazar had both assumed that his betrothed would be a lady of *normal* sensibilities. There had been no way for them to know that she was a creature of nature, more comfortable outdoors than in, and apparently that was true at any time of the year. She wouldn't complain of a snowstorm any more than she had of being continuously in the saddle for the past three and a half weeks.

It was still early in the afternoon the day they finally reached the mountain pass and began their descent. The sun had been shining for most of the morning during the last of their climb. And with the worst of the danger at least half over now, they all began to relax somewhat, despite the gloomy clouds that blew in and hovered over the western face of the mountain.

But the snow arrived less than an hour later

and ended their run of good luck. Within thirty minutes, it was snowing so hard they could no longer see the trail in front of them and were forced to make camp.

While the tents were being erected, Alexandra worked frantically to create a windbreak and shelter for the horses, which were her main concern. She made use of the wagons, all of their contents, and at least half of the extra blankets she had brought along for precisely such an emergency. And she cursed Vasili beneath her breath all the while, blaming him and his wasted week with Countess Shevchenko for stranding them on top of a mountain, far from any decent shelter.

She was given pause, however, and reason to think she must be going snow-blind, when she saw Vasili helping her rather than seeing to his own tent and comfort. She continued to curse him, but she didn't get as much pleasure out of it as she usually did, and stopped altogether when she felt something suspiciously like guilt.

So he could perform one unselfish act. That didn't make much of a dent in all of his bad qualities—except he was helping her to protect *her* horses, her babies. She'd have to at least thank him—when she had the time.

The storm continued to unleash its fury all afternoon, and Alexandra continued to worry about her horses. They were as used to the cold as she was, but they usually had a warm stable to return to after being out in it. This situation was different, and her need to reassure them as much as herself was why she couldn't remain in her tent for longer than an hour without checking on them.

She'd already done so twice. The third time she found someone else there ahead of her and heard him say, "Oh, Jesus," before she realized it was Vasili huddled in a long fur cloak. She thought he was grumbling over the weather until she reached his side and saw that the shelter she'd fought to erect was half empty.

"What have you done?" she asked in a horrified whisper, blaming him automatically.

"I wish I could take credit, but I can't." The derision in his voice was also automatic, but at her stricken look, Vasili wished he could take it back. "Damn, I knew this was going to happen. You can't expect to bring such valuable horses into these bandit-infested hills and not lose a few of them."

"A few? All my whites are gone!" she cried, and then: "Oh, God, this is my fault. I called in the guards. I didn't think there would be any trouble in the middle of a storm."

"When all this snow offers the perfect cover and these mountain people are used to it?"

He might as well have said he'd never heard of anything so stupid. She got the message. She even agreed. She hadn't been thinking about bandits, only about the storm, and she'd wanted to spare her men, as well as his, from standing guard during the worst of it, at least until evening, when it might have blown over.

But that was no excuse, so she didn't bother explaining. And she'd already dismissed Vasili from her mind as she bent under the rope that had restrained the animals and moved to the back of the temporary corral where the rope had been cut.

None of the remaining horses had bothered to wander off, preferring to stay close to what little shelter had been provided. And with as many that were still there, including the roan stallion, it appeared that only her rare whites had been the target.

The trail was wide, but barely discernible, and filling up with new snow even as she stared at it. It would be gone in a matter of minutes. There was no time to summon her people or his. Even a shout wouldn't be heard over the keening of the wind. She had to follow the trail to find out where the horses had been taken, then come back . . .

"Where do you think you're going?"

She had started to mount one of the horses—all those that had been wearing saddles still had them on for added warmth—when Vasili yanked her back to the ground to answer his idiotic question. "There's no time for this, Petroff."

"I'll get your horses back."

"How?"

"I'll buy them back. My cousin and I have had run-ins with these hill bandits before, or at least with similar ones. They're always willing to turn a profit."

"Don't be absurd," she replied. "And leave me beholden to you? I'll get them back, and it won't cost anything but a few lives—theirs."

"The odds are, you're talking about a whole village of thieves, Alex, not just a few."

"I'm talking about getting my horses back, *my* horses, *my* responsibility. And the trail they've left is disappearing even as we speak. If you want to help, get the others and follow, but I'm leaving now."

She had to shove him slightly to get him to let go of her. And it was infuriating to know that the shove wouldn't have worked if he hadn't lost his balance in the snow they'd just trampled. His high-handedness was intolerable, and she wished she had time to tell him so, but she didn't.

Vasili didn't fall, but by the time he steadied himself, Alexandra was already at the end of the corral, disappearing into the swirling white beyond the camp. He shouted for the others, but only in the time it took him to mount his stallion and ride after her.

Whether anyone heard him was doubtful, but he didn't particularly care at the moment. When he caught up with that fool woman, he was going to wring her neck, and he didn't need any help for that.

20

Vasili couldn't quite manage to catch up to Alexandra. He wasn't following the trail as she was; he was keeping her in his sights instead. But more than once the snow became so thick, she was lost from his view and he panicked and shouted at her, even though he knew damn well she couldn't hear him.

Although the mountain road was no more visible than anything else, Vasili was sure they were on it and that the thieves had circled around the camp to get back to it. After all, it would be the safest route for them to take, especially if they thought no one was following them, and with nightfall coming on fast.

When it did start to get dark, he panicked again because he had nothing to light a torch with, even if he could find something dry to use, and no time to do either. He tried to coax a little more speed from the roan, but the descent was too steep in places, making it too treacherous because of the snow. The stallion balked, having already gone to his knees once, where he actually slid several feet. He refused to go any faster.

When night finally did fall, Vasili found that he had panicked for no reason. The only advantage that the snow provided him was that the pristine white landscape kept complete darkness at bay, allowing him to still see ahead—when the swirling gusts weren't blinding him.

Hours passed; he didn't know how many. But he knew he was going to die. He was slowly freezing to death, his extremities already numb. He remained in the saddle only by sheer determination, keeping one thing in mind: he was going to murder that fool woman . . . no, he would make love to her first and then murder her.

And then the wind suddenly stopped, and within moments, the snow also stopped falling. The temperature might have become less severe, too, but Vasili was in no condition to tell. What was obvious was that the growth of oak and fir trees on either side of him had become thicker. Somehow he had nearly reached the foothills on the lower slopes. People lived in the foothills, entire villages, with fires and warm, cozy huts, hot food and drink. If he could just continue for a mile or so more, he might not die after all.

Before he had even finished the thought, he saw Alexandra veer abruptly south off the road, and he groaned. Moments earlier, he might not have noticed, might have gone right past where the trail left the road and lost her entirely.

With the wind quiet now, he tried shouting again, but she was already gone from sight. When he reached the same point, he could see her again, but she was as far ahead of him as she had been all along. And she was no longer descending. The trail was actually rising gradually as it followed a narrow path along the slope.

Again he shouted her name. She heard him this time. Her head turned. She looked right at him. But she didn't stop. She dug her heels into her horse instead.

That did it! He really *was* going to murder her as soon as he got his hands on her—if they both didn't freeze first. Fortunately, her borrowed horse wasn't any more eager for a gallop than his stallion was, so she didn't gain on him. But she continued to maintain the same distance that kept him from reaching her.

He wondered if a shot from the pistol he'd stuck in his belt earlier would stop her or spur her on. If he'd brought more than one, he'd be tempted to find out. Then again, she might have one of her own and fire back at him, thinking he was trying to kill her. She had good reason to think so. Besides, he didn't trust her not to shoot at him in retaliation. Her horses were involved, after all, and there was no doubt whatsoever that they meant more to her than he did. Damned horses. He wouldn't be out here freezing if— Torches suddenly flickered far ahead. Either they'd found the thieves or a village, or both. But Alexandra didn't slow down to let him catch up to her. She kept charging straight for the lights, and after another few moments, he could see why. Her horses. She'd seen her horses, and she was probably too furious even to think of the danger that lay ahead, and she was certainly too furious to be sensible.

And, because he couldn't stop it or her, he had to watch her ride right into the midst of a half-dozen men and start wielding the horsewhip that she had taken to carrying on her hip ever since *the fight.* She scattered the men. Horses were rearing. One man was thrown from his mount and slid and tumbled down the slope a good twenty feet. Another raised a pistol and had it whipped from his hand. The rest were dismounting. The path was too narrow a space for so many horses to converge, and the men obviously intended to bring Alexandra down before she did any serious damage.

Vasili drew his pistol and fired, but it was good for only one shot, and once it was discharged, he threw it away to draw his sword. He was still too late to keep Alexandra from being yanked off her mount, and with the torches having been dropped to the ground and the snow swiftly extinguishing them, he couldn't see what had happened to her.

Another shot was fired, this one at Vasili. But he was still so numb with cold that he doubted he'd feel it if he were hit. He trusted he wasn't, and when he finally reached the group on the ground, he started swinging his sword to prove it.

The bandits scattered again, a bit more leery of his sword than they'd been of the whip, though they didn't go far. They brandished an assortment of weapons that he took note of—a dagger, two swords, a club, but no other pistols that he could see. And he could also see Alexandra now.

She was on the ground, fighting with one of the men, who was trying to hold her down and get a rope around her. That he had his hands on her at all made Vasili a little crazy, and without considering that he'd be giving up his advantage on horseback, he dove at the man, slamming against him, rolling on the ground until he managed enough purchase to smash his sword hilt against the fellow's head.

He got back to his feet swiftly, slipping only a little in the snow, and faced three more men. The fourth had taken over with Alexandra before she'd had a chance to get up; he had her face down in the snow with a knee in her back, tying her hands. He'd be joining the fray in moments.

Vasili had his shocking burst of rage under control now. He wouldn't even have minded the odds he was facing; he considered them paltry against his own sword skill. But slippery ground had a way of evening odds, and he couldn't help but remember the one time he'd trained with Stefan in snow, and how they'd spent more time on their backsides than on their feet, a learning experience which he couldn't use to his advantage when facing more than one opponent.

He was still ready and eager for the first assault, and it came swiftly. Vasili held his ground, deciding that the least movement would be the best defense under these circumstances, and it worked for a while. He disarmed one man, wounded another, and had found an opening on the third when he was forced to stop, to go perfectly still. The blade digging into his back— sword or dagger, he couldn't tell—had pierced through his cloak, jacket, and shirt, telling him without a doubt that he wasn't too numb to feel a wound after all.

21

"A wise choice, Count Petroff. Now tell me, will my good friend Stefan be joining us as well?"

Vasili knew that deep voice. Pavel, the man was called, and he was anything but Stefan's friend. He was as tall as Vasili but more muscular, with raw-boned features and a swarthy complexion, and a perpetually belligerent attitude. And when Vasili glanced back to confirm the speaker's identity, he saw that Pavel wasn't alone, that nearly a dozen men were ranged behind him, some sporting firearms that were trained directly at Vasili.

"A pleasure to see you again, Pavel," he said so dryly that only an idiot would believe him, "and no, Stefan didn't join me on this trip."

"I'm disappointed," Pavel replied, and he did, in fact, sound it. "When I recognized you just now, I had such hope for another challenge— but perhaps you will stand for your cousin, eh?"

Vasili wasn't surprised. Pavel's attitude hadn't changed.

"Perhaps," was all he would commit to. "But first I'd like to take advantage of your famous hospitality. I trust your village isn't far?"

"Not far at all, or we wouldn't have heard those shots and come to investigate."

And Vasili could blame Alexandra for that. If she had stopped, they would have seen where her horses were being taken, he would have recognized the village, and they could have returned with the others in their party, in a position of power rather than as prisoners.

At least Latzko, the leader of these hill bandits, was an easy man to deal with. Greed was his guiding principle, and everything had a price.

"Would you mind getting that knife out of my back, Pavel? Latzko won't appreciate damaged goods."

"Latzko is not your worry. He's gone to Austria to the bitch's wedding. I am your worry, aristo. I rule in Latzko's absence."

Just what Vasili needed to hear. He had a madman to deal with instead of the reasonable Latzko. The "bitch" he assumed was Latzko's daughter, Arina. Pavel had loved her and lost her to Stefan a number of years ago, which was one reason Pavel hated Stefan so much. The other reason was because Stefan had fought him and beat him, twice. And that was why Pavel hated all aristocrats.

"Congratulations on the promotion, Pavel, but can we continue this discussion in your village, preferably before a warm fire? I happen to be freezing."

Pavel laughed. At least half of his men joined in. But the knife was finally removed from Vasili's back. A few orders were given and Vasili's sword was taken. Then Pavel noticed Alexandra.

"Another woman?" Pavel came around and approached Alexandra until he was standing in front of her. But after one quick look, he glanced back at Vasili for a little gloating. "This day's work has turned out much better than I expected. Will she be worth as much as the other one?"

He was referring to Tanya, who had been captured last year and whose retrieval had cost Stefan five hundred rubles. Vasili was already going to have to pay a fortune to get Alexandra's horses back. Their value was obvious. Hers wasn't, and he needed to establish her worthlessness then and there, not only to keep her cost down, but because Pavel was a vengeful bastard. But he wouldn't have done it the way he did if she hadn't been glaring at him at that exact moment. He was already angry with her, and that only inflamed him.

With just enough annoyance in his voice to sound sincere, he said, "Keep her. You'd be doing me a favor."

Even with several feet separating them, Vasili heard Alexandra draw in a sharp breath. Pavel couldn't help but hear the indignant sound himself. It was obvious he'd had no real interest in her. Bundled up in her Cossack garb, she hardly presented an alluring package. But the sound drew his attention back to her, and he lifted her chin for a better look at her.

Nothing should have happened. Her hands were tied behind her back. She was surrounded by bandits.

But she kicked him, hard.

Pavel howled. Some of his men laughed, adding insult to injury. When he got done hopping around on one leg while he massaged his aching shin—it was incredible how he did it without slipping—he looked positively murderous, and Alexandra was going to catch the brunt of his fury.

Vasili had begun stepping closer, but not soon enough. He wasn't close enough to stop Pavel's raised fist from connecting with Alexandra's face. He had to tackle him to manage it, which was what he did.

When they stopped sliding in the snow, Pavel was looking up at him incredulously. Vasili felt exactly the same. The cold had obviously numbed his mind as well as his extremities. There was no other excuse for doing something so stupid. The only reason he hadn't been shot already was because Pavel's men couldn't believe he was that stupid either, and were immobilized by surprise.

That gave him time to help Pavel to his feet, dust him off a bit, and say, "Sorry, but no one hits her except me. An idiosyncrasy of mine."

He should have switched to Cardinian, which Pavel understood well enough, because Alexandra chose that moment to prove she hadn't lost her voice. "You're going to regret that, Petroff."

He didn't glance her way when he replied, "You've been silent until now, wench. Keep it that way."

Pavel was glaring between the two of them, but suddenly his humor took an upward swing and he was almost smiling when he told Vasili, "That—whatever you called it—is going to cost you, Cardinian."

Vasili sighed. "I figured as much."

22

The food was hearty, but Vasili was only interested in its warmth. He was still chilled to the bone, despite the clay-mounded oven in the center of the room that seemed to be keeping everyone else warm. Latzko's house was a large, one-room building that served as a sort of meeting hall for the village and a barracks for the single men in the village.

Vasili's hands were no longer numb, but snow had seeped into his boots to soak his feet, which were still freezing. He wasn't going to feel truly warm until he could get out of his damp clothes, and he doubted Alexandra was, either.

Not that she'd made any comment about it. She was ignoring everyone, including him, especially him. She was sitting cross-legged on one of the many cots in the room. She was holding her plate on her lap, picking at the food on it with her fingers. The spoon that had been supplied for her lay on the blanket by her knee. Heaven forbid she should actually know what to do with it.

Vasili was almost accustomed to her eating habits by now, but she had surprised their hosts. Even hill bandits had better table manners than his betrothed. But for once he was glad it was so, because they took her for a peasant and dismissed her as unimportant. He would have wrung her neck if she had suddenly developed proper manners.

She was still wearing her thick woolen coat fastened up to her neck. With ample light in the room, he could see that the front of it was soaked from when she'd been shoved facedown in the snow. Her lovely breasts had to be icy cold beneath that dampness, the nipples hard little nubs just waiting for him to . . .

Vasili covered his eyes with his hand, groaning inwardly. What the hell was he doing? He had Pavel sitting across from him, two of his men on either side of him, one of the village women moving around behind them, filling mugs with ale and congratulating the locals on their bravery and cunning. And what was he doing instead of listening for a piece of information he could use to his advantage?

The only thing of interest that he'd heard so far was that the bandits hadn't just stumbled across his party, as might be supposed, but had known about the travelers and the horses well in advance. Apparently they had men in their pay who lived in the village on the other side of the mountain, where Vasili's group had taken shelter the previous night.

It was an ideal arrangement that kept the bandits informed whenever a rich party was crossing the mountains. Shortcuts connected the two villages in a matter of hours. And today, the storm had merely been an added boon, allowing them to take what they wanted without a confrontation.

"What is she to you?"

Alexandra was suddenly looking straight at Vasili, proving she'd been listening to every word even if he hadn't been. But he wasn't going to make the mistake of giving an inflammatory answer in Russian again. She was too unpredictable. He couldn't depend on her to help them get out of this mess she had gotten them into. Make her angry, and she'd just as soon attack him as the bandits.

So Vasili switched to Cardinian to say, "Her father gave her to me. I've decided to amuse myself with her for a while."

The look Alexandra gave him before her eyes returned to her food said she didn't appreciate one little bit being excluded from that answer. Vasili was relieved. There had been the possibility that she might know Cardinian. It hadn't been likely, but it was possible.

"And you amuse yourself by beating her?"

Pavel was sticking with Russian, deliberately to discomfit Vasili, he didn't doubt. And Alexandra's head had snapped back up. Vasili could try again in Cardinian, he supposed, but as Pavel had already given the wrong impression with that question, the odds were he'd do the same again, so Vasili might as well stick with Russian. If Alexandra was going to be foolish enough to draw attention to herself with an interruption, it would be her own fault.

Vasili's golden eyes settled on Pavel and stayed there, refusing to look in Alexandra's direction again. "I believe my earlier words were that no one hits her except me. I don't find amusement in that, merely necessity. She does so often deserve it, after all."

"But you mean to keep her, eh?"

"I'm not bored yet, so yes, for a little while longer I'll keep her. But during that time she remains mine exclusively—or I lose interest."

Pavel's shrug said he understood perfectly. Used goods lost their value. And now they could get down to the business at hand.

"Fifty rubles, no more," Vasili offered, and his expression implied that he was being generous. Then he sat back, lifting one arm over the back of his chair. "Wasn't that the price Stefan had to pay to get Arina back that time?"

It was a calculated risk, bringing Arina into the conversation. But he'd already guessed that the woman serving them was Pavel's woman, simply by the expressions passing between them, and because the other men kept their hands off her. Pavel could either explode with jealousy as he usually did whenever Arina was mentioned, or quickly get the subject of women out of the way, since his own was listening.

"You would compare Latzko's daughter with this peasant?" he demanded, waving a hand toward Alexandra.

Indignation? Vasili couldn't have asked for a better reaction. "You're right, of course. What would you suggest, then? Twenty-five?"

"Forty-five," Pavel replied, obviously having realized his mistake.

"I suppose that keeps anyone from being insulted," Vasili remarked dryly. *Except for*

Alexandra. "Agreed, and by the way, who is Arina marrying?"

Pavel spit on the floor before he said in disgust, "She got tired of her Austrian duke and took up with a count. He's crazy enough to marry her."

Vasili knew he shouldn't, but he simply couldn't resist rubbing it in a little. "Latzko must be pleased to have a count in the family."

"Latzko just wants her married," Pavel half growled, half mumbled. "He don't care to who. Now for you, Count Petroff. I know my good friend Stefan will pay plenty for you. The horses, of course, I keep for myself. But you—"

"Horses like that would be useless in these mountains and you know it, Pavel. I'll give you three hundred for the lot of them."

Pavel laughed. "You think I don't know horses that fine are for your cousin? If he wants them, he'll have to pay the price I ask, or I keep them."

Vasili couldn't imagine where *that* notion had come from, but he'd have to disabuse him of it quickly or he'd never get the horses back. "They happen to be a gift to me from my betrothed. Stefan doesn't even like whites. He calls them bloodless, temperamental creatures, not worth the effort to feed them. Having traveled with them, I'm inclined to agree, though I may still start a breeding farm with them, as I had planned to do. However, since they cost me nothing, I really don't care one way or the other. Three hundred rubles for the lot, and not a ruble more."

"One thousand rubles each, and not a ruble less," Pavel countered belligerently.

Vasili could feel Alexandra's midnight eyes

slicing into him like daggers. He'd just insulted her "babies." He was surprised she hadn't thrown her plate at him. And he wasn't finished.

"Absolutely ridiculous," he said in his most derisive tone. "If you can't be serious, then we have nothing further to discuss."

"It is Stefan who will pay, aristo," Pavel replied confidently. "As for what he will pay for you, five thousand rubles, I think—no, ten thousand."

"You're crazy."

Pavel's fist slammed down on the table. "He owes me! If he does not pay, believe me, I will be happy to send you back to him in pieces."

Vasili had tried to be reasonable. He was tired. He was cold. Now he was angry.

He leaned forward, his arms crossed on the table, pinning Pavel's eyes with the heat in his. And he said very softly, "You shouldn't make threats you don't dare follow through with, Pavel. It weakens your position."

"And why wouldn't I do as I say?"

"Because we both know that if anything happens to me, Stefan will come here with his soldiers and this village will be no more. Death or profit. Which was it you had in mind when you stole my horses?"

Pavel had gone red in the face, either from fury or from embarrassment, because he was going to have to back down. The power of being leader for a while might have gone to his head, but Latzko would be returning, and Latzko would demand an accounting.

Vasili decided to make it a little easier for him to back down. "Forget about Stefan, Pavel. It's

I who will pay, not Stefan, and it's me you are dealing with, not Stefan. I would suggest you sleep on that, and perhaps we can get back to negotiations in the morning. In the meantime, the wench and I require quarters where we can dry off—in private."

One of the other men chuckled, a reaction Vasili had counted on. Pavel was still red-faced, though, and it was a long, tense moment before he joined in the laughter, albeit with a hollow sound.

"By all means. You will want to be *dry* while the rest of us celebrate our good fortune."

23

They were shown to a ramshackle, vacant hut that belonged to one of the men who had accompanied Latzko on his journey to Austria. It contained the basics—a few chairs and a table, a narrow bed, some dishes, and some blankets—but nothing of a personal nature, since the owner hadn't seemed to trust his comrades enough to leave his valuables behind. It was also nearly as cold inside the one-room hut as it was outside, because the oven hadn't been used for several weeks.

There was one window, but it was boarded up from the outside. The door had no lock, so their escort had nailed a plank to it before he departed. It wouldn't be opened again until it was pried loose in the morning.

The best Vasili could say for the accommodations was that they were private. The one candle they'd been left with gave off a warm glow. There was a small stack of firewood in a corner, and the reason it was so small was because the oven was small. It was going to take hours for a fire to take the chill off the room, and he didn't intend to wait that long to get dry. But a fire was his first priority.

As soon as he was assured a guard hadn't been left outside, Vasili headed for the firewood. A wooden bowl glanced off his shoulder before he got there.

"What the—?"

He swung about, but had to duck as a plate flew past his head. Alexandra had moved to a cupboard against the wall where she had a wide assortment of missiles at her disposal, and she gave the impression that she intended to use every one of them. Considering the distance separating them, Vasili decided to talk quickly.

"Whatever I said about your horses, Alexandra, it was merely to get Pavel's price down. Or don't you want your animals back?"

Her answer was a glass mug that came damn close to his cheek. So it wasn't the horses?

He started moving slowly toward her as he tried again. "I also had to say what I did about you, and it had nothing to do with price. If Pavel thought you meant something to me, he could well decide to hurt you before selling you back to me, he's that unpredictable and vindictive. In his mind, what hurts me would hurt Stefan, and he'll do anything to hurt Stefan, whom he hates."

Vasili had to duck again, but he sensed that he was getting closer to what was bothering her. However, he obviously hadn't touched on her sore point yet, and her aim was improving.

His voice dropped to a menacing tone. "Spit it out, Alex, before I lose my patience."

Another plate came at his head, but also the shouted reminder: "Twenty-five rubles?"

Jesus, he should have known that was what she would take exception to the most. Women and their damn sensibilities. And he'd thought hers weren't normal—but, of course, they were only normal when he could have wished they weren't.

"You also heard that Stefan paid only fifty for Arina," he pointed out.

"Arina obviously gets passed around a lot, so that hardly counts. Who was the other woman, and how much did you pay for her?"

That question was accompanied by a bread-board hitting him squarely in the chest. He was so surprised by the impact, it took him several moments to realize that Alexandra had left the area of the cupboard and was heading for weightier missiles in the form of firewood.

Vasili shot across the room and caught her from behind, lifting her off her feet, his arms tight around her waist. She screeched. He shook her. She kicked backward, aiming for his knees. He shook her again. Her hat had come off, her hair spilling into his face. It was cold and silky and smelled of spring flowers.

He didn't dare hold her for long. "What other woman are you talking about?"

"Put me down!"

"When you've calmed down, I will," he replied. "What other woman?"

"The one your friend mentioned—"

"He's not my friend."

"—when he asked if I will be worth as much as the other one!"

She sounded so furious, it finally occurred to him why she might have been glaring at him out in the snow when Pavel had posed that question. "Were you jealous, Alex?" he asked softly by her ear.

He imagined he could feel her squirming in his arms; however, her reply, when it came, was a stubborn "Answer my question, Petroff."

"Answer mine first—or I might recall a promise I made to you about inflicting violence upon me—"

"You son of a—!"

His arms tightened around her waist just enough to shut her up so he could add, "I was going to suspend that promise temporarily, since these do happen to be unusual circumstances, but—"

"I wasn't jealous," she cut in quickly. "It's only the women you attempt to bed now who will feel the point of my blade. And I told you why."

"Yes, yes, because I'm yours," he said in a tone that implied he'd heard that too often. "That smacks of jealousy to me, sweetheart."

"What it is, is your loss," she growled. "Now, who was she?"

"Queen Tatiana."

"Who?"

"My cousin's wife, though she was merely a princess at the time. She was raised in America, was lost there in fact, but that's a long story I'm sure you're not interested in. Now, aren't you ashamed of your suspicions?"

"Of a man who has no shame? I don't think so," she retorted. "How much was paid for her?"

Vasili sighed. "Five hundred rubles, and before you go comparing yourself with a princess, you should know that that was a ridiculously high price to demand for a woman and that Latzko expected to have it haggled down. My cousin, however, was too angry to haggle. He just wanted his bride back. But he set a bad precedent by paying it, which is why Pavel is being ridiculous in his own demands."

Her tone became excessively haughty. "The price he asks for my horses is not ridiculous."

"You're missing the point, Alex. These are simple people with simple needs. The reason they survive up here in the mountains is that they never take too much. The people they rob or ransom are merely annoyed by the inconvenience. But if the bandits start taking too much, someone will get angry enough to do something about them. Latzko understands that. Pavel doesn't have enough sense to."

"Are you saying there is no danger?"

"If Latzko were here, I might say that. However, with Pavel in charge, nothing is certain, particularly where we're concerned. And that's as I said, because he hates Stefan so much."

"You can put me down now, Petroff."

Vasili certainly hoped so. Holding her this long was giving his body ideas that his mind was trying desperately to ignore.

"No more throwing things?"

"I believe I can restrain myself for a while."

The sarcasm in her tone was actually more reassuring than a straight answer would have been, at least from her. He had found that when she was angry, she was extremely direct in her responses.

He set her down carefully. With the loss of her

warmth, a chill went through him, and he turned immediately toward the firewood again.

He wasn't sure how she was going to take his next suggestion, but it had to be made. "We have to get out of these wet clothes."

"I know," she said in a small voice behind him.

She could be sensible? Thank God for small favors. And then it hit him. She was going to take her clothes off. And they were in a locked room, alone—with a bed. He was fully aroused within seconds and groaning.

"What's wrong?" she asked.

"Nothing," he replied, but he had gone perfectly still, bent over the firewood.

"The fire, Petroff," she prompted impatiently. "Or do you think we can survive the night without one?"

He wasn't going to survive the night either way, so what did he care? But he got a grip on himself and went through the motions of starting the oven.

"Tell me why Pavel dislikes your cousin so much," she said.

Excellent. Something else to think about— besides what she was going to be doing soon.

"Pavel was in love with Latzko's daughter, Arina, and possibly still is. But she had higher aspirations. She met Stefan some eight years ago when he was the Crown Prince, and she became his mistress for a time. Then they had a fight and she came back here. Stefan followed her to make amends, and ended up having to pay Latzko the fifty rubles before he would allow her to leave with Stefan. Pavel also insisted that Stefan fight for the privilege."

"Did he?"

"Yes."

"That sounds rather romantic."

Vasili snorted. "There was nothing romantic about it. Pavel fought dirty, but still lost. The trouble was, he's a bad loser. When Tanya was captured—"

"Who is *Tanya?*"

He ignored the fact that her voice had gone sharp again. " 'Tanya' is what Tatiana insists she be called. As I said, she was raised in America and that was the name she was known by there. She didn't learn her true name until we found her last year . . . but I digress. As I was saying, when she was captured, Stefan had to come here again, and Pavel saw it as an opportunity to have revenge. He challenged Stefan again, this time with knives, with the sole intent of killing him."

"I'm going to assume he lost that fight, too?"

"Indeed, but you heard him. He's still not satisfied, even though Latzko warned him the last time that he'd kill him himself if he ever challenged Stefan again."

"Ah, but Latzko isn't here to enforce that warning and . . . you think he's going to challenge you before this is over, don't you?"

Did he hear concern in her voice? Jesus, now he was imagining things. Alexandra concerned for him? Maybe when cows learned to dance.

"He'd be an idiot to challenge me," Vasili scoffed.

213

"He strikes you as having some sort of intelligence, does he?"

Her tone was so dry, he almost chuckled. And that surprised him. When the hell had he started to find her wit amusing?

The fire had finally caught, and it wasn't as weak as he'd feared it would be. The clay oven would still take a while to warm the room completely, but surely not the hours he'd first thought.

He turned to suggest that Alexandra move closer to the oven before she took off her clothes. He wasn't prepared to find her already with a blanket wrapped around her, her coat, pants, and shirt draped over the back of one of the two chairs next to her, even her feet bare. He was breathless. His mind went blank, then abruptly focused on one thing. Was she completely naked under that blanket, or did she still have on some sort of underwear? Did she even wear underwear? He was about to embarrass himself by asking, when he knew damn well he didn't dare find out.

He looked away from her, but he couldn't find anything to settle his gaze on that would help him to ignore the reaction of his body. Had he been the one to ask for private quarters? He must have been out of his mind.

"You can take the bed," he blurted out. "I'll sleep on the floor."

"Don't be absurd. I'm not going to make any pretense of liking this situation—"

He whipped his head back around and interrupted her with an emphatic "We are in complete accord."

"—but we are adults, there is only one bed, and once you remove your boots, you will discover that the cold happens to be seeping through the floorboards. You would be extremely ill come morning if you attempted—"

"I get the point, Alex!" he snapped, albeit a bit too loudly.

She drew herself up stiffly because of his tone. "You can try to get someone's attention to ask for separate quarters, but from the distant sounds of revelry and music, our bandits are apparently barrel-deep in their celebration. I seriously doubt anyone will hear you."

He doubted it as well, but this wasn't going to work. He wanted her—well, he didn't, certainly he didn't, but his body did, and he was a man who too often allowed his body to govern him. But he couldn't allow it this time. He absolutely refused to let her find out how intensely she'd aroused him.

"You're right on all counts. I simply didn't expect you to be—sophisticated about this."

The stiffness didn't leave her posture. If anything, her chin had gone up a notch, and her spine was actually a little more stiff.

"There's nothing sophisticated about having the sense to share body heat on a night like this," she informed him. "So don't get the wrong idea, Petroff. I'd much rather sleep next to any other body than yours, but since yours happens to be the only one here—"

"Get in the damn bed and go to sleep," he growled. "Morning can't come soon enough for me."

24

Vasili felt her eyes on him as he stood near the oven, about to disrobe. He knew it wasn't so, that his imagination was running amok, because Alexandra had no interest whatsoever in his body. And she should be asleep. He'd waited long enough to ensure that she would be. Yet he imagined her watching him and he became so hard he ached.

It was pure self-torture, getting in that bed to lie beside her. She was tightly wrapped in her blanket, had piled every other one she'd been able to find on top of the bed, and the second he lay down, he could feel the heat radiating from her body.

As chilled as he still was, he was drawn to that heat as strongly as he'd ever been drawn to a female body, and it wasn't sexual attraction. The sexual need was there, too, pulling just as strongly, but this was another need, just as basic, a simple need for warmth.

And yet he didn't dare gratify that need. She'd said they must share body heat, *she'd* said it, not he. But because of the state of his arousal, if he gave in to the one need, he'd lose control of the other. So he lay there, beginning to shiver, gritting his teeth to keep them from chattering, being torn apart by both needs.

Logically, Vasili knew that he would eventually

warm up just as Alexandra had. Eventually his arousal would quiet down, too. And eventually he might even fall asleep. In the meantime, he was going to suffer through the worst night of his life; what he wanted was within his reach, yet it might as well be miles away because he was unable to take it.

But he could at least get as close to her as possible without actually touching her. The bed was narrow. Lying on his side, facing her, he was already close. Just a few inches more . . .

Alexandra sucked in a breath and sat bolt upright when his foot accidentally brushed against hers. "God, your feet are *freezing!*"

In the next moment, she reached beneath the covers, pulled his nearest foot onto her lap, and began to rub it briskly with her warm hands. Her blanket opened in the front, held only by her shoulders, but he was in the wrong position to see what it revealed.

"Didn't you have sense enough to stick them in front of the fire?" she continued, her tone abrasive. "Don't you know that if your feet are cold, the rest of you doesn't stand a chance of warming up?"

There was a part of him that was burning hot, completely disputing that remark. He didn't mention it to her. He also didn't mention that he had sat before the fire, still in his damp clothes, and that the warmth had failed to penetrate them, reaching only a few parts of him.

But the cold hadn't been on his mind then; she had. He had been thinking of her lying naked in that bed, thinking about joining her there, just as naked, imagining her turning to him—and what would naturally occur after that. He hadn't thought of her scolding him, and sitting there warming his foot with her hands, as if it were the most natural thing in the world for her to be doing.

It was a bit of a shock, being treated like a child. But the mere fact that she was touching him, albeit in a nonsexual way, gave him anything but childlike thoughts. And it was even more of a shock that she was touching him at all.

He couldn't figure out why she was doing it. For that matter, why had she practically insisted that they share the same bed? Had she merely suspended their differences for the duration of this misadventure, or . . .

The other reason that occurred to him started his heart pumping to a nearly audible tempo. Could Alexandra want him, yet be too bashful to say so after all that had passed between them?

The numbness was rapidly receding from his foot. After a few moments more, she said in that impatient tone of hers, "Give me the other one."

He was quick to comply, and it wasn't long before he felt warm all over, from either her ministrations or his own thoughts.

"Thank you," he said when she finally stopped.

All she did was give him a curt nod of acknowledgment before she lay down again, turning away from him as she'd been before.

Vasili threw caution to the wind and lied. "I'm still chilled, Alex. I believe you said something about sharing body heat—"

She turned onto her belly and pounded her

pillow. She was also groaning. Ironically, Vasili found that to be quite an encouraging sign.

"You've changed your mind?" he queried, trying for a blend of indifference and disappointment, no easy feat.

She sighed. "No, go ahead." And then she added sternly, "As long as you keep your hands to yourself."

Now, *that* wasn't encouraging. But she turned onto her side again and moved slightly backward, while he moved forward. They connected, back to chest. She would have given no more, but he wanted it all, buttocks to loins, thigh to thigh. He edged closer until they were a perfect fit. She protested by scooting away. He followed until she could move no farther and gave up. She sighed again.

He had to fight down his own sighs of pleasure. He also had to keep his hands tightly fisted, or he'd be touching her all over. But if he couldn't use his hands as he wanted to, he could and did use his body, though he wasn't obvious about it, was in fact quite devious.

It was a subtle seduction. A caress here, a rub there, a shift, a stretch, warm breath on her neck, nothing overt, nothing threatening. And it was working. He could feel her relaxing into him— until that part of him that had a mind of its own pressed against her buttocks.

She stiffened. "It occurs to me that your body has warmed up sufficiently, Petroff."

That was an understatement, but he maneuvered himself to whisper in her ear, "Then why am I still trembling?"

"I don't feel—"

He was quick to interrupt. "Of course you don't, bundled up in that blanket as you are, when all you need are the top ones—and me."

"Petroff—"

He cut her off again. "If you don't believe I'm trembling, come closer."

"No, I'll take your word for it."

"Which is what I did, took you at your word, yet you're not giving me all of your heat." His voice sounded accusing now. "Or is it that you don't have anything on underneath that blanket?"

"Yes, but—"

"Then what's the difference if you remove it? I don't call that sharing—"

"All *right!*"

Beneath the top blankets, she shoved down the one she'd been wrapped in, but no lower than her hips. Actually, she doubled it over her backside, as a sort of shield against what she'd felt.

Vasili almost laughed. She now knew that he wanted her, she couldn't not know, but she wouldn't mention it. He knew this game very well. Instead of leaving the bed, offended or outraged, she was playing the game, making the traditional huffs and puffs of supposed protest. The moves would continue to be his, while she continued to pretend she didn't know what he was doing. It would be a game well played, with a satisfactory conclusion for them both.

And he refused to listen to the voice that warned him that his Alexandra was too direct and straightforward to countenance such games.

Instead he ran through his favorite lines for seduction—and realized that none were appropriate for this particular woman. Honesty, plain and simple, was what was needed and for once, honesty was going to win the game.

But not yet, that voice cautioned. This woman required patience, even if it killed him, and it just might.

Still without touching her, he surrounded her with his body. He hadn't seen what she was wearing, but he could feel it now, some sort of sleeveless camisole, thick and sturdy, nothing frilly. He imagined her in silk and lace and nearly groaned.

After a moment more, he pressed his face to the back of her neck, rubbing it against her hair and skin. He felt her shiver and pounced on this reaction.

"If you're getting cold," he said huskily, "my arms might help."

"No! I'm not!" she assured him. "In fact, I'm getting too wa—"

"I can't tell you how much I appreciate this, Alex," he replied.

Another sigh, exasperated in tone. He wanted her relaxed again, but she wasn't cooperating.

"Am I making you nervous?"

"Of course not."

"Good, because I don't think this is going to work until you—"

Vasili said no more, waiting for her curiosity to get the better of her. Tactics like these rarely failed, and they didn't now, but it took nearly ten seconds, much longer than he would have figured.

"*What?*"

"Until you lie on top of me."

The tension was almost palpable, right up until she exploded with "That does it!" and sat up, throwing back the blankets to get out of bed.

Desperation made Vasili much quicker, his arm snaking around her waist to pull her back down, his chest moving over hers to hold her there, his mouth catching her protest, hushing it for the moment. He had only seconds to win her over, he knew; he could feel her pushing against his shoulders. If he lost this time . . .

Alexandra was lost. She'd fought it from the moment he had removed his shirt and revealed all that golden skin, and contours more masculine than she could have imagined. She'd closed her eyes to fight it, appalled by what the mere sight of his naked chest had done to her. And she'd almost told him to sleep on the floor after all.

But she hadn't. She should have, but she hadn't. And when he'd curled his body to hers, the desire had built inside her, had nearly taken over twice, and now was beyond her control. And he hadn't let her run from it. Had he known what she was feeling, what he'd made her feel?

He held her cheeks with both hands while he kissed her. He was gentle. He was thorough. He was at his persuasive best. And he was driving her mad with . . .

"Your body is driving me mad, sweetheart. I'm sorry, but I can't lie here beside you and *not* make love to you."

Had she said that? No, he had. And for once his "sweetheart" hadn't sounded mocking; it had sounded like the endearment it was supposed to be. But he wasn't giving her a chance to answer him. He was kissing her again, more deeply now, and she was drowning in sensations, the heat, the churning—him. She was drowning in him, with him.

"Yes," she gasped out when she could.

"What?"

"Yes, now."

"Oh, God, thank you," he whispered, covering her face with kisses, not missing an inch of it.

She smiled, not sure what God had to do with it. He didn't notice, moving on to her neck, her shoulders, leaving a moist, hot trail that caused shiver after shiver to pass down her arms, down her spine, down her legs.

The covers were gone. He was her cover now, and she didn't feel the cold at all. On the contrary, she was so hot, a dousing in the snow would have been welcome. Vasili was more welcome, though, when he moved farther over her and settled between her legs, not his hips but his waist, because he'd moved down as his mouth had, following the deep scoop of her camisole, his teeth pulling at the strings that laced it together, opening it inch by agonizing inch.

Her own hands were not idle, were learning the texture and hardness of his skin, the broadness of his shoulders, the thickness of his neck, the unruly hair that was so soft running through her fingers.

"Oh, Jesus, thank you. They're more perfect than I imagined," he said reverently.

223

He had revealed her breasts completely, was staring at them in something akin to awe, and she was finally embarrassed, because she considered them her worst feature. They were too large, frequently having to be bound when she worked and exercised her horses, certainly more trouble than they were worth.

Yet Vasili didn't seem to think so, and she stared at him oddly as he buried his face between them, turning slowly from side to side to share his lips with each. And then his words penetrated. He didn't find her breasts unusual, he found them beautiful, and he proved that over and over again in the minutes that followed. He held them, he caressed and suckled on them, he wouldn't leave them alone. And what that sensual onslaught did to Alexandra, coupled with his hard belly pressed to the center of her loins, was to take her so near the precipice, the tiniest push would have sent her over.

Vasili was aware of that. He knew the female body as well as his own, knew all the pleasure points and how to maximize a woman's enjoyment. And he knew that Alexandra had gone beyond that. Her breathing told him, her fingers digging into his scalp, the arching, the thrusting, her legs squeezing against his waist with more strength than he'd ever felt before. Much as he would have loved to continue his exploration of her body, he wanted even more to feel her climax surrounding him. And if he didn't enter her now, she'd have it without him.

His lips returned to hers to try to calm her with light nibbles while he removed the rest of her underwear, but she was beyond calming. And she was as demanding and passionate in lovemaking as she was in everything else, pulling him to her as soon as she was bare, her hands gripping his buttocks, pressing him forward.

It was mere luck that he was positioned accurately, because she wasn't waiting, was already thrusting upward, and he slid home, into so much moist heat, such incredible tightness, and an unexpected barrier that he broke through before there was even time for him to realize what it was.

There was a barely perceptible stiffening of her body that didn't last, a gasp that she cut off. He leaned upward, disbelieving, but whatever he would have said was forgotten as he watched the pleasure suddenly wash over her, felt the pulse-beat surround him and draw him deeper into her, and in the next heartbeat, incredibly, he soared over the edge himself, caught in the most powerful climax of his experience.

25

It didn't take long for them to feel the chill in the room again once their bodies cooled. Vasili was the first to retrieve the blankets that had been kicked aside. Alexandra said nothing when he covered her.

She was in a state of shock over what she'd done, and it got worse when she realized that not once had she thought of Christopher tonight. Not once had she considered that she was being unfaithful to him. Those damn feelings had just taken over, leaving her uncaring of anything except gratifying them.

She'd never known that passions could be so powerful and all-consuming. She wished she'd never found out. She wished also that she could blame Vasili in some way, but she couldn't. Seducing women was what he did. As far as she could tell, it was his only occupation. She'd known that. And as for his being irresistible, that was God's gift, not something he'd arranged for personally.

The blame was hers and hers alone. She'd known exactly what he was doing, fought it as long as she could, then given up and enjoyed it. And the enjoyment—she wasn't going to think about that. Pleasant feelings had no place beside her present self-loathing. But, oh, God, it had been nice, better than nice, too nice.

For a first experience of such things, Alexandra had to allow she'd had the best, certainly more than she could ever have imagined. But she wished that were otherwise, too. At least she'd be feeling better right now if it hadn't been so damned wonderful.

Vasili couldn't stop thinking about it, and no wonder, since he'd never experienced anything like it before. If he hadn't broken all records on the speed of his first climax, there was no comparison on the second one. But that first time, to come after only one thrust, when had that ever happened to him before? For that matter, when had it ever been that powerful before?

But what he still found unbelievable was that it hadn't ended there. While he had lain on top of her, trying to recover, trying to figure out what had just happened, it had happened again, without any effort on his part, without warning, merely because he'd still been buried in that tight, hot sheath. No, not merely. That in itself was too ordinary to have anything to do with it. It had to be that virgin barrier that he'd found so stimulating, the one thing in his vast sexual experience that he'd always denied himself.

And that was another thing. How could he not have known? Virgins were too easy to spot. They had qualities that were uniquely their own. Alexandra was too bold, too frank, too passionate in her emotions, and there was nothing even remotely virginal in the way she kissed. The typical signs hadn't been there and he felt—deceived, tricked, and about as gullible as a sixteen-year-old.

But at the same time, there was another feeling that was too primitive even to examine, and certainly made no sense. As if it would matter to him that no man had ever been there before him. That *never* mattered to him, only the pleasure mattered.

With such turbulent thoughts on both sides of the bed, the tension in the room was building fast. Vasili felt the need to complain about the gift he'd been given, a gift he would have refused had he been offered a chance to—at least he wanted to think he would have refused it. And Alexandra knew she'd never be able to sleep until she assured Vasili that their making love changed nothing between them—at least she wanted to *think* it didn't.

For her, the easiest way was to tell him. "What I said once about this sealing your fate—forget I said it."

He reared up on his elbow so quickly, it was obvious he'd been about to make some provocative statement of his own. She was relieved to know she'd beaten him to it. He wasn't.

"Am I also supposed to forget you were a virgin?" he demanded.

"Yes."

An impossibility if he'd ever heard one. "Why the hell didn't you tell me, Alex? Whatever you might think of me, I am not in the habit of bedding virgins. In fact, I never have, and I don't appreciate your happening to be the first."

That statement came out sounding so indignant, she nearly laughed. As redeeming qualities went, this one she considered minuscule, but wished to hell he didn't have it at all. He shouldn't care, dammit.

"Why didn't I tell you? Why did I have to?" she countered. "What made you assume otherwise when I've never been married?"

"You're Russian," he said without thinking, but realized his mistake immediately. If that wasn't an insult to get himself shot over, he didn't know what was, and he quickly amended his words. "That is to say, I've been to your Russian court. I found out firsthand how promiscuous you ladies are, including the unwed ones. If there was a virgin there, she was kept well under wraps."

"Or hidden from you for obvious reasons," she replied dryly.

Alexandra wished she could be more offended than she was, but in fact, she'd been to the same court and knew just how jaded and licentious some of the aristocrats were. *His* kind of people. He must have felt right at home.

"But of course," she continued in the same dry tone, "I so reminded you of those court ladies you met, what else were you to think?"

Even in the dim light, she could see the color mounting his cheeks, because he'd just realized his mistake, and it was so obvious an idiot could have seen it. She might carry the title, but when had she ever behaved like a lady or, for that matter, even looked like one?

He didn't apologize, however. She would have been amazed if he had.

"As I recall," he said, "you had your chance to correct that impression."

She remembered the time he was referring to, when he'd asked her what one more lover could mean to her, since she'd already had so many. She also recalled why she hadn't corrected him. Impressions. She'd wanted all of his impressions of her to be bad, and that was just one more to add to the list. But to be called on the carpet for it now? She certainly didn't want him thinking that if he'd been wrong about one, he might be wrong about others.

So she said, indifferently, "Why would I bother correcting you? It's not as if I care what you think of me." And then to be on the safe side, she lied to put the fault back in his corner. "Besides, I didn't think you *really* believed that nonsense about my having lovers."

She might as well have said that no one could be that stupid. Which was exactly how he was feeling. He'd labeled her before he'd even met her, then forgot to change that opinion once he did meet her. Of course, the label fit now, didn't it? Thanks to him. And he still didn't like that fact.

But she wasn't giving him much chance to express his displeasure, and she went on the attack again. "By the way, I've been meaning to ask, Petroff. What is it you do, besides seduce women?"

The fact that he'd managed to give her such a low opinion of him should have delighted him. So why did he feel like defending himself? He wouldn't. He would use her own logic, and he told himself that it wasn't as if he cared what she thought of him.

So he retaliated instead. "I get invited to share their beds without asking for the favor. Care to explain why *you* made that offer?"

"Not for the reason you're thinking, you conceited popinjay," she retorted.

He took it as a good sign that she was resorting to name-calling—though he resented "popinjay" as much as he had resented Tanya's calling him a peacock. But if she had no answer—that she was willing to own up to—then he had *his* answer, and he wasn't going to let her avoid it.

"Well?" he prompted.

"You know exactly why. So stop looking for ulterior motives. There were none."

"Weren't there?"

She glared at him now, but just as quickly she shrugged, then sighed. "I was trying to spare you, but if you want it spelled out, by all means you can have it. This kind of cold is nothing to take lightly. People have been known to die from exposure to temperatures like these, and I'm sorry, but you don't strike me as a hardy individual. Your body seems strong enough, but you court dandies are too used to being pampered by your servants and your luxuries. And dying isn't how I want to get rid of you."

That was *not* what he was expecting to hear, and it infuriated him that she had a legitimate excuse that sounded too true to be anything but the truth. A pampered court dandy? She'd said it once too often.

"I should have let them have you," he growled as he got up and stalked to the oven, where his clothes were drying. "I can't imagine why I didn't."

Alexandra sat up to watch him yank his pants on. The sight of those long legs and firm buttocks before they were covered held her breathless for a moment. And for her to be caught like that again, after what had happened, was galling in the extreme.

So the disgust in her voice was very real, if just for herself, when she said, "Don't worry, Petroff. It will take more than your blundering into a bunch of bandits and getting caught yourself for me to see you in a heroic light. You're still a despicable lecher as far as I'm concerned."

He turned to give her a mock bow. "How good of you to say so."

She sat there bristling, unable to think of a rejoinder that would be insulting enough for him. But by the time he had his coat on and was reaching for his boots, she felt a smidgen of unwanted concern. If he was still thinking about sleeping on the floor . . .

"Just what do you think you're doing, Petroff? Those clothes can't be completely dry yet."

"It doesn't matter," he replied, stomping his foot into one of the boots, "since I'm leaving."

Her brows angled upward. "Oh? You know how to walk through walls, do you?"

"In a manner of speaking."

Fully dressed now, he stalked to the door and, without breaking stride, slammed his shoulder into it. Nothing happened, of course. He must have been rather deflated. Alexandra grinned smugly to herself.

She was about to make some taunting remark when his shoulder hit the door again. To her disgust, the nailed plank gave way this time and the door wobbled open. Old wood, obviously.

"You couldn't have thought of that sooner?" she said scathingly.

"Sorry, but I wasn't angry enough then."

He gritted his teeth against the blast of cold and stepped outside to have a look around. Latzko's main hall was lit up, but none of the other buildings were. Apparently everyone was still celebrating.

Vasili came back to stand in the open doorway. "Are you coming?"

"I'm certainly not staying here with a broken door," she said and started to throw off the blanket before she caught his eyes on her. "Do you mind?"

"As a matter of fact, I do." And he crossed his arms, leaned against the doorframe, and grinned. "Call it recompense for my getting you out of here—so *unheroically.*"

So that dig had struck home? Well, what did she care if he watched? He'd already done much worse.

"Have it your way," she said with blatant unconcern and headed for her clothes, not even bringing a blanket along for partial modesty.

Before she got her drawers on, Vasili had turned away. He was going to add "No shame whatsoever" to his list of her bad points. She was forced to add one more redeeming quality to hers, but hoped that would be the last one.

Before long, they were tromping through the

snow again. The stable was easy to locate, but it was an old building, with crumbling walls that did nothing to keep out the cold. Vasili's roan was there. So was the horse Alexandra had borrowed, and most of the villagers' mountain ponies. But not one of the white herd.

"Where would they have taken them?" she asked.

Vasili was still smarting over how easily his manhood had come to life again at the sight of her naked body, which was why he replied curtly, "I could not care less."

"I'm not leaving here without my horses, Petroff," she warned.

"Suit yourself."

"Don't think I won't," she snapped and led her mount out of the stable.

Vasili gritted his teeth and followed. "Dammit, that celebration could break up at any minute. We don't have time to go searching."

"Nobody's asking you to help."

He felt like shaking her, but knew it wouldn't do any good. And it would take less time to find her horses than it would to argue with her, she was so damn stubborn.

"All right," he conceded. "There will be a new stable around here somewhere. It's doubtful that the old one is even used anymore, except for emergencies like this. Look to the outskirts—"

She'd already spotted it. "Over there, on the edge of the village farthest from the direction we entered."

"It would be," he grumbled, looking in the

234

same direction. "Well, let's at least be quick about this."

He needn't have bothered with the suggestion. She was already heading that way, leaving him to follow again.

The new stable was closed up tight, and a yank on the doors proved it was also barred from the inside, which meant the animals were being guarded. So much for leaving without notice. But this time Vasili didn't bother to point out to the stubborn woman at his side that he'd have to do some bodily harm to someone in order to get her horses back. He knew by now that she'd just tell him to get on with it.

So he pounded on the door and called out in a tone that wouldn't carry beyond the immediate area, "Open up."

It took a moment before a voice came from the other side. "Who is that?"

Vasili made a guess at a common name for the area and supplied it. Apparently it worked, but it did not yield the results they wanted.

"Ain't you heard?" the guard shouted back. "Pavel, he said I don't open to no one but him, and you ain't him. You'll have to wait until morning to get a look at these beauties, just like everyone else."

"He thinks you're one of the villagers," Alexandra whispered. "Play on that."

Vasili considered it a waste of time, but made one more effort. "You're missing the celebration," he called out. "I've come to relieve you."

There was a chuckle. "Nice try, but I've got my own jug of ale and my orders."

The last words were barely heard as the guard moved farther back into the stable. "Do something," Alexandra ordered.

"What would you suggest?"

"You got through the last door."

Vasili snorted. "Forget it. This happens to be new wood, not old, and I'm not damaging my shoulder for your damn horses. We tried; now we're leaving. And you can be toted out of here if you insist."

"But—"

"Your horses aren't going anywhere, *and,* I might add, they're a hell of a lot warmer than we are. They'll be here in the morning, Alex. Now, we can either return to that shack they stuck us in and continue at a disadvantage, or show up tomorrow with an armed escort and get your horses back—one way or another. You choose."

She took her time deciding, but finally said, "I don't like leaving my babies with strangers for even one night, but I suppose it wouldn't hurt to start the bargaining tomorrow with some leverage on our side. Very well, let's find our people."

Vasili sighed. Considering that the cold was getting to him again, he'd almost hoped she would have chosen to return to the shack instead.

26

As it turned out, they might have been rescued if they had stayed in the village a little while longer. At least that was what Alexandra wanted to think, because she hated being beholden to Vasili for getting them out of there. But Lazar and three of Vasili's guards met them on the narrow mountain path not far from the village.

"It took you long enough," was Vasili's surly greeting, which had his friend's brows shooting up.

"Was I supposed to follow a trail buried under a half foot of snow? Even that Russian wolfhound of Alexandra's couldn't pick up your scent. What makes you think I could?"

"Then what led you this way?"

"I remembered where Latzko's village was. I was going to ask for his help, or buy it, as was more likely to be the case. I didn't expect to find you here."

"I don't know why not," Vasili replied. "He does consider these hills his territory, after all."

"But I didn't think he was crazy enough to provoke Cardinia's royal house again."

Vasili was forced to agree. "He's probably not, but Pavel sure as hell is, and unfortunately, Pavel's ruling the roost temporarily."

"Well, that explains it," Lazar said. "I suppose he was hoping Stefan was in our party?"

"Actually, all he was after was the horses. He had no idea who was transporting them."

Lazar frowned. "Then how did he get you and Alexandra as well?"

Vasili's golden gaze lit on Alexandra before he answered sardonically, "Because my sweet little betrothed here thought nothing of attacking six bandits single-handedly, right on their doorstep."

"I didn't know we had reached their village," Alexandra mumbled in her defense.

Vasili said nothing to that, which was saying a lot, since he continued to stare at her. Lazar made an attempt to conceal his grin, but gave up when he saw that the guards were doing the same thing. Alexandra was aware of it, and the heat already climbing her cheeks went up a few more degrees.

Lazar cleared his throat to regain Vasili's attention. "So where are the horses?"

"Locked up for the night."

"But not for long," Alexandra added. "Between the five of you—"

"Give it a rest, Alex," Vasili cut in, clearly at the end of his patience. "You may not be exhausted after fighting through that storm today, but I most certainly am."

"It figures," she replied in disgust.

The black look she got for that remark should have knocked her off her horse. She merely raised her chin a notch and glowered right back. Vasili was too cold to waste time staring her down—if it were even possible.

He sighed. "I'll allow that Pavel might be too drunk to notice that we are so few in number, but he'll also be too drunk to have the sense to lower his price. And if you think I'm going to pay what he's asking for those animals, you're out of your mind."

She didn't want him paying anything that would make her any more beholden to him. "What happened to getting them back 'one way or another'?"

"Jesus, sheathe your claws, woman. Cardinia happens to be one of the richest countries in Europe. We're in the habit of using money first, arms only as a last resort. And we haven't reached our last resort yet. Returning in the morning, when they'd rather be sleeping off all the ale they drank tonight, is still our best bet."

"And if I happen to disagree with that?" she asked stubbornly.

"Wouldn't you prefer that your *babies* spend the night in that nice warm stable they're presently enjoying, rather than be exposed to the elements?" It was rotten of him to play on her concern again, but he wasn't finished making his point. "We can reach one of Stefan's hunting lodges by tomorrow night, so we'll have some proper shelter again. This is the last night that we'll have to rough it outdoors, but this happens to be the coldest night we've seen yet, which you pointed out to me, if you'll recall. And for all we know, that storm could return before morning."

All she'd heard was that his cousin owned property near here. And just as the heat of her embarrassment had gone undetected in the dark a few moments ago, so did the abrupt loss of all her coloring now.

"We're that close to Cardinia?" she whispered.

239

He didn't notice her subdued tone. "Another few days should see us there, as long as we don't encounter any more storms—or bandits. Now we're going to find our tents and get some sleep, and I really don't want to hear any more arguments about it." He turned to Lazar. "I hope to hell you're not camped where we left you."

Lazar was startled to be drawn back into the conversation so abruptly, having been engrossed in that fascinating exchange. "We're about thirty minutes from here, where this path leaves the main trail." But then he couldn't resist goading. "Are you certain you want to head in that direction?"

When Alexandra immediately perked up upon hearing that, Vasili hissed, "He was *joking!*" and gave Lazar a look that promised he'd get even with him for that, before he headed for their camp.

27

Early the next morning, they left one man behind with Nina and the wagons. The rest of the party, all fully armed, rode into Latzko's village, and Alexandra had to admit they were an impressive sight. She also had to admit, though grudgingly and only to herself, that Vasili had had the right idea. Returning triumphant, so to speak, inspired confidence. She *would* get her horses back, "one way or another."

Only a few of the villagers were up and about after their long night of celebration, but that quickly changed as Vasili's men slowly approached the main building. Someone had run ahead to inform Pavel of their arrival, because he stumbled out onto the porch just as they drew abreast of it. No one dismounted. Guns were held at the ready.

Pavel was still shrugging a coat on. That he had no shirt on under it and was barefoot indicated he'd been pulled from his warm bed. He certainly didn't seem to be happy to see Vasili mounted and surrounded by his own people, instead of how he'd left him last night.

"Who let you out?" he demanded.

"I let myself out—and now I want the horses," Vasili replied.

The reminder that all was not lost changed Pavel's demeanor abruptly. "Ah, yes." He

241

flashed a toothy grin. "King Stefan's very valuable horses. I can assume they didn't let themselves out?"

Vasili waited while the bandit and his cohorts laughed over his little joke. He wasn't amused. He wanted to get this over with. The sooner they were out of these mountains, the sooner they'd be back to temperatures he could at least tolerate. Never again would he cross the Carpathians this late in the year.

"The horses aren't for Stefan, as I believe I already told you," Vasili informed the bandit. "However, I did stretch the truth a bit yesterday, since they aren't mine either—at least not yet. They belong to the wench here, and she doesn't have the amount you're asking. But I've promised to get them back for her. One hundred rubles each—and no one dies. Think about it before you answer."

Pavel didn't take that advice, saying immediately, "Double or nothing and you accept my challenge."

"How fortunate that I can afford not to waste my time," Vasili replied in a bored tone.

"You fight me, aristo, or I keep one of the horses for myself."

Vasili nearly rolled his eyes. Why had he known this was coming? Because Pavel was so damn predictable in some ways, and this was certainly one of them. He looked at Alexandra, but her mulish expression said she wasn't going to leave a single one of her precious babies behind, and that didn't surprise him either.

But she did manage to do the unexpected by

interfering, telling Pavel, "The horses are mine. The choice of who fights you should be mine."

Pavel glanced at the three Cossacks surrounding her and laughed. "Pavel is not stupid, woman."

That was certainly debatable and she started to say so. Vasili, guessing as much, said quickly, "All right, Pavel, but indoors, if you don't mind. And the choice of weapons is mine, so have someone fetch the sword that I surrendered last night." When Pavel just stared at him, looking a little green around the gills, he remarked, "No sword skill? Well, never let it be said I took advantage. You choose, then, but I should warn you, Stefan and I shared the same instructors. How is your shoulder, by the way?"

Pavel had become red in the face by that point. Vasili supposed he'd gone a little overboard, reminding Pavel of the knife wound Stefan had given him. But he was a man so *easy* to goad, Vasili hadn't been able to resist. However, he regretted it in the next moment.

"Whips," Pavel said.

There were some collective gasps over the bandit's unexpected choice. Vasili barely managed to contain his. "You call that a weapon?"

"Mine is going to cut you to ribbons. You *don't* call that a weapon?" Pavel countered with a chuckle.

"The choice of weapons was yours, Petroff," Alexandra interjected. "Take it back."

Vasili knew she didn't think he could win with whips. That was obvious. Hell, she hadn't thought he could win against the brawny bandit period, no matter the weapon, which was why she had tried to interfere earlier. Just as he'd labeled her promiscuous, she'd labeled him a useless, helpless court dandy, and refused to see him any other way. And thanks to his moment of generosity with Pavel—he should have stuck with swords—he wasn't going to be able to prove otherwise, because he, too, doubted he could win with a weapon he'd never had occasion to use before.

But he couldn't, honorably, do as she was suggesting either, much as he'd like to. That she thought he would was still another indication of how low her opinion of him was. That was fine, exactly what he had been striving for. But he *seriously* objected to the label of court dandy.

Damn Pavel anyway, and his quest for one-upmanship. Whips, for God's sake. How were you supposed to fight with whips? Take turns slashing at each other and see who could withstand the pain the longest?

Pavel had already sent someone for whips and had reentered Latzko's hall to wait. On Vasili's right, Lazar caught his friend's arm as he started to dismount.

"This is ridiculous. He's using you as a substitute for Stefan."

"Tell me something I don't know," Vasili replied with a sound of disgust.

"How about, 'You don't have to do this'?"

Vasili was quite aware of that. He was willing to pay the ransom, even though he'd end up with nothing to show for it once the betrothal was broken and Alexandra took herself and her horses back to Russia. He certainly wasn't after her gratitude, which could only hurt his campaign. And to say that he refused to let Pavel take one of the thoroughbreds was pretty lame. So why had he accepted the challenge? Payment for that gift he'd received last night?

Disgusted with himself and the whole situation, Vasili dismounted. But he confided in an aside to Lazar, "Relax, my friend. If it gets too painful, I'll concede and pay the double ransom."

"Well, at least you haven't gone *completely* crazy," Lazar remarked.

That was another thing that was debatable, but Vasili didn't say so and headed for the house. Alexandra had also slipped off her mount, and she was practically blocking the entrance to the hall as he neared it. She hadn't heard his exchange with Lazar, which was fortunate, since he didn't feel like arguing anymore, and she'd no doubt insist he hang in there until the bitter end.

"Petroff—"

"Concerned for me, sweetheart?" He'd cut her off, the sarcasm in his tone saying he wouldn't believe it if she tried to pretend she was.

And that sarcasm had her hissing, "Certainly not," regardless of her true feelings.

"Then stay out of it. Whether I win or lose, you still get your horses back."

He said no more, stepped around her to enter the house, and promptly closed the door in her face. But if he thought that would keep her out, he should have known better. She'd want to see him lose the fight, to have something to gloat

245

over. If Lazar hadn't followed her in, along with a half-dozen others, Vasili would have made an issue of it, insisting she leave. Now he merely shrugged mentally. Maybe she deserved this, too, for last night.

Pavel had removed his coat and was presently shoving the sleeping cots out of the way to clear an area. He was apparently going to remain shirtless. A prerequisite? Whether it was or not, Vasili supposed he ought to strip down himself, just to keep things sporting.

He had seen Pavel fight twice before with Stefan, and each time he had fought dirty. Vasili's advantage would have been that Pavel had never seen him fight. With whips, though, he had no advantage, and was really at a disadvantage. Why the hell had he agreed to this?

Killing Pavel would have been an ideal solution, because he didn't have Latzko's sense of honor and couldn't be trusted to stand by his word if he lost. But Vasili simply didn't feel like killing him, even if they were going to use *normal* weapons. The bandit was a bitter man, and a woman had made him that way. Vasili could certainly sympathize with him about that.

Knocking him out was another solution, since there was the possibility that if Pavel lost—for the third time to an aristocrat—and was still conscious at the end, he might be enraged enough to order them all shot. Some of the bandits wouldn't follow that order, but some might, and the risk wasn't worth the taking.

Since his skill with a whip wasn't likely to get him either of those solutions, it seemed his only other alternative, intentional or not, was to lose, let Pavel have his moment of glory, and get the hell out of there. And he'd already assured Lazar that he would concede if it looked like he couldn't win. But this option went against every instinct he possessed . . .

"Finally," Pavel said.

Vasili turned to see a man coming through the door, holding a coiled whip in each hand. The whips seemed nearly identical, but they weren't. He didn't know how he recognized it, since he'd never given it more than a cursory glance when she'd worn it, but he knew which one was Alexandra's. A glance her way proved she had no trouble identifying it either.

Without questioning why he wanted it, Vasili stepped forward to say, "I believe the choice of weapons is mine again, and I'll take the wench's whip."

"What wench?" Pavel demanded, but his eyes sought out Alexandra even as he asked the question.

"You weren't told it was taken from her last night?" Vasili countered.

The frown was there before Pavel's suspicious gaze returned to Vasili. "Did you teach her how to use it, aristo?"

It was a toss-up between lying to benefit himself in the fight and lying to benefit his campaign against Alexandra. Vasili found the choice an easy one.

"Lucky for you," he told the bandit, "I haven't known the wench long enough to teach her anything—of importance."

247

It was a dig for Alexandra alone. Vasili didn't look at her again to see how she had received it, which was fortunate, because he might have made an ass of himself and apologized if he had.

To insinuate that what had passed between them was nothing significant was no more than Alexandra herself had done, yet to hear him say it struck her painfully, and her expression briefly revealed that emotion before she managed to conceal it beneath a mask of indifference.

Fortunately, no one else read anything into Vasili's remark, and when he added, "Shall we get this over with?" Pavel was quick to comply.

Whips in hand, uncoiled and dragging on the rough floor, they circled each other, Vasili waiting to be shown the rudiments by example, Pavel waiting for the ideal opening so that his first strike would be an excruciating one.

Neither got what he was after.

When Pavel finally released his first snap, Vasili was too busy dodging to notice how it was done. The crack of that whip was demoralizing, though, even with its only striking air. And his own first swing was laughable. His coil was dropping to the floor before it even got close to Pavel.

Vasili didn't know it, but he was holding his whip as if it were a sword, and also swinging it like a sword, which might have worked if his target had remained stationary. That wasn't the case, however. Apparently the object was for him to hit, and for him to avoid getting hit in return. So far he was managing to do one, but not the other.

Alexandra was disgusted, watching them dance

around each other. Pavel didn't know much about wielding a whip, but he sure as hell knew more about it than Vasili, and it was only sheer luck and quick reflexes that had kept Vasili out of the whip's path thus far.

And then he was hit. It wasn't a solid hit. Pavel's coil curved over Vasili's back, around his side, and up his chest, where the worst damage was inflicted by the tail, leaving a red, diagonal streak to mar his golden skin. He barely winced, but Alexandra hadn't counted on what the sight of that mark would do to her.

The urge that came over her, nearly over-whelming her, was to snatch her whip from Vasili and make mincemeat out of the bandit. To do that would take her only a minute or two. She knew every place on the body that was most susceptible to pain, and her aim was unerring. Pavel would be writhing on the floor in seconds . . .

She literally had to stuff her hands in her coat pockets and concentrate on keeping them there. She had to spare some of that concentration to remain standing where she was. But she was too angry to keep quiet.

"The snap is in your wrist!" she shouted at Vasili. "Flick it!"

Vasili heard her. He couldn't help but hear her. And it was galling to realize that if she were participating in this fight instead of him, it would probably be over already. Of all the weapons Pavel could have chosen, why did he have to pick her weapon, her sphere of expertise?

249

And Vasili had no idea what she was talking about.

The second strike snaked across his tender belly. He felt as if he'd been ripped open and his guts were about to spill out, but when he glanced down he saw no more than a red welt raised across his skin. Yet that was enough for him to put an end to this, more than enough.

He was about to tell Pavel just that when Alexandra shouted at him again. "That's not a sword, dammit! Don't use it like one!"

Vasili gritted his teeth and tried again. But his lash still did no more than brush teasingly against Pavel, like a worrisome gnat rather than a stinging bee. Pavel, of course, didn't have that problem, and he got in another two flashing, burning hot strikes, the one on the back of Vasili's shoulder drawing blood.

At that point, Alexandra yelled, "Give it up, Petroff—you can't win!" And at that point, Vasili decided to prove her wrong.

Not with a whip, however. He couldn't be expected to use the damn thing with any proficiency without the benefit of a few lessons first, and in the middle of a fight was no time to get them. So his whip coiled next to his feet and stayed there in supposed readiness, and when Pavel's next swing came at him, Vasili didn't try to dodge it. He caught it instead, gave it a hard jerk, dropped his own whip at the same time, and slammed his fist into Pavel's face.

Pavel's feet went up as he went down. His nose was definitely broken, but he wasn't aware of it at the moment. He was out cold, and Vasili felt completely vindicated, having downed the man with only one punch—at least he felt that way until he recalled his own throbbing aches.

"If you were going to do that, Petroff, why the hell didn't you do it sooner?"

Alexandra had come up behind him, and her tone was about as castigating as it could get. He didn't turn around, was going to ignore her completely, but the words came out anyway when she appeared on his left side. "Shut up, Alex."

Lazar came around his other side. "The shoulder isn't bleeding bad, but you should have it cleaned and bandaged before we leave."

Alexandra had retrieved her whip from where Vasili had dropped it, and he knew it was too much to hope that she would have heeded his advice.

"And this is a flick," she said and demonstrated.

The coil flashed across the room, the tail curling around the leg of a chair, and the chair came sliding across the floor, to bump into Vasili's knees. His frown was turning thunderous, but she didn't seem to notice.

"Sit down and let your friend tend you," she told him, *ordered* was more like it, and still in that bossy, chastising tone.

"Shut up, Alex!"

She was treating him like a child again, and in front of Lazar and everyone else this time. And her angry advice during the fight might not have come only because she thought him so inept, as he had assumed at the time. It could also have come from concern, and the mere possibility,

251

unlikely as it was, was making him panic, which didn't help him handle the situation at all well. If she showed the least bit of gratitude on top of the rest, he'd probably murder her.

Alexandra was experiencing her own emotional upheaval that was two-thirds panic, but hers had started last night, when she'd heard they were so close to Cardinia. What was turning her irrational and bitchy now was her actually having been afraid for Vasili during the fight, and that absolutely infuriated her. And it didn't help that she was definitely beholden to him now. Feelings of gratitude in connection with this man just didn't sit well with her. And that she was going to have to own up to it was galling.

But the worst of it was her knowing that he was in pain, and having the ridiculous urge to ease it for him somehow, not knowing how, and not daring even to try. All in all, her emotions were making her crazy, and she had about as much control of them as he did right now, which was none.

If it were otherwise, she might have noticed that he wasn't himself, that it wasn't the pain making him testy, but Alexandra herself. She really should have heeded him and said no more. Stubbornness definitely had its pitfalls.

"I have to thank—"

Vasili stopped her before she went any further. He knew one sure way to get rid of the gratitude he didn't want from her, and short of murdering her, as had been his earlier thought, he didn't hesitate to use it.

"Before you say something you'll regret, Alex,

you should know that I didn't get those horses back for you. If the worst comes to pass and we end up married to each other, I wasn't going to lose the profit they'll bring me when I sell them."

She took that news exactly as he'd expected. For a moment, he was in danger of her using the whip in her hand on him, and with a skill he wasn't likely to appreciate. He knew it. Even Lazar knew it. Vasili had never seen her more furious.

Yet amazingly, she answered him with a degree of calm, for all that each word was gritted out. "You're not selling my horses."

"I don't believe you'll have any say in the matter," he replied.

The dam broke then, her voice raised to the rafters. "I'll see you in hell first!"

He responded in kind. "You'll be putting me in hell if you don't end this damn betrothal!"

"I told you, I can't. I made a promise!"

"Jesus, women break promises every day. What makes you so different?"

"Honor," she said acidly. "Something I'm not surprised you aren't familiar with."

Having delivered that deadly insult, Alexandra stalked off. Lazar had to pull Vasili back when his fury made him start after her.

"For God's sake, let it go, before you end up with worse welts than you've already got."

Vasili turned on him, demanding, "Did you hear what she said?"

"Yes, and you asked for it, if you want my opinion," Lazar said bluntly. "What the hell possessed you to tell her you'd sell her horses?"

"That was necessary, or didn't you hear her? She was about to shower me with gratitude."

"Well, heaven forbid."

"Gratitude and hate don't go hand in hand," Vasili said, trying to explain his reasoning, but then he sighed. He even sat down in the chair Alexandra had fetched for him, suddenly exhausted. "You know, Lazar, this damn feeling I have of being trapped isn't going away."

The change in subject and Vasili's sudden deflation made Lazar wary, yet he replied, "Possibly because you're depending on your mother to now settle this matter, and you don't quite trust her to react to Alexandra as you hope."

"No, she'll be horrified by Alex, I have no doubt, so it's not that. It's as if something's trying to tell me I'm never going to escape the wench."

28

The royal city of Cardinia was a jewel in a fog-shrouded valley, glittering brightly despite its present gloomy setting. That was how Alexandra saw it from afar, and the dismal weather on the day of their arrival matched her mood perfectly. Even when the fog lifted long before they reached the first cobbled streets, and the sun actually made an appearance, her mood didn't improve.

It was a large city that had spread far beyond its original walls, which were so old they were crumbling in places and showed evidence of removal rather than repair. Out with the old, in with the new. Too bad betrothals didn't fall into that category, she mused.

The fog had appeared the morning they'd left the Carpathian foothills, after having spent the night in King Stefan's private hunting lodge. "Private" described that dwelling well, since it turned out to be a place the king visited when he wanted to be alone, and its one and only bedroom assured he wouldn't be bringing friends or family along with him. He had other lodges, of course, that were much larger, but this one was nearest to the mountains.

The stable hadn't been large enough to accommodate all of the horses, but the snow hadn't reached the lowest foothills, where the lodge was nestled, and the climate wasn't much worse than what they had experienced on the Russian plains. As for so many people to bed down, it had been fortunate the hall of the lodge was large.

Alexandra, still in a simmering rage over Vasili's revelation about selling her horses, hadn't asked if she could have the single bedroom for the night; she'd simply informed him she was taking it.

He hadn't been in the best of moods himself and had seemed inclined to argue. "Is that so?"

"You might as well get used to being inconvenienced," she'd told him. "You'll have a wife soon."

"At which time we'll share—"

"Don't count on it!" And she'd slammed the door in his face.

She hadn't spoken to him since. But her anger hadn't lasted very long and had soon turned into dejection. The past few days had been gloomy, with the fog following them and her mood at its lowest point since she'd begun the journey to Cardinia.

Nina and her brothers hadn't been able to cheer her up either, even though Konrad was of the opinion that Vasili hadn't meant what he'd said about her horses.

"He's too rich to need or want the profit the whites would bring. Why would he sell them?"

"To get even with me for not saving him from a fate worse than death," had been her rejoinder.

Konrad had simply said, "If he wants to be saved, he can do the saving himself."

"You think I haven't pointed that out to him?"

And Nina hadn't helped yesterday by

informing her, "Lazar asked me why you don't want to marry Vasili."

"You didn't tell him, did you?"

With the most innocent of expressions, Nina had replied, "Was it supposed to be a secret?"

"It's none of their damn business."

To which Nina had snorted. "It most certainly is Vasili's business, and you should have told him."

"He never asked—you didn't tell Lazar everything, did you?"

"You mean about all those wasted years—?" At Alexandra's blush, Nina had lied, "Of course not. I told him to ask you."

And Alexandra had to assume that since he hadn't approached her, he'd lost interest in the matter. And she could only hope he wouldn't mention it to Vasili. But she wasn't even sure why she felt that way.

It wasn't as if Vasili's learning about Christopher would make any difference. If he was going to do the noble thing and bow out because of another man, he would have done it for his own sake. And it wasn't as if she was worried that he might care. He wouldn't.

She supposed it was her own embarrassment. She simply didn't want him to know that she'd waited seven years for a man—and was still waiting.

Now, as they rode through the city that Alexandra had been so sure she would never reach, she was more despondent than ever. She had done everything she could think of to get

Vasili to cry off, but she was still betrothed to him, and her time was running out.

She was being taken to his family home. Someone had mentioned that to her, she wasn't sure who. But she knew she'd be meeting Vasili's mother there, and she was dreading the meeting because it was going to make the betrothal so final.

And she hadn't decided yet if she was going to continue her rustic ruse for the countess or give it up, since it certainly hadn't made much difference to Vasili that she acted like an uncouth provincial. Would it matter to his mother? If it did, did she have enough sway with her son to get him to change his mind? Probably not, but Alexandra supposed that if there was even the smallest chance, she'd have to take it. Yet it was going to be so much more difficult to be outrageously ill-mannered in the presence of another noblewoman, rather than just Vasili and his men. And this noblewoman had been the wife of her father's best friend.

And then there was a small, wicked voice inside her that had been intruding ever since they'd left the bandit village in the mountains, telling her that she ought to stop fighting it and marry the man. Of course, she refused to listen. There were a hundred reasons she couldn't marry him or didn't want to, and only one reason she wouldn't mind doing that, and *that* reason she shouldn't have learned about at all, at least not before the wedding.

She could chide herself for thinking about it, even ignore it—most of the time—when Vasili kept his distance. But when he was near, or when she caught herself staring at him, she would remember his lovemaking so vividly, it would almost render her breathless. And at night, with nothing else to distract her, she was assailed by the memory. What was increasing her despondency was her fear that if the worst happened and she was forced to marry him, she might forget about all the reasons he would make a terrible husband, and compromise herself for mere pleasure.

She could tell herself it wouldn't happen, but she would have been the first to deny that she'd ever succumb to the temptations of the flesh, yet she'd already done so once. So it could happen, and not wanting it to didn't seem to be much consolation for her lately.

She didn't want to be in Cardinia either, yet here she was, soon to be married. When would the wedding take place? She didn't even know that. In days, or a week? No matter when, it was going to be too soon for her. And whatever delays she came up with wouldn't last for long.

One of those delays was more than likely going to be legitimate, because she was actually making herself sick, worrying about it. Or was it nervousness over meeting Vasili's mother? If that lady welcomed her with open arms, she'd probably puke all over her.

Alexandra shuddered, imagining it, and decided that the meeting, at least, could be delayed right now with a little detour. With that objective in mind, she moved Sultan's Pride up beside Vasili's roan.

"Do you live with your mother, Petroff?"

He looked surprised, which was feigned, she was sure. "You're speaking to me again?"

She could play that game. "You actually noticed that I wasn't?"

He gave up too quickly, sighing. "I wish I hadn't noticed that you are again."

"My question?"

"No, I don't live with her."

"Then show me where you live."

This time he looked genuinely surprised. "Now?"

"Certainly now."

He thought of Fatima and her exuberant welcomes whenever he had been away for even a short time, and shook his head. "It's a bachelor residence. It wouldn't be proper to take you there before we're married."

Being told no only made Alexandra more determined. "If you were worried about 'proper,' you wouldn't be marrying me. Show me your house or I'll camp right here in the street."

"That will get you arrested."

"Really?" she asked with interest. "You think I wouldn't prefer a jail cell—"

He was getting angry. "How about a dungeon cell? That can be arranged."

Cardinia didn't happen to have any dungeons, but at the moment, Vasili was thinking about having one built just for her. And she was beginning to get suspicious of the prevaricating he was doing over a simple little request.

"Is there something about your house you don't want me to know?"

"I merely have a great many things to do today, now that I'm home, and they don't include giving you a guided tour—"

"Fine!" she cut in sharply. "Then I'll view it some other day, when you're not around to be bothered. I'm sure someone at your mother's house can direct me."

Any one of his mother's servants could do just that, and nothing might happen if Alexandra showed up at his house when he wasn't there. Then again, she had threatened to cut off too many ears for him to take the chance.

"Are you always going to be this difficult?" he asked, not trying to hide his vexation.

She gave him a tight little smile. "For you, Petroff, I will certainly try."

"Then by all means, welcome to my humble abode," he said dryly, and his extended arm indicated the house they had just passed.

She gave him a sour look at that point. "This was really going to take *so* much of your time, wasn't it?" she said with frosty sarcasm, and turned her mount toward the not-so-humble town house.

Vasili didn't answer. He was shouting at Lazar, who had ridden up ahead, to continue with the wagons and the horses. When Alexandra realized she was going to be left there alone with him, she nearly changed her mind. But the large, three-story house undoubtedly contained servants. Anyone who claimed to be as wealthy as Vasili wouldn't dismiss his retainers just because he was going to be gone for a month or two.

And she was proven correct when he joined

her at the front door and knocked for entrance. While they waited, she sensed that he was more than just annoyed about her putting him to this bother. He seemed . . . nervous? Was he actually worried about what she would think of his home?

Highly doubtful. She must be imagining it, and what did she care anyway? She was too disappointed that his house had been so close and that visiting it wouldn't take as much time as she had hoped it would. Her despondency was returning, and with it, some self-defensive apathy. What difference did it make if his mother didn't like her? What did it matter if her father was mortified when he learned of her behavior? So what if Christopher would be lost to her if this marriage took place?

The door opened, and Vasili was being greeted by a crusty-voiced servant who surprised Alexandra by his very size. He was the tallest, largest man she'd ever encountered, a giant, really, and ancient, with white hair and wrinkles. By the look of him, he should have been retired twenty or thirty years ago. He was certainly too old to be a butler, which he apparently was since he began directing several waiting footmen, including sending one out to see to the horses. But she had to allow that in his day he must have had no problem keeping out unwanted visitors— What was she thinking? He still wouldn't have any problem.

Vasili was telling him—Maurus, he called him—that he wasn't staying now, but would be back late that evening. He didn't bother to introduce Alexandra, so she ignored them and glanced around one of the loveliest entrance halls she'd ever stepped into.

The white marble floor reflected the jewel tones of the mammoth stained-glass window above the door, which cast a rainbow of colors that turned even the three large crystal chandeliers hanging from the second-floor ceiling into glittering gems. It was a long hall, and quite wide, with a grand staircase centered at the end and corridors on either side of it going deeper into the house.

Many closed doors lined the left side of the hall; only two sets of double doors were on the right, the first set open, revealing a glimpse of white carpeting. She could also see a few pieces of furniture in rosewood, and light-blue-and-gold upholstery on a sofa and some chairs, indicating a drawing room.

Along with an array of paintings in all sizes that filled the high walls, there were a number of ornate mirrors in thick frames, with hothouse flowers on pedestals or long wall tables set before them. The flowers were such a welcome sight in winter. Above some pink roses, Alexandra caught a glimpse of herself in one of the mirrors and winced.

She wasn't as dusty as usual—the roads they had traveled since yesterday had been well maintained—but as always with her fine locks, she had hair escaping from under her fur hat. She'd also picked up a black smudge on her chin, she couldn't imagine from what. Her clothes, of course, were wrinkled, and she looked tired—exhausted, actually—but that wasn't surprising either. A trip that could have taken three weeks had taken five because of the wagons, but Vasili had still managed to keep them on the road for most of the daylight hours of each day. The circles under her eyes, though, were caused by lack of sleep—that little voice that had been bothering her the past couple of days did so mostly late at night.

She wondered whether she should be glad that she looked so terrible for her first meeting with Vasili's mother, or if she ought to take a few minutes while she was here to improve her appearance. She couldn't do anything about the circles under her eyes, but Vasili apparently had a typical staff which would include someone who could give her clothes a quick press. And her hair was easy to— "Master!"

Alexandra turned abruptly. She first saw Vasili rolling his eyes, then followed the sound of the rushing footsteps to the staircase, where a small, black-haired woman in a flowing silk caftan of floral print—a thin garment more suited to the bedroom—was running down the stairs. She appeared to be in her early twenties and was exquisitely lovely, her long black hair nearly reaching her knees, her dark brown eyes large, her body delicate, graceful even in her rush, her features exotic and sensual.

Alexandra merely lifted a brow and said to Vasili while the woman was still a distance away, "Master?"

"Fatima was a slave when she was given to me," he said in exasperation. "I freed her, but she was born in a harem and persists in calling me—"

Alexandra had to interrupt at that point because Fatima had reached them and was about to throw herself at Vasili. "Hold it right there," she said, her voice so commanding it would have stopped a battalion. The ex-slave obeyed instantly.

Oddly enough, Alexandra wasn't angry, though the woman's position in the house was pretty obvious. She should have been angry, probably would have been mere days ago. But today her mood was so gloomy with hopelessness that it didn't leave much room for any other emotions.

If she didn't have to remain consistent for Vasili's benefit, she might not have stopped the girl at all, might have just quietly left so the two lovers could enjoy their happy reunion. At least she understood now why he hadn't wanted to bring her here. And she could see that he was braced for her attack, expecting the worst.

She surprised him instead, merely telling Fatima, "You'll have to find somewhere else to work."

"But I live here, mistress."

"Not anymore. Your *master* is getting married."

Fatima turned to Vasili, apparently thinking that, as the man, he was going to have the last word on the subject. And to make sure his decision would be in her favor, great fat tears appeared in her pretty eyes.

That was when Alexandra got angry. Of all the rotten, female things to do, to use tears to appeal to his protective instincts. As if he had any. It

265

was his rutting instincts that were going to be swayed, but not while Alexandra was there to witness it.

Vasili saw her unhook the whip from her belt, but she'd already snapped it once before he could reach her. The sound brought back to him the painful memory of the welts he still wore, but that wouldn't have stopped him if her intent had been to do damage. Since all she'd done was crack the lash to regain Fatima's wide-eyed attention, and was even now rewinding it, he decided not to tempt her further . . . the hell he wouldn't.

He snatched the whip from her hand, but she merely gave him a disgusted look and chided, "You should recall that I always give fair warning first, Petroff—and I have other whips." Then her expression turned positively menacing as she fixed her dark blue gaze on Fatima to say, "You want to share his bed some more, you're going to pay a price for it. Are you sure you want to?"

Fatima was too frightened to answer. She simply shrieked and ran toward the back of the house. Vasili was torn between going after her to assure her that she wasn't in danger of losing any skin, at least not yet, and wringing Alexandra's neck. He took a step toward Alexandra.

She backed up, but her expression didn't change. If anything, she looked like she was about to scratch his eyes out now that they were alone, but it was a verbal attack she unleashed first.

"You are the most perfidious, lecherous, despicable man in creation! You went to collect a bride, but kept your mistress installed in your own house? You couldn't even move her to another house?"

She was shouting at him. He answered her almost too quietly as he forced her to retreat another step. "I went to Russia to get rid of a bride, not bring her home with me. You were supposed to have sense enough to see that we wouldn't possibly suit. But rest assured, my other mistresses are in other houses, and Fatima will be installed elsewhere before the end of the day."

"But you won't get rid of them?"

"I warned you I wouldn't, sweetheart. So why don't you rejoice and realize that that gives you grounds to end this thing?"

"I'm not just bound by that betrothal contract, you fool, I'm bound by my own word to marry you. When are *you* going to realize that that means it's going to happen no matter what you do, with only one exception? Refuse to marry me, and that will end it."

Another step had her backed up against a wall, and he braced his arms on both sides of her. "I'm beginning to look forward to this marriage, just so I can spend the rest of my life making you miserable."

Alexandra was too angry to be intimidated. "Misery loves company, *sweetheart*," she shot back. "So don't think I'll be suffering mine alone." She slipped out from under his arm and marched out the door.

29

Bojik had been waiting on Vasili's doorstep for Alexandra to appear. She chided herself for forgetting about him. Ever since the snowstorm when he had been unable to find her, he hadn't let her far from his sight . . . and what could have possessed her to lose her temper like that again? She really didn't care how many women Vasili had. Others? He'd said *others,* the son of a . . . no, dammit, she didn't care. It was necessary to do something, yes, to remain consistent, but she didn't have to *mean* it.

She could only be thankful that he hadn't remembered what he'd warned her he would do if she ever threatened another one of his women. She could also be thankful she had gotten out of there just in time, because he had been too close physically. Those feelings that now seemed to well up within her anytime he came near her had definitely been on the rise. And she was afraid she knew what would happen if she lost control of them again.

Vasili kept his eyes squeezed shut, but he could still smell the scent of her, still see the fury in her midnight-blue eyes, such passion, such . . .

He groaned and banged his head on the wall again; he hadn't moved from there since she'd slipped away from him. He could control this, he really could. He just had to keep his distance from her. He'd managed to until today. And what had possessed him to give in to her demand? He should have called her bluff and let her camp in the street. If she got arrested, he wouldn't say a word to prevent it. But when she came before the magistrate, he'd arrange to have her placed in his custody—and the fantasy that that inspired had him groaning again.

His mother was his only hope now, and this hell he was caught up in could conceivably be over by the end of the day. Maria's first encounter with Alexandra could do it and . . . Jesus, she'd left, slammed out of here, and she was too angry to wait for him outside. He had visions of her lost in the city. The way she was dressed, and alone, men wouldn't think twice about accosting her. And he had her whip. He'd left her defense-less.

He felt such fear, he broke out in a sweat, and sure enough, when he got outside he saw that the footman held only his horse. Alexandra's was gone. "Did the lady at least ask you for directions to my mother's house?" he asked the man as he mounted, but was met with confusion.

"The lady?"

"The wench who arrived with me!" Vasili snapped.

"No, sir—but I heard her tell her dog to find Nina, whoever that is."

That news didn't exactly relieve Vasili, and he took off, hoping he could catch up with Alexandra before she got into trouble. But he arrived at his family home without sighting her, and by the time he located his mother in the conservatory, he was out of breath from running.

He also shouted without realizing it. "Where is she?"

Maria, wide-eyed and indignant, said, "Three months' absence and this is the greeting I—"

"Mother, is Alexandra here?"

"No, she isn't," she huffed. "And why isn't she with you? Only her servants have arrived so far, the last one just minutes ago."

That gave him pause. "Was the last one a woman?"

Maria frowned. "I suppose that's possible. I mean, now that you mention it, yes."

The fear was gone instantly, leaving him so weak he had to sit down on a nearby bench. Maria, observing him closely, said suspiciously, "You aren't going to tell me that woman was Baroness Rubliov."

Anger should have overtaken him by now, for what he'd just gone through, but instead Vasili found himself grinning. "I'm afraid so."

Maria was horrified. "And I sent her to the servants' quarters!"

At which point he started to laugh.

"I've never been so embarrassed," Maria later told Vasili. "Why didn't she say anything?"

They were in the drawing room, waiting for Alexandra to join them for dinner. Vasili had gone to the palace to let his cousin know he was back, but Stefan had been in conference with his ministers, so he'd left word that he would see him tomorrow. By then, he'd had only enough

270

time to return home and change for dinner with his mother, which he wasn't going to miss for the world, and to try to calm Fatima.

That had been a lesson in exasperation. She hadn't stopped crying, and while he'd always given in to her tears before, he couldn't this time, not when he knew Alexandra had her ways of finding out things—her people were too clever by half. And he'd found it much easier to send Fatima away for the time being than to deal with Alexandra's temper again. Yet even when he'd told Fatima that her leaving would just be temporary—he hoped—she had not been relieved.

He supposed the easiest way to have assured her that everything would be all right would have been to make love to her, but incredibly, he couldn't dredge up the least desire to do so. Fatima's small, delicate body simply didn't tempt him the way it used to, not when all he could think of was lush curves and breasts so large his hands couldn't contain them . . . Jesus, not again!

He dragged his mind back to his mother's question. "Alexandra didn't say anything because she doesn't care about such things. You probably could have put her in the stable and she would have been happy."

"What a ridiculous thing to say," Maria admonished. "And why was she dressed that way? Did something happen to her clothes?"

He shrugged. "She came with a mountain of trunks, but if there's a dress in one of them, I wouldn't know. The way you saw her is the only way I've ever seen her dressed."

Maria narrowed her eyes so he wouldn't

mistake her displeasure with him. "You're determined to persist in teasing me, aren't you? Really, Vasili, I don't find it the least bit amusing."

"I can't tell you how glad I am to know that, Mother. In fact, I can guarantee that you aren't going to find anything amusing tonight."

"And just *what* is that supposed to mean?"

"He would be referring to me, madam," Alexandra said from the doorway. "Since he can barely tolerate me, he must assume that you won't be able to either."

"My dear girl, whatever gave you that . . . idea?"

Vasili barely managed to keep from laughing. His mother's hesitation came from finally noticing that Alexandra was still wearing the clothes she had arrived in, minus the coat and hat. And Maria was remembering what he'd said about never seeing her in a dress, if the sharp glance she gave him was any indication.

But Alexandra ignored their silent communication to address Maria's question. "If you don't believe me, madam, you have only to ask him. He quite despises me."

Vasili should have known that this evening wouldn't go *entirely* as he had hoped it would. Alexandra's frankness was going to shock his mother, yes, but he wasn't going to escape unscathed from it.

Maria was now indignant again. "Vasili, tell her that isn't true."

He obliged. He even did so with a lazy smile. "Of course it isn't true. Whatever I feel for you, Alex, I could never despise you. That's such a cold emotion, and mine run much—warmer—where you're concerned."

She ignored his allusion to passion completely, and provoked him with an arched brow. "So we are to lie for your mother's sake?"

"I don't despise you, dammit!"

"Vasili!" Maria admonished.

He sighed. If he was going to lose his temper this soon, he'd never get through the evening. And Alexandra's smug look was designed to make him lose it again. The little witch. She was deliberately putting him on the spot.

"Forgive me, Mother. Why don't we assume the subject is exhausted and go in to dinner?"

Maria quickly acquiesced. "An excellent suggestion—except, Alexandra, wouldn't you like to change first?"

Vasili had never seen a more feigned look of innocence as the one Alexandra wore when she replied, "Change what?"

And his mother accepted it. "Your clothes, dear. We dress for dinner here."

Alexandra glanced down at herself. "But I am dressed."

"No, I mean—"

"Give it up, Mother," Vasili cut in. "I honestly don't think she owns any dresses."

"Of course I do," Alexandra said. "What do you think was in all those trunks we carted here?"

"Whips and daggers," he said, straight-faced.

She actually laughed. That it was genuine surprised him. It also warmed him and brought a smile to his own lips. Maria wasn't amused.

Sternly, she said, "We will continue this discus-

273

sion of clothes tomorrow, Alexandra. For now, Vasili, escort us to the dining room."

He did, but he wondered if maybe he should have given his mother some previous warning of Alexandra's eating habits. If Maria happened to insult Alexandra in her shock, the girl could lose her temper with her, and there was no telling where that would lead.

As it happened, he needn't have worried about it. He should have recalled that Alexandra rarely took offense about her unusual habits. And some time actually passed before Maria noticed that Alexandra was eating with her fingers. When she did, she wasn't so much shocked as embarrassed, though she wasn't very careful about broaching the subject. Maria could be direct at times herself.

"Didn't anyone teach you proper table manners, dear?"

Alexandra shrugged. "I suppose they did, but it's been so long, I forget."

"Why didn't you continue the lessons?"

"You must be joking." Alexandra laughed. "To deal with so many utensils is a waste of time, when I could be spending that time with my babies instead."

Now Maria was shocked, and her honey-gold eyes turned on Vasili. "Her *babies?*"

"Horses, Mother."

More shock. "You call her babies horses?"

"No," he replied patiently. "She calls her *horses* her babies. She breeds them."

"That isn't funny, Vasili."

"It wasn't meant to be."

Alexandra could feel Maria's incredulous gaze

274

on her again, but she didn't care. Keeping up the pretense for Maria's benefit was much easier than she'd thought it would be, with Vasili present. Of course, he wouldn't remain here. After dinner, he would return to his own house and . . .

"Just how many *others* do you have besides that concubine at your house, Petroff?"

Maria gasped. Vasili nearly choked. He couldn't believe that even Alexandra, as frank as she was, would bring up such a topic in front of his mother, and where the hell had it come from anyway? But at least she was losing her temper with him, and not with his mother. He really couldn't have arranged it better himself. *This* was going to be the crowning touch, the coin to tip the scales.

"Only three others," he answered, aware that his mother's gaze had just swung back to him, but he kept his own eyes on Alexandra. And Alexandra was gloriously furious. This could only get better. And it did.

"*Only* three others? And you keep them all, pay for them all, fornicate with them all?"

He nearly choked again. His mother sounded as if she were also choking. He didn't dare look in her direction. Even expecting something of the sort, he could still feel heat rising in his cheeks. And he'd thought Alexandra couldn't shock him anymore.

Somehow he managed to answer calmly, "Something like that."

"I'll find them, Petroff, each one of them, don't think I won't. You won't be enjoying them much longer."

"Then I suppose I will be visiting you quite often, won't I?"

"In your mother's house?" she countered triumphantly. "I don't think so."

"You really don't think that will stop me from keeping my promise, do you, Alex?" he asked in a softly warning tone.

"For a lecher like you, no, I suppose not. But Bojik will, and he'll be sleeping with me from now on."

Maria finally found her voice, and it came out quite loudly. "Who . . . is . . . Bojik?"

More color mounted Vasili's cheeks. Alexandra so aggravated him, he had actually forgotten, briefly, that his mother was still sitting there with them. And finally looking at her, he was afraid that he'd managed to shock her as much as Alexandra had.

"Bojik is her dog, Mother."

"There will be no dogs in my—on second thought—oh, God." Maria started fanning herself. "You will *not* go sneaking into her room, Vasili, until after the—oh, God. This can't be—she's—oh, God."

"I know, Mother," Vasili commiserated.

"Did you know?" Her voice was accusing.

"Not everything, certainly. The trip was quite an eye-opening experience."

"And you didn't return her?"

"I believe you told me that wasn't an option," he reminded her.

"No, of course, but—oh, God, this is too unexpected. A lady who thinks horses are more important than—"

Vasili wished his mother hadn't begun her complaints there, because now he had to stop her before she got too far along. But he knew Alexandra wouldn't tolerate any complaints that included her horses.

"She has a mind of her own, Mother." And then he grinned at Alexandra. "Isn't that right, sweetheart?"

"I must have misplaced it, to be sitting here listening to you two dissect me," Alexandra replied as she stood up. But there was no anger in her tone. She even licked her fingers, loudly, before adding, "If you have anything more to say to me, Petroff, I'll be in the stable. Don't bother if it's not what I want to hear."

At that moment, watching her leave the room, he realized that she expected him to end the betrothal tonight, that just about everything she'd said tonight had been deliberate. Jesus, had she figured out what he had, that his mother could end this thing for them? No, she was guessing, testing the waters, so to speak. When he recalled some of the language he'd heard her use on the trip, he knew she could have been even more outrageous than she'd been. Perhaps she'd merely been trying to show Maria her worst so she wouldn't be shocked by her on a regular basis—as he'd been.

"My God, Vasili, that girl is barbaric," Maria said as soon as they were alone.

"Yes, splendidly so."

"You can't marry her as she is."

"Can't I?"

"Of course not. She'd disgrace us both. She'll have to be taught proper behavior first."

He wasn't expecting that. But his surprise quickly turned to amusement. Teach Alexandra to be a lady? It would never happen.

"You don't know what you'd be letting yourself in for, Mother. Don't you think sending her home would be the wisest course?"

She thought for a moment, he'd give her that. But he knew the way her mind worked. This was the closest she'd ever come to getting him married. She wasn't going to give up yet.

"No, the girl needs a little help is all. She was undoubtedly taught better at some point—she's a baroness, after all. She's just forgotten, as she said. Her father must have let her run wild after his wife died."

Her father had a live-in mistress. Why hadn't *she* done something about Alexandra's behavior?

"She swears like a drunken sailor, she wields a whip, she threatens to cut off the ears of any woman who comes near me. And you're going to turn her into a lady?"

He could tell by his mother's expression that she didn't believe a word he'd just said. She wouldn't even address it, asking instead, "Why has Alexandra gone to the stable at this time of night?"

He sighed. "Because she spends every spare moment with her horses. I wasn't joking when I said she breeds them. She also trains them and cares for them, and she's brought her whole herd with her."

"Well, that will have to stop. I've never heard of anything *more* unladylike."

"Those horses mean everything to her, Mother. She gets violent where they're concerned. Go ahead and try to turn her into a lady, but I would advise you not to even mention keeping her from her babies."

"We'll see about that," Maria huffed, but only to maintain her position. She would take his warning to heart and work around the animals for the time being. But she wasn't going to work around him, so she added sternly, "And you, my boy, will stay out of her bedroom. Don't think I didn't understand that byplay between you."

He smiled, remembering her aborted "on second thought." "If you haven't seen her dog yet, Mother, I assure you, I'm not going to tangle with it."

"See that you don't." And then she sighed. "Dogs in my house. The things I do to . . ."

She didn't finish. She didn't have to.

30

Vasili had not intended to go to the stable. Alexandra had said not to bother if he wasn't going to tell her what she wanted to hear, and he wasn't. But instead of sending a servant around to collect his horse as he always did, he went himself.

It was a large stable, though it still wouldn't have been able to accommodate all of Alexandra's whites, plus her servants' mounts, if his mother didn't keep so few animals herself, no more than her carriage horses, and a few extras for running errands. The stable was so large that, standing just inside the door, he couldn't see anyone down the dimly lit aisle, and could barely hear voices deep inside, then laughter.

Following the sound, he soon realized the laughter was Alexandra's, and it gave him a warm feeling, just as it had earlier at dinner. He had so rarely heard her laugh, and usually she did so only in mockery. But this was a sweet sound, full of real humor, and he wished . . .

Vasili turned around abruptly when he realized the direction of his thoughts. He had to be crazy to come in here to see her when he didn't have to. And she was enjoying herself. He would only ruin that and . . . who the hell was she enjoying herself with?

He turned around again and, taking long, angry strides, reached the large, well-lit stall in moments. What he found, however, deflated the hot emotions that had just assailed him.

Four of her mares were in the stall, and Alexandra was applying a poultice to the foreleg of one of them, on a scratch that appeared too minor to fool with. Of course, this was one of her babies and she treated them all as such. And helping her was the Cossack Stenka, who was doing anything but helping, which was why she was laughing. He was lifting the mare's leg, but maneuvering it so that every time she tried to place the poultice, the leg would move out of her way.

"Enough, Stenka," Alexandra said, still chuckling. "Go away now, or I will put this on you instead, and then you will stink so bad, none of the maids will—"

She didn't finish. One of the mares had greeted Vasili with a nicker, and she turned in that direction and saw him standing at the entrance to the stall. Her entire demeanor changed, as he'd known it would, the humor gone, her expression becoming carefully blank.

"It's over, then?" she asked.

It hadn't occurred to him that she would immediately assume that by his presence. "Sorry, sweetheart, but we're still very much betrothed."

Alexandra could breathe again. It had felt as if the bottom had dropped out of her stomach when she'd seen him there. Now she felt queazy, as if she'd just experienced fear. But that made no sense.

She turned back to the mare. She was going to ignore him. He was probably here only to complain about her behavior at dinner, and she could do without that.

"Leave us."

Her head snapped back around. Vasili was staring at Stenka, and Stenka wasn't budging. Her friend was angry, and no wonder. He'd just spent the better part of the past hour trying to lighten her mood with the most ridiculous antics, and having finally managed it, he didn't appreciate Vasili ruining the effect. But she'd succeeded in keeping Vasili and her friends from one another's throats for the past five weeks. She wasn't going to let them have at each other now.

"It's all right, Stenka," she said, her voice firm. "I'll see you in the morning."

Stenka nodded curtly and she finished applying the poultice to the mare. So she missed the looks that passed between the two men. Stenka's expression said clearly, Hurt her and I'll kill you. Vasili's said, just as clearly, She belongs to me now, so don't interfere.

Not that he really felt that way. He certainly didn't. But he'd been compelled to give that impression to the Cossack.

His gaze came back to Alexandra as soon as the Cossack left the stall. And Vasili had to wonder why she'd let the man go when he knew she didn't like to be alone with him. But they were definitely alone now. His arousal came immediately with the thought. Oddly, it didn't annoy him this time. He must be getting used to it. But then, wanting her was so easy—and it happened so damn often.

Alexandra washed her hands in a bucket of

water. When she deigned to notice Vasili again, she sighed. "You might as well get it over with."

Could she possibly have been having the same thoughts as he? "What?"

"The complaints," she said. "That's why you're here, isn't it?"

"Actually, no," he replied. "I thought the dinner went rather well, all things considered."

"Your mother's not furious?"

" 'Determined' would better describe her."

He didn't elaborate, but he smiled, and she was always suspicious of a smile from him. "Then why did you come?"

"To get my horse."

"You came to get your horse, instead of sending someone?" she said, her tone going beyond skeptical to the realm of disbelief.

"Don't make it sound as if I never do anything for myself, Alex."

"You don't."

Now he sighed. "Do you think we could have a conversation for once without arguing?"

"Probably not."

"Could we *try?*"

Her look was wary, but after a moment she shrugged indifferently and asked, "Do you have something in particular you want to talk about?"

He didn't. He simply didn't want to leave yet. But he knew why, or thought he did. His body was hoping he'd do something about the state it was now in. He wasn't going to. Making love to her again could be nothing but a bad idea, leading to complications—and addiction.

But for want of a subject, he said, "I noticed

the wagons outside are still full. Aren't you going to unpack?"

"I took a few trunks into the house. I don't see any reason to unpack the rest."

She was making it very easy for herself to leave on the spur of the moment. He found he didn't like that idea. His body liked it even less, going into something of a panic as he thought of her never being available again to— "I should go," he said abruptly.

"About today," she said at the same time, but she'd heard what he'd said. "Never mind."

He'd tried, he really had. But if *she* was going to bring up his promise of making love to her if she committed any violence, what chance did he have of letting it pass?

"Come home with me, Alex, now."

Her eyes flared, not so much because of the unexpected request, but because he had slowly started to move toward her. She started to back away.

"Why?"

"Because I don't want to make love to you in a stable."

"Stop it, Petroff! I was going to apologize. I wouldn't have lost my temper this afternoon if that woman hadn't used tears to try and sway you."

"A common enough ploy, though I suppose it's not one that you would use, is it?" He was still coming forward.

"Certainly not. But the point is, I was not going to threaten her. I would only have told her she had to leave, which I tried to do—"

"And you ended up threatening her anyway."

"But that wasn't my intention! Your ridiculous promise shouldn't apply!"

"Yet what I saw was what you have repeatedly told me. You don't want me, but nobody else can have me. Isn't that about the gist of it?"

If she wasn't panicking—her back had come up against the wall, and he was nearly upon her— she wouldn't have gotten angry enough to snap at him. "Exactly! I *don't* want you, but for the time being, you're mine."

He was beginning to like the sound of that. "That can go both ways."

"But it doesn't."

"Who says it doesn't?"

And he leaned into her, holding her there against the wall with his body, his mouth seeking hers, leaving her so little room to avoid it, taking what he could get when she did. And she still nearly lost it.

For long, breathless moments she was over- come by the feel of his hard muscles, his rampant desire, his lips on her cheek, and her own unbri- dled response. For long moments she savored the feel of him, and those thrilling, wild sensations that only he could inspire. She wanted so much to give in, to pretend . . .

But she didn't lose control this time. She retained the painful knowledge that this would lead them nowhere, would serve no purpose other than brief—albeit wonderful—gratification. And that was not something she wanted to get used to, when he had no intention of turning this into a habit for either one of them.

So she said the one thing that would stop him, before she lost the will to say it. And she spoke in a tone guaranteed to get results.

"Bojik!"

The dog growled instantly. Vasili hadn't even noticed the wolfhound, since it had been curled up on the other side of the horses. But he knew now why Alexandra hadn't been worried about being left alone with him.

He leaned away from her to say, "You don't play fair, sweetheart."

"Neither do you, Petroff."

Hearing that, he grinned, understanding that it hadn't been easy for her to resist him. She'd had a hard time just getting that reply out. And he wasn't going to let them both suffer when a little charm and skillful persuasion would crumble her defenses—or so he thought.

As his luck would have it, he didn't get the chance to find out. His name was shouted from the front of the stable, and he recognized that blustering tone as belonging to his friend Serge Lehar, whom he would have been delighted to see any time—except now.

Stifling a sound of frustration, he called out, "I'll be there in a moment, Serge."

To which a reply came. "They're as magnificent as Lazar said."

"A friend of mine," Vasili said in a whisper to Alexandra. "He's come to admire your horses, apparently."

"I won't sell to him if he asks."

The unexpected statement didn't surprise

Vasili as much as the stubbornness he heard behind it. "Why not?"

"Because I remember every horse I've sold and still think of them often, and think of their owners caring for them. I won't want to think of one belonging to a friend of yours, because I want no reminder of you once I leave here."

Considering what had just passed between them, he found her reasoning amusing. "You don't think we're going to be married, do you? You've never really thought so."

That might have been true a few weeks back, but the hopelessness Alexandra had carried with her into town today had destroyed that confidence. She wasn't going to admit that to him, though.

"I know what kind of man you are, Petroff," she told him plainly. "A lecher like you married? You'll panic at the last minute and do what you should have done before you took me from my home."

"It's interesting that you should think so," he replied, his fingers brushing softly against her cheek before he stepped back even farther. "I rather think we're going to be married—or not. But the decision won't be made at the altar, I can promise you that."

He left her with those cryptic words. He could have told her what his mother intended. He could have told her that if she didn't cooperate and learn some proper behavior, she'd get her wish, that there would be no marriage. But he didn't tell her. He left it to fate, and he was damned if he knew why.

287

31

The next morning, Vasili found himself in his mother's stable again, but with Stefan this time. "You were right," Stefan was saying as he moved to another stall down the aisle. "I've never seen finer blooded whites. Are you sure she wouldn't sell me one for Tanya?"

"I know my Alex," Vasili replied. "She's as stubborn as a mule. I'd love to have one for myself, but I knew from the beginning that I didn't dare ask. She doesn't even know how much I admire her babies, and I certainly wouldn't let her know how much I want Prince Micha."

"But you, cousin, are a mere count, while I happen to be a king. With all the headaches the title gives me, it ought to afford me a few benefits to go with it."

Stefan might be teasing, but Vasili took the subject seriously. "Don't count on it. If she wasn't impressed by my being related to royalty, what makes you think she'll be impressed by you? And I'd really hate to see you ask, Stefan, and get told no."

Stefan chuckled. "Don't make it sound as if it never happens. I'll have you know Tanya has no qualms about telling me no quite frequently."

"Ah, but Tanya has special privileges. I never heard the rest of us daring to so offend you, Your Majesty."

For that, Vasili got a punch that produced only a half-joking wince. "And who are you trying to impress with that bull? Shall I name you times and dates when *you* have refused to do what I ordered?"

"Only in your best interest."

Stefan snorted. Vasili grinned and rubbed his shoulder. They had spent the morning together, catching up. But Lazar had gotten to Stefan last night, and he'd filled him in on a number of things Vasili would rather not have had repeated. As a result, he'd been suffering quite a bit of ribbing this morning, and Stefan had decided he had to meet this "little barbarian" who thought one of his elite personal guards was no more than a court dandy.

But arriving at the house, Vasili had found that although Alexandra had sat through several hours of his mother's lecturing this morning, she'd finally escaped to the stable. And at the stable, he had been told she and the Razin brothers were exercising some of her horses at the nearby park.

"I suppose I can wait until you marry the girl," Stefan said now, "then buy one of the mares from you."

"Not a chance. *If* I end up marrying her, the horses will remain solely hers."

"That's not the way Lazar tells it."

"Lazar knows damn well I didn't mean what I told her about selling them, and *you* know me better than that, Stefan. Besides, my life would be in danger if I made any claim to those horses, and don't think I'm joking. I'm not."

"She can't be that—well, never mind." Stefan

shrugged. "I suppose if I want one, I can buy one from her father, as Lazar did."

"Hers are better," Vasili said with an unmistakable note of pride.

"Don't rub it in, when you've assured me I can't have one. Now, if I'm going to meet the lady, I suppose we should take a ride through that park on the way back to the— Jesus, is that her?"

Vasili swung around, and he had to wonder just how long Alexandra had been standing behind them. Considering some of the things he'd said to Stefan, he had color mounting his cheeks. Yet her expression was completely bland. She couldn't have heard anything, or she'd be showing some definite signs of anger.

Stefan's surprise was for obvious reasons. He'd been told she wore nothing but breeches, but seeing a woman of her attributes so abundantly displayed would give any man pause. She had removed her coat and was holding it over one shoulder with a finger. Her other hand was thrust in a pocket. Her cheeks were rosy from the cold outside. And as usual, long strands of her ash-blond hair had escaped from under her hat. She looked adorably disreputable—for a baroness.

"Come here, Alex, and meet my illustrious cousin," Vasili said.

She stepped closer, though she did so rather slowly. "Do I call you Your Majesty, or, since we're apparently going to be related through marriage, do I call you Stefan?"

"I would prefer Stefan."

"What about curtsying?"

Vasili answered. "Without a skirt? Perhaps a bow would suit you better."

She didn't rise to the bait, and Stefan said quickly, "Neither is necessary. I've been looking forward to meeting you, Alexandra. My wife is even more eager and has invited you to come to the palace this afternoon."

"I'll be bus—"

"She'll be there," Vasili cut in, and his look was full of warning for her not to contradict him.

She didn't bother, though she had no intention of complying. It would be too embarrassing to maintain her rustic ruse at the Cardinian court. Besides, just as she had held herself aloof from his friends on the trip, she intended to maintain a distance from his royal relatives. At least she would try. But she wasn't crazy. She had as much healthy wariness for royalty as anyone with any sense did. And King Stefan of Cardinia, with those scars on his cheek and his golden eyes, which were so much more prominent than Vasili's, would have intimidated her even if he weren't a king. The less she had to do with him and his wife, the better.

He must have sensed her wariness, or was so accustomed to inspiring it that he had made it a habit to keep introductions brief. He took her hand—he had to lift it from her pocket—and kissed the knuckles, saying, "It is my hope that I will soon welcome you to the family, Alexandra. But now I must return to the palace, though I would like to view your stallions first. I assume they have returned with you?"

She merely nodded, and with a parting smile,

Stefan headed outside to where the stallions were being walked after their brisk ride. She stared after him, uncomfortable with the feeling that she could like him if she let herself. It took her a moment to realize that Vasili hadn't followed him out.

She wished that weren't the case. She wasn't at all happy with him at the moment, though when had she ever been? But now she was confused by what she'd overheard. He'd lied about intending to sell her horses. He'd concealed from her his admiration for them, and that he was as much a connoisseur of fine horse-flesh as Lazar was. Had he guessed that it would raise him in her estimation if she'd known, that she could never hate anyone who loved horses as much as she did?

She wasn't going to mention what she'd heard. She needed time to figure out his motives for deceiving her. And she had to wonder what else about him wasn't true. Even hearing him call her "my Alex," which was what had stopped her in her approach, made no sense to her, and she was alarmed by the thrilling pleasure it had given her.

Refusing to examine her feelings for him, she could only conclude that it had been so much easier when she had been able to hold him in complete contempt.

"You'll have to dig out one of those dresses you claim to have for this afternoon," he told her.

"No, I won't. Convey my apologies—"

"You're going, Alex. You don't refuse an invitation from a queen any more than you would one from a king. Even you have to know that."

Again she didn't rise to the bait, which his condescending tone only made more tempting. "Your mother is determined to monopolize my mornings with nonsense, Petroff, leaving me no time to waste on visiting. You can tell that to your queen."

"I'll tell her no such thing. Did you lose your temper with my mother?"

"No, I was kind enough to humor her, though I don't know how long I'll be able to keep my patience. For now, she thinks she made some progress."

"Did she?"

Alexandra snorted. "What do you think?"

He grinned at her. "I think you will do what you want, despite well-meaning advice—except for today. Be ready and dressed appropriately, Alex, by two o'clock. I'll pick you up in my carriage—"

"No—"

"Or Stefan's soldiers can escort you."

32

Alexandra compromised. She was ready to leave at the appointed hour, but she was dressed in her usual attire. She had an excuse for Vasili which wasn't exactly the truth, but she was sure she could make him believe it.

And she gave it to him the moment he arrived, before his expression turned too thunderous. "It's your fault, Petroff." Her tone was deliberately accusatory. "Not allowing me enough time to pack properly. It's no wonder all my gowns are ruined. Even your mother was scandalized when I told her how you rushed me into leaving with less than a day's notice. You owe me a new wardrobe."

That bit about her telling his mother was an underhanded tactic and it actually had him blushing. Why had he never considered that Alexandra's frankness could extend to his own outrageous behavior on the trip? She could, if she realized it, win Maria completely over to her side, and he'd never hear the end of it if that happened. But that wasn't what Alexandra wanted. She had to be aware of that.

For now, he addressed only her demand for clothes. "If you were hoping I would balk at supplying you with a new wardrobe, I'll have to disappoint you. It will be my pleasure. But for today, couldn't my mother give you something . . . ?" At her lifted brow, Vasili was forced to correct himself. "No, I suppose you are too dissimilar in size." But then he snapped, "Dammit Alex, stop looking so pleased about this! It doesn't cancel your trip to the palace, not when the queen is waiting."

"I didn't imagine it would."

"Then you're probably thinking this is going to embarrass me, but you're wrong," he said as he ushered her out the door. "You're the only one who is going to feel conspicuous, dressed as you are. I happen to enjoy looking at you no matter what you're wearing."

Vasili hadn't meant to say that, couldn't imagine where it had come from. But before he put his foot further in his mouth, he dropped the subject completely. And because Alexandra had been disturbed by his remark as well, both of them were silent during their trip to the palace, which was fortunately only a few blocks away.

Alexandra had been to a reception at the Czar's palace in St. Petersburg, but nothing could have prepared her for the opulence of the Cardinian palace. It covered an entire city square and was three stories high; the halls alone contained more solid gold in frames and statues than she'd ever imagined to see in a lifetime. Every floor was polished marble, every window adorned in rich velvet or silk, every wall lamp tiered with crystal, all in quiet elegance rather than the Russian preference for grandiose display.

It wouldn't have been so bad if the long hallways they had to traverse had been empty, but they weren't. Besides the liveried servants standing on duty outside doorways, there were courtiers in abundance, coming and going, gathered in groups talking, all in their fancy court finery. And every single one seemed to stare rudely at Alexandra, either in avid curiosity or in outright disdain.

But even that wouldn't have been so bad if the ladies, one after the other, hadn't greeted or hailed Vasili with such pleasure, and too many of them did so with an intimate familiarity that spoke of past association. Alexandra was able to remain quiet the first two times Vasili was stopped, because he broke away quickly with the excuse that the queen was waiting for them.

But the third time she saw a woman reaching for him to detain him, Alexandra stepped between them and declared, "He's soon to be married, madam. You can still talk to him, but from now on you will refrain from putting your hands on him, however innocent your intent."

Vasili was whisking her away from the open-mouthed woman before she had got the last word out. "And here I thought you were actually going to behave yourself," he said.

"It's going to get worse if they don't keep their hands off you."

"I suppose you're going to tell me now that only you have the right to touch me."

"I see we understand each other."

Then when the hell are you going to start? he wondered, but to her, he kept in form by complaining, "You're pushing it, Alex."

"You were given fair warning, Petroff."

"So were you," he reminded her, and was

pleased to note that whatever she'd been about to reply to that, she thought better of it. "And," he added, *"you'll* have to deal with my mother when she hears about this, and I can guarantee you that she will. I don't think she'll accept jealousy as an excuse for scandal."

"You know very well jealousy doesn't come into this," Alexandra said crossly.

"Certainly, but no one else is going to believe that, sweetheart, least of all my mother. And she happens to be of the old school that agrees a wife should ignore her husband's little indiscretions, and jealousy is the height of foolishness."

"I'm not jealous!"

"I think enough people heard you—but they still won't believe it."

"Now who's pushing it?" she gritted out.

He chuckled, amazed that he was actually enjoying this verbal battle, probably because, for once, he was coming out ahead with her. "I would suggest you contain that temper of yours, Alex. You're about to meet the queen."

"Thanks to you, I'll probably end up insulting her," she retorted.

"I hate to say it, but what you're *wearing* is going to insult her."

"Damn you, Petroff!"

"Shh. We've arrived."

They had indeed, and he apparently didn't have to be announced, because he opened the door to the queen's receiving chamber and walked right in, the guards at the door merely nodding at him. And since he was still holding Alexandra's arm from when he'd forcibly pulled her away from that woman, she didn't get the opportunity to hang back so she could try to compose herself.

The room wasn't as large as she might have expected, and the three women in it were informally dressed in day gowns that were obviously of fine quality. Two of the women were Tanya's favorite ladies-in-waiting, Alexandra was to learn, both married and in love with their husbands as the queen was with hers, which was probably why Alexandra sensed immediately that she wouldn't have to do battle here, and she began to relax.

The two ladies merely nodded at Vasili and Alexandra on their way out, but Tanya hadn't seen Vasili since his return, and her greeting in English was warm as she approached him with open arms. It was automatic for him to accept her hug, which he started to do until he recalled who was with him and backed off in alarm.

Alexandra noticed, and said in English for the queen's benefit, "She can."

He didn't have to ask her what she was talking about, but after the alarm he'd just experienced, he was annoyed enough to demand, "Why can she?"

"Because she's happily married and doesn't have designs on you."

Tanya lifted her brows. Vasili said, "You don't want to know, Tanya, believe me."

Alexandra shot him a baleful look for that. Tanya laughed and said, "Maybe I don't. So introduce us instead." He did, and after a moment of studying Alexandra, she added,

"You're luckier than you deserve, Vasili. She's beautiful."

The statement made both Alexandra and Vasili uncomfortable. He knew Alexandra was beautiful, but he wasn't about to own up to it in her presence. And she never did like hearing it.

But Tanya didn't notice, and went on to say, "Come, I've ordered refreshments and—"

"We've both eaten," Vasili said so fast, Tanya raised a brow again.

Alexandra had to bite back a laugh that he was so horrified at the thought of her eating in front of the queen, and she decided to tease him. "Actually—"

"You're *not* hungry, Alex, believe me you're not," he stated emphatically.

At which point Tanya placed both hands on her hips and demanded, *"What* is going on?"

"Nothing, just a private joke," he assured her, and to change the subject, he added, "I must say you're looking pleasantly plump—quite different from the last time I saw you."

It was a subject guaranteed to lighten the queen's mood and she grinned. "I am, aren't I? Which reminds me. Before I get any more plump, I want to arrange a ball to introduce Alexandra to—"

"No!"

He'd actually shouted, and Tanya said in exasperation, "Why ever not?"

He didn't bother to prevaricate this time. "Because Alex would find some reason to show up just as she is."

"Oh, come now," Tanya scoffed, but she

looked at Alexandra to deny it, and found an expression that was just too inscrutable. After a thoughtful moment, Tanya suggested, "Vasili, why don't you go find Stefan? I believe he's on the training field—and from what I've heard, you could use some practice yourself."

"Lazar and his big mouth," Vasili grumbled. "You make it sound as if I *chose* whips. And besides, I don't dare leave you alone with—"

"Run along, Petroff," Alexandra cut in dryly. "I'm not going to murder your queen, but *you* aren't going to be so lucky if you say another word."

He winced, and she was right. By trying to keep her from embarrassing herself, he was doing it for her, which hadn't been his intention.

He tried to make amends. "I'm sorry, Tanya, if I've given the wrong impression. She's really very . . ." He had to pause to think of something nice to say other than "kind to animals."

"Go!"

That from Tanya, in complete annoyance now, and he sighed and went. The two women shared a moment of silent communion, having found something in common—easy exasperation where Vasili was concerned. And yet they were still strangers, Tanya hoping to change that, Alexandra wary of trying.

Accordingly, Alexandra offered an innocuous subject as Tanya led them to a group of comfortable chairs. "You speak English very well."

"I was raised in America. It's pretty common over there. And you?"

"My tutor insisted I learn French and English,

though my English was not so good until—much later."

Tanya didn't notice the pause and said, "What little French I know, I learned from the patrons where I used to work, though not enough to manage a decent conversation. But I'm delighted we won't need an interpreter. So often I do require one, though I'm learning Cardinian. I understand it's very similar to Russian, so you should have much less difficulty learning it than I."

Alexandra had no intention of learning it, but she didn't say so, and her curiosity had been aroused despite her determination to remain aloof. "You used to work?"

"Didn't Vasili tell you? I was raised in a tavern without any knowledge of who I was. When Stefan and his friends found me and tried to convince me I was a princess from this country, betrothed from birth to the Crown Prince, I didn't believe a word of it. I thought they were playing some elaborate practical joke at first, and then when they insisted I come along with them, I'm afraid I thought they were planning to sell me to some brothel. Such things were known to happen along the Mississippi."

Alexandra's eyes had gone wide during Tanya's story, but now she burst out laughing. "A brothel?"

Tanya grinned. "I know how farfetched that sounds, but it happened to be much more believable than my marrying the king of some country I'd never heard of."

301

"I see your point. What finally convinced you they were telling the truth?"

"When they had me on a ship bound for Europe, they finally admitted that Stefan was the king, rather than Vasili."

"Vasili?"

Tanya snorted in remembrance. "That was Stefan's idea. I was giving them trouble right from the beginning, and he thought I'd come along with them more willingly if I was told Vasili was the king I was to marry."

"I can't imagine why."

"Neither could I. I positively detested the man at the time, he was so condescending and downright insufferable, but I have to admit I'm quite fond of him now."

"You mean it's possible to get used to his arrogance?" Alexandra asked doubtfully.

Tanya chose not to answer that, at least not until she had clarified what she had begun to suspect. "Can I ask you why he didn't want you to eat anything?"

"Will my answer get back to him?"

"Not if you don't want it to."

"Very well. He didn't want *you* to see me eat anything. He thinks I eat like a pig."

She said it with enough amusement in her tone that Tanya felt free to ask, "Do you?"

"Only when he's around."

"I begin to understand. Lazar told us about the trip, but mostly about Vasili's behavior. You really *don't* want to marry him, do you?"

"Would *you* want to marry a lecher like him?" Alexandra countered.

Tanya laughed. "I agree he indulges in excess, but he's too handsome for his own good, and women tend to make fools of themselves over him. I had intended to warn my ladies that he is no longer available."

"Well, that will save me the trouble of cutting off any more ears." Alexandra snorted.

Tanya was startled. Lazar hadn't mentioned that, merely that there had been threats. "Would you really?"

"No, but women tend to prefer not to find out."

Tanya laughed again. "I suppose not. But, you know, Vasili has never had a reason *not* to be a libertine. And as I understand it, you told him you didn't want to marry him when you first met him, which wouldn't have encouraged him to change *that* aspect of his nature."

"I had only learned of this damn betrothal a few hours before I met him."

"You must be joking!"

"Not at all," Alexandra said in remembered disgust. "My father kept it a well-guarded secret. He was afraid that if he gave me prior warning, I wouldn't be there to meet Vasili at all, which was likely, considering how furious I was."

"Was that the only reason you didn't want to marry him—because you were angry?" Tanya asked gently.

"No . . . but I'd rather not discuss the other reason." Alexandra was already blushing, just imagining the queen's reaction to someone's waiting seven years for a man to get around to proposing. "It's—well, I find it embarrassing."

"Then don't think of it. But I have to ask, since I'm so fond of Vasili, if you still feel nothing for him."

Alexandra wasn't sure how to answer, considering that the woman *was* so fond of him. "I have sensed, just recently, that he might have a few good qualities, though he rarely shows them. But—whatever I feel for him, it doesn't matter. You said it yourself, how contemptuous and insufferable he can be, and that's about all I've seen from him. I could never get along with someone like that."

"And how does he get along with you—as you are?"

Alexandra blushed. "I may have pretended to be something I'm not, but I was trying to make it easy for him to end the betrothal, since I can't."

And that put Tanya in something of a dilemma, wondering if she should tell Alexandra the truth about Vasili, or if it wouldn't make any difference if she knew. Lazar had told them some surprising things, about Vasili calling her "his" without realizing it, and asking Lazar to seduce her, then changing his mind, and displaying some obvious signs of jealousy over the girl. That pointed to something other than indifference as far as Tanya was concerned.

"Would you be surprised to know that Vasili has done exactly what you have?"

"What do you mean?"

"He hasn't shown you his true self. When I said I detested him—and I really did—it was because he was doing everything possible to *make* me detest him, and he did it all deliberately."

"Why?"

"Because women tend to fall in love with him before they even know him—it's that face of his—and he was afraid I would do the same when I was to be Stefan's wife, not his. He loves Stefan, you see. They are more like brothers than cousins. And he'd do anything to assure Stefan's happiness, including acting like the most despicable, condescending jackass imaginable, when he's not like that at all."

Alexandra had gone very still. "He's not?"

"Not at all—well, perhaps a little arrogant—no, make that very. I believe arrogance runs in the family. And maybe he does occasionally belittle things that he deems unworthy with that diabolical wit of his, but he more than makes up for that with his loyalty and dedication to duty."

"What duty? He's no more than—"

"One of the king's personal bodyguards, his elite guard, and quite deadly with numerous weapons, which you can see for yourself if you care to take a stroll by the training field before you leave. You know"—Tanya took a moment to reflect—"Vasili didn't like me either when we first met. He thought I wasn't good enough for Stefan. But when he could have let me escape—I tried to more than once—he didn't. 'Duty before preference' was how he put it, and he meant it. And there's something else you probably don't know. He's also incredibly charming when he's not *trying* to be nasty."

"You're right, I wouldn't know," Alexandra said in a hollow tone.

"Please, you weren't supposed to be hurt by what I've told you."

"I'm not," Alexandra insisted, if a little stiffly.

"If Vasili has shown you the worst he can be, it's because he didn't want to get married. He was very upset when he learned of this betrothal. He went to Russia to—"

"Get rid of me."

Tanya winced. "He told you?"

"Yes; he's been quite honest about that at least."

"But the point I was trying to make was, I'm not so sure he still feels that way. Yet he's locked himself into this role he's playing for you—just as you have."

Alexandra wasn't so sure Vasili *was* playing a role, but if she was to believe it, then that made the whole thing even worse. He was so against marriage he had to pretend—just as she did. And what would happen if she showed her true self? Would it matter? No, he had been against marriage before he'd met her, and again after, and Tanya might not be sure, but she was—he was still against it. And he *was* a lecher. The queen hadn't contradicted that. And *she* had to be crazy even to think about it.

"Vasili might have some noble virtues I would never have guessed at," Alexandra said. "But he's still a lecher."

"Yes, and probably will be—until he falls in love."

33

Alexandra decided she wasn't going to wait for Vasili to collect her from the receiving chamber. She would use his carriage, then send it back for him, and hopefully she wouldn't see him again for a while. She needed time to digest everything she'd been told before she spoke with him again—*if* she ever spoke with him again. At the moment, she couldn't imagine her reaction if she had to listen to another taunting, derisive remark from him, when she knew now that it was all for effect, because he *wanted* her to despise him.

But it wasn't all lies. What he'd told her about the way their marriage would be was undoubtedly the truth. As Nina had pointed out, most aristocratic marriages were exactly like that, though usually the terms weren't spelled out, just mutually understood. And every time he'd pushed her to break the betrothal, he'd been expressing his true feelings. And his lecherous inclinations were also all true.

She did stop by the training field before she left the palace. She'd been unable to resist, and in the space of minutes, she watched Vasili defeat one opponent after another with his sword skill. Some court dandy, she thought in disgust. And yet the signs that he was really quite different from that had been there all along, the military physique and bearing, the way he rode a horse, his quick reflexes, how easily he'd ended that fight with Pavel when he'd got fed up, even the way he'd gallantly declined the use of swords, because he'd known Pavel wouldn't have stood a chance with them. She'd seen only what she'd wanted to see because she hadn't *wanted* to be impressed.

She really wished the queen hadn't felt the need for confessions. On the return trip to the Petroff home, she recalled their parting words.

"I'd like you to be one of my ladies," the queen had told her.

"I thank you for the offer, but I couldn't possibly accept. I have an image to maintain for Vasili, and it isn't exactly ladylike."

Tanya had frowned. "Then you're not going to tell him the truth?"

"I don't see any point in doing so. It would cause one hell of a fight. He'd be furious with me; then I'd throw it back at him that he hasn't been honest either. And we'd still be right where we are now, neither of us wanting to marry the other."

The queen hadn't been very happy with her decision, but Alexandra wasn't going to be budged from it. Nor was she going to delve any further into her own feelings. How she felt about Vasili simply didn't matter when he still didn't want to marry her. It occurred to her that there was one more thing she could do to help them both get out of this approaching marriage. She could refuse to cooperate with his mother's training program.

Maria was already displeased with her.

"Disgusted" might be a better word. And it was Vasili's mother who'd told him he couldn't go against his father's wishes. That was the reason he'd given for being unable to break the betrothal. But if Maria changed her mind . . .

Vasili received yet another summons from his mother. He'd managed to ignore it for a day and a half, but Maria's messengers kept showing up at his house, and finally one was sent to the palace and caught him when he was with his cousin. And Stefan's saying, "I hope she's not going to appeal to me again," told him he'd better take care of it before she did.

But he knew what the countess wanted this time. After her first note of complaint had been delivered to him two weeks ago, telling him, "The girl is impossible," and, "You're going to have to talk to her," he hadn't bothered to read the others that had been sent nearly every other day. He'd merely jotted off encouraging replies such as "You can do it, Mother," and "I'm counting on you, Mother." And once, still without reading the message, but because he *knew* Alexandra and he was starting to be amused by the whole thing, he'd advised, "Ignore her temper, it's mostly hot air."

His only surprise was that Alexandra hadn't sent him some complaints as well. But expecting them was one of the reasons he had decided to stay away from her until her transformation was complete—or had failed. Having to deal with her temper would most likely provoke his own, which would lead to his wanting her again—and he was having enough difficulty dealing with that *without* seeing her. Fate was going to decide this thing, one way or another.

But his mother was determined to interfere with what he'd thought was an excellent plan. Still, it was possible that he might be able to see his mother, listen to her harangue, convince her that she couldn't expect miracles in only two weeks, then leave before running into Alexandra. Now, if he could just resist the *urge* to see her . . .

At least his mother was alone when she joined him in her drawing room. He'd half expected her to have Alexandra in tow, dressed in one of her new gowns that she would hate wearing. But the scene was more reminiscent of the night he'd first learned of the betrothal, except it was afternoon and Maria wasn't dressed for a social engagement—and she definitely wasn't smiling this time.

He tried to forestall his mother's complaints by asking, "How is the new wardrobe coming along?"

Unfortunately, that topic happened to be on Maria's list. "The girl refuses to 'waste any more time,' as she puts it, with fittings, and she won't wear the several gowns that have been completed for her already."

"Why not?"

"They are either the wrong color, or too tight, or too loose—she never lacks for excuses."

Vasili managed to keep from grinning. "I have the feeling she's worn her breeches and shirts too long. She probably finds dresses too constraining now."

"A lady can*not* go about dressed as she does!"

"I know, Mother."

"She can't hold a fork or a knife without dropping it. The most disgusting words come out of her mouth when she gets the least bit frustrated. And she threatened to roast my cook!"

That one caught his interest. "She got angry with Monsieur Garrard? Why?"

"Because I thought she could benefit from the experience of a seven-course meal," Maria replied stiffly.

"But that would take hours," he pointed out.

"Exactly, and before the sixth course arrived, she marched into the kitchen and told Monsieur Garrard that if he sent out one more course, she'd make sure he was in it. He quit."

"I never liked his soufflé anyway," Vasili managed to say straight-faced before he burst out laughing.

Maria glared at him, but that didn't curb his amusement. He wished he could have seen Alexandra in the kitchen. She must have been magnificent with her midnight eyes flashing, her breasts heaving . . .

"How can you laugh?" Maria demanded. "She's no longer even pretending to try to correct her behavior. She claims we have no right to change her."

That sobered him, and he said quietly, "She's right, you know. We don't have the right to try to change her."

Apparently that wasn't what his mother was

hoping to hear, because she said, in an offended tone, "You're going to make me say it, aren't you?"

"What?"

"That I made a mistake, that I never should have insisted you collect a bride sight unseen."

"*Is* that what you're saying?"

"I'm telling you that you can't marry this girl. She doesn't want to learn how to be a lady. All she wants to do is muck about in a stable. Stefan will agree. We can't have someone like that in the family."

"Stefan won't care one way or the other—what about my father's honor?"

"Vasili, I promise you, your father would break that betrothal himself if he were alive today. He made a contract in good faith, but Baron Rubliov broke that faith by allowing his girl to turn out as she has. And you needn't hide your relief for my sake. I *know* this is what you've been waiting to hear."

It was indeed, but now that he'd heard it, he wasn't reacting as he'd imagined he would. Instead he felt as if the bottom had dropped out of his belly.

"Where is she?"

"Locked in her room," Maria replied. "She has been there since early yesterday morning, which is why I sent for you. She won't open the door. She won't even answer inquiries. I've never known anyone who could be so willfully stubborn."

Neither had he. "I'll take care of it," he said on his way out of the room.

"Good," she huffed. "And you can also make the arrangements to send her home. I've already told . . ."

He didn't hear the rest of what she was saying because he had already started to run. Even as a child, he'd never reached the upper floors so quickly. That he didn't know which room was Alexandra's didn't slow him down, but it was fortunate that an upstairs maid appeared to point him in the right direction, or he would have broken down every closed door in the house, locked or not.

Hers was still locked and she wouldn't answer his demands to open it. It didn't take him long to break it down, because his fury was mounting at what he knew he would find. His Alex had too much courage to hide behind locked doors. And he was right. She wasn't there. The room was empty of her possessions, too. Then he saw the letter propped against the pillows on the bed. And next to it lay the ring he had given her.

Your mother has told me that you can't marry me, Petroff, so I am released from my promise. In your happiness over this news, I hope you will grant me a favor. It is too soon for my horses to travel again, so I ask that you allow them to remain in your stable until I send for them. I have left their grooms to see to their care. If you don't agree, inform the head groom, Bulavin, and he will make other arrangements.

Now I must tell you how sorry I am for all the trouble I put you through. Please be

*assured that I bear you no grudge. In fact, I
wish you well, Petroff.*

Vasili read the letter a second time, then a
third, but it still didn't sound like Alexandra. The
words were too stiff, and the sentiment? She bore
him no grudge, was sorry, actually wished him
well? Not his Alex. And how did she dare to
leave? How did she dare to assume that his
mother's word was the final word? *He* hadn't
released her from her promise.

To hell with fate. Give it a chance, and damned
if it didn't suit you.

34

"She left her horses with me, even the two stallions," Vasili said, his voice still expressing disbelief. "They mean everything to her. How could she leave them?"

Stefan led Vasili to a chair in the audience room, where his closest friends were gathered; he even pushed him down into it, but this was the second time he had done so, and he doubted his cousin would remain there for long this time either. Vasili was angry, yet he was bewildered, too, and it wasn't a combination that sat well with him.

"Try thinking about it logically," Stefan suggested. "She would leave them because she *does* care so much for them, and it's the middle of winter."

Stefan had been allowed to read the note Alexandra had left; he'd had it thrust into his hands, actually. They had all read it, though Vasili hadn't noticed it being passed between Serge and Lazar, he'd been pacing so hard.

"Besides the weather," Lazar added, "the reason she gives is a sound one. It's too soon to take them on another long, grueling trip."

Vasili shot back to his feet for some more pacing. "Then she would have stayed with them until they could travel with her."

"When your mother told her that there would

be no marriage?" Serge reminded him. "The girl probably assumed she was no longer welcome."

"Then perhaps she didn't go far," Stefan said. "She could still be in the city."

Vasili shook his head. "No, her man, Bulavin, said she left Cardinia, that she won't be back, not even to collect the horses. She's going to send for them."

Tanya had just finished reading the note and looked up. "Obviously Alexandra trusts you to keep them safe for her, Vasili."

He snorted. "She doesn't."

"I have reason to believe she does," Tanya said.

That arrested him, and his golden eyes settled on her intently. "What reason?"

"It's just an . . . impression I got, after talking to her," she said evasively.

"You mean she didn't drag my name through the mud?" he asked sarcastically.

She smiled gently at his remark. "Actually, your name might have gotten a few sprinkles of dirt on it. After all, she can't help thinking you're a lecher, when it's a well-established fact that you are."

His reply was indignant. "I'll have you know I haven't touched another woman since I met her."

It was Serge who caught the implication in that. "*Another* woman?"

"Oh, Vasili." Tanya sighed now in disappointment. "Don't tell me you seduced that innocent girl when you had no intention of marrying her."

And from Lazar: "Jesus, Vasili, when did you

316

manage that, as cramped as the accommodations were on the whole trip?"

Vasili was flushing with heat by then. "It was hardly a seduction when—never mind. It doesn't matter, since I *am* going to marry her."

"You are?" more than one of them asked incredulously.

And Stefan said calmly, if a bit dryly, "I suppose this means you're leaving again."

Vasili nodded. "Within the hour. I only came here to tell you."

"It's late afternoon," Lazar said. "Shouldn't we wait until morning?"

"Not when she left early yesterday—and I wasn't inviting you," Vasili retorted.

"But you'll take him," Stefan said in a tone that would brook no argument, "and an extra complement of men with him. There's no point in inviting more trouble from our annoying friends in the mountains."

"That's *if* she's gone home," Vasili said.

"What makes you think she hasn't?" Serge asked.

"Because her groom wouldn't give me a straight answer about it, even after I threatened to rearrange his face for him. And she left her trunks behind, every one of them. She's traveling light this time, taking only the Cossacks and her maid with her."

"Which could mean she's merely in a hurry to get home," Serge said.

"Then why not make arrangements to have the wagons follow her?"

"I wouldn't say that's conclusive," Stefan pointed out.

"I know," Vasili agreed. "Which is why I'll be looking for her trail. I wish she *had* taken the stallions, though. At least people notice and remember them."

"You're not suggesting she knew you would follow her, are you?" Lazar asked in surprise. "That she's going to be covering her tracks?"

"She knows we're not finished. Maybe she won't admit it, but deep down she—"

"Vasili, she doesn't *want* to marry you," Lazar cut in to remind him. "And she assumed you felt the same way, since that's the only impression you've given her. If she's thinking anything, it's that your mother did you both a favor. That's what *you* were counting on, if you'll recall."

The reminder just got Lazar a glower, at which point Tanya asked, "Vasili, do you know *why* she didn't want to marry you, even before she met you? I asked her, but she said the reason was too embarrassing for her to mention."

Vasili was shaking his head, but Lazar supplied the answer. "She's in love with some Englishman she met on her coming out in St. Petersburg— or at least she says she is."

Vasili received that news with a mixture of incredulity and raging jealousy, and both had him shouting, "How the *hell* do you know that?"

"Unlike you, I was curious why she didn't fall at your feet the way most women do, so I asked."

"*She* told you that?"

"Of course not," Lazar replied. "You know she rarely even spoke to me in passing. No, I asked her maid, Nina, one day, and she treated the subject as if it were a long-standing point of contention."

"Meaning?"

"Her disgust was pretty obvious. Nina thinks that whatever it is Alexandra feels for this Christopher Leighton, it certainly can't be true love. And she's of the opinion that it's only Alexandra's stubbornness that has had her maintaining loyalty to this fellow after so many years."

"Did the maid give a reason for these opinions, Lazar?" Stefan questioned.

"Because Alexandra simply went on with her life, without a single bit of pining."

"Just how many years are we talking about?" Serge asked next.

"Seven."

"Jesus," Vasili groaned.

"Well, that explains her embarrassment," Tanya said. "And I'm inclined to agree with the maid."

Vasili glanced her way. "Why?"

"Oh, just the impression I got," Tanya said evasively once again.

"Now, don't be giving my wife hot looks, cousin," Stefan said, trying not to find any humor in Vasili's predicament, though it really was priceless. The man who could have almost any woman he wanted couldn't keep track of the one he had decided to settle down with, or get a declaration from her other than that she *didn't* want him. "If Tanya found out something in confidence, you can't expect her to tell you about it."

The hell he couldn't. Vasili demanded, "Whose side is she on, anyway?"

"Yours," Tanya assured him with a grin. "Which is why I'm delighted that you've decided you want to marry her. I think she'll make you a splendid wife, Vasili."

He gave her a reproachful look. "But you aren't going to tell me why you think so, are you?"

"No. But I'm sure it won't take you long to find out from Alexandra—if you can find her."

35

Alexandra found another month of traveling a daunting prospect. That was about how long it was going to take her to reach England. Nor did she like riding unfamiliar horses on this trip. They'd no sooner left Cardinia than she began to miss her own. So she was as relieved as Nina was to meet up with Lady Beatrice Haversham in Warsaw and be invited to continue their journey in her carriage.

Lady Beatrice was in her mid-forties, was wide of girth, and still wore her blond hair in the fashion of her youth, which wasn't as ridiculous-looking as it might have been, thanks to her laughing gray eyes. Amazingly, she had recognized Alexandra from her one season in St. Petersburg. The English lady and her husband, who was now deceased, had been visiting the city with friends at the time, and she had noted Alexandra at several functions, including Olga Romanovsky's lavish dinner party, the disastrous one which had led to Alexandra's unofficial ousting from St. Petersburg.

But it was that very party that was responsible for Lady Beatrice's recognizing Alexandra. To hear her say it, "I've never laughed so hard, my dear, and I hope you don't mind, but I regaled all my friends at home with that story. You were so wonderfully ingenious to sound so sincere when you told Princess Olga how she might lose some weight. All my friends found it hilarious, and I do so love to make people laugh."

Alexandra didn't bother to mention that she *had* been sincere in her suggestion, nor did she relate the repercussions that had followed. And although she had no memory of the Englishwoman herself, she grew fond of her as they traveled to England together. Beatrice really did love to laugh, and she found humor in just about everything. She even mistook Alexandra's frankness for a droll wit and claimed the *ton* was going to adore her. And another benefit the lady supplied was that her presence put an end to, or at least subdued, all the complaints Alexandra had been receiving from Nina and her brothers about her decision to find Christopher, complaints she refused to listen to.

Beatrice only vaguely remembered meeting Christopher while in Russia, and didn't know him personally. Yet she assured Alexandra that she was acquainted with people who would know him; and as it happened, it took her only two days after they finally arrived in London to show up at Alexandra's hotel with his address.

Checking with the embassy herself, since that was the only address he had ever used on his letters from England, had gained Alexandra nothing. He was presently between assignments, was all she could get out of the harried clerk she'd spoken to, and no, they weren't in the habit of handing out personal information about their diplomats. Try the *ton* directory, like everyone else.

Thanks to Lady Beatrice, she didn't have to deal with any more rude officials. And sooner than she might have expected, she was on her way to Christopher's aunt's home, where he was living, which was fortunately right there in London.

Nina had suggested she wait until the next morning to go, because it was evening by the time she was ready, but Alexandra couldn't afford to wait. Before they had left the Continent to sail for England—which had been a nightmare of sickness for her—she had known she was going to have Vasili's baby. And that baby needed a father. She would, of course, be honest about it with Christopher. And although that might complicate things, she didn't for a moment regret her condition. She was, in fact, absolutely thrilled about it.

The aunt's town house was ablaze with lights, and the numerous carriages dropping off their occupants indicated that some type of entertainment was going on, the fancy clothes suggesting something formal. Alexandra had had several days to shop while waiting for their ship to sail, and had found three partial-made dresses to add to the few she had stuffed into her valise for the trip. Nina had finished them on the voyage— her own sewing skills were atrocious. One was a lovely evening gown in rose and navy silk. She hadn't thought she would need it tonight, however, and she was barely let in the door in her green wool dress, despite the sable fur trim on her coat.

The dress was suitable for visiting, but not for

a ball, which was what the Leightons were giving. It got her stiffly escorted to an empty room away from the guests, a library by the looks of it, where she was told to wait.

And she waited. An hour passed and still she waited. But she didn't mind. Now that she was about to see Christopher again after all these years, she wasn't impatient. She wasn't much of anything, actually, not nervous, not even excited.

She found that rather strange, but attributed it to the deep melancholy she had fallen into since leaving Cardinia, and she attributed *that* to having to leave her horses behind. It certainly wasn't because she missed Vasili, because she didn't. She rarely even thought of him more than a dozen times a day anymore. But considering the hopelessness she had experienced in Cardinia and the melancholy she was feeling now, it was no wonder she was drained of emotion.

Lady Beatrice had kept Alexandra's sadness at bay with her gregarious good cheer, and so did Alexandra's own thoughts of the baby. But not much else did. Yet the fact that she was about to see Christopher again should have given her such joy. Why didn't it?

"Alexandra, is that really you?"

She hadn't heard the door opening and closing behind her, but she turned to find Christopher coming toward her with open arms, his expression proclaiming his delight at seeing her again. The years had barely changed him, though he would be thirty-five now. And he was perhaps even more handsome than she remembered, the extra fullness in his face and body improving his appearance—he'd been too lean before. He looked as distinguished as she recalled, with his dark brown hair and eyes, and his impeccable black evening attire. But his height of five feet ten inches seemed not so tall to her now, and . . .

He was hugging her too tightly. And before she had caught her breath from that, he was kissing her, and all she wanted to do was push away from him. What was wrong with her? This was Christopher, whom she loved, and apparently he was overjoyed that she had come to him, so everything was going to be all right. Then why didn't she *feel* as if it was? And she had always been thrilled by his kisses, yet nothing stirred within her, not even a flicker of the desire Vasili could spark. But she *wouldn't* think of him now—not now.

She managed to extricate her lips long enough to ask, "So you still love me?"

"Of course I still love you, darling. How could you doubt it?"

She could give a number of reasons, but decided sarcasm wasn't called for. Her frankness was, however, and she asked the question that should have been asked years ago. "Then are you prepared to marry me?"

He let go of her in surprise, but then he laughed. "I see you haven't changed. You still say exactly what's on your mind, no matter the consequences."

She could have told him that wasn't exactly true anymore. Some things she'd been managing to keep to herself recently. The Razins didn't know about the baby yet. And Vasili never knew how she really felt about him—She was doing it again, letting him into her thoughts when he should be the farthest thing from her mind right now.

"You haven't answered my question, Christopher."

"But you can't be serious," he said in a gentle, though no less scoffing, tone. "I was hoping you were going to tell me you *were* married, so we could finally be together."

Since that didn't make the least bit of sense to her, she was forced to ask, "What exactly does that mean?"

"Come now, Alexandra, you know love and marriage are rarely compatible. And I learned firsthand how promiscuous and amoral you Russian ladies are. I had hoped you would marry so we could have an affair. I thought you understood we could only be lovers."

She didn't need him to clarify that, since it was perfectly clear, but the mild shock she experienced made her remark, "Actually, I expected us to marry."

"Good God, you can't be that stupid."

She winced. "Oh, but I—was, obviously."

"But, my dear, you must know you're too unconventional. That habit you have of saying exactly what you think or feel would be ruinous to my career."

"I must still be rather stupid, because I don't understand why you continued to write me, to send me poetry and words of love."

He had the grace to blush. "I don't believe in

burning my bridges, darling. I still hoped we would one day end up in bed together."

Why wasn't she furious, or slapping him, or crying? "You should have said so," she replied flatly. "I probably would have been quite willing at the time."

"But you were an innocent and I don't—" He paused, and his expression changed to a curious, hopeful look. "Are you still?"

Alexandra decided a lie was appropriate at that point. "Yes."

"A shame." He sighed. "But tell me, what are you doing here in London? I hope you didn't come all this way just to see me."

Another lie, for her pride's sake. "No, I didn't. I just ended an engagement to a Cardinian count and decided to travel a while before returning home."

"A Cardinian?" He was suddenly excited. "Is there no hope of patching that up?"

"Why?"

"Because that would be ideal for us, darling. I've just learned that I'm going to be assigned to the embassy in Cardinia in a few months. And if you're there, and married—"

"That would be an excellent idea, Christopher, except . . . even if I did marry my Cardinian, and did find the need for a lover, which would, in fact, be likely"—she patted his cheek before ending—"I am absolutely certain that I wouldn't choose you." And she walked out of the room with her pride intact, if a little bruised.

36

Nina was waiting for her when she returned to her hotel room, and one look at Alexandra's expression made Nina say, "He wasn't there, was he?"

Alexandra removed her coat and sat down carefully on the bed. "Oh, he was there," she replied dryly. "And we had quite an interesting conversation. Apparently lechers aren't exclusive to Cardinia."

"I never thought they were." Then Nina's eyes flared in understanding. "You mean the Honorable Christopher Leighton isn't so honorable?"

Alexandra nodded and, as briefly as she could manage it, related what had happened. When she had finished, Nina was furious.

"That rotten bastard! That miserable deceiver, to give you no indication of his true motives, to deliberately let you think—"

"He said he assumed I understood."

"That's a lie and you know it, Alex—and don't you even think about trying to defend him."

"I wasn't."

"Good, because—" Nina broke off when she finally realized that she was doing all the yelling and Alexandra wasn't doing any. "Why aren't you angry?"

"I suppose I am."

The lackluster answer had Nina rolling her eyes. "You don't sound it. You don't even sound upset. In fact, you sound no different from when you left here."

"I'm still adjusting to the fact that Christopher isn't the man I thought he was." And then Alexandra frowned thoughtfully. "But you're right, I should be more upset about this than I am, shouldn't I? After all, I've loved him for so long—"

Nina's snort announced her opinion on that, yet she responded, "You say that from habit only."

"Nina—" Alexandra began defensively, but that, too, was out of habit, and her friend wasn't going to let her trot out the same old, lame excuses this time.

"I'm telling you, you didn't love him!" Nina interrupted hotly. "Not then and not now. I've always said it, but now you're going to believe it." Then she said, less severely, "You wanted him when you met him, but you were young and romantic then, and you needed a name for what you were feeling, so you called it love."

"And all these years—"

"All these years you simply haven't cared one way or the other, Alex, or you would have done something about it. Think about it. If you had really loved him, would you have been content to sit at home and wait?"

Put that way, the question demanded an obvious answer. Alexandra didn't have the temperament to be that patient, not if her emotions were involved. So why had she been deceiving herself? From habit, as Nina had said? Or because she had mistaken infatuation for love and was too stubborn to admit she'd made a mistake?

But Nina wasn't finished. "Even if you didn't love him, you still ought to be angry about what he's done to you. If it weren't for him, you would have been more favorably disposed to Count Petroff and would be married to him by now."

Would she? No, what she would have been was angrier at Vasili for not giving them a chance, because *his* sentiments wouldn't have been any different. He would have turned on his contempt no matter how she'd felt about him.

"My being more agreeable to him, Nina, would only have led to hurt." And hadn't she been hurt? Hadn't she been sick with regret? In a tone of annoyance she said, "I'm going to bed. Maybe tomorrow I'll be angry. Now I'm just tired."

But the next day didn't bring anything except a return of her melancholy—with the addition of knowing that she had to make a difficult decision. She was still pregnant, and she still needed a husband, quickly. And with Christopher no longer a candidate for the position, she was going to have to settle for a stranger.

That actually wasn't as daunting as it sounded. Alexandra had been quite happy with her life these past few years, with only one exception— her desire for children. But she had her baby now, and she still had her horses, and she could be content with that. And there was even the possibility that she might like whomever she chose to marry, might even one day come to love her husband. It wasn't *that* unlikely. But it didn't really matter to her if love happened or not.

She wished she didn't *need* a husband just because she was pregnant. It would be so much easier if she could settle somewhere and raise her child by herself. Her horses would support her quite adequately, would even make her rich if she decided to race them. But her child would suffer for that, would be branded illegitimate, and that was *not* an option she cared to exercise.

She didn't even consider going home, since she hadn't forgiven her father and doubted that she ever would. It still hurt even to think about him and what he'd done to her—what she was now suffering because of it.

Her only other option was Vasili. If the distance weren't so great, she'd return to Cardinia and insist that he marry her. But she was already seven weeks along in her pregnancy. It would take another month just to get back to Cardinia; then more time would be wasted arguing with Vasili in order to get him to agree, which wouldn't be easy after he'd been reprieved from the "hated state of matrimony." She would probably be showing her condition by then. Of course, a baby being on its way before marriage would be no more than anyone would expect from him.

The stirring of excitement she felt from merely considering the idea infuriated her. She still didn't want the kind of marriage he would give her. If she hadn't found out how wonderful those marital rights could be with him—which he intended to deny her—her decision might have been different. But she did know, and she would come to hate him after a while, might even toss her pride away and . . . no!

A stranger was much better. No emotional involvement and something in common, because the man would have to be an avid horseman, and from conversations she had overheard, she knew that many Englishmen were.

He would also have to have a strong penchant for horse racing, since that was probably the only thing that was going to get her a husband quickly. Although she had enough money to keep her comfortable for some time to come, even if she didn't sell another horse, she could in no way be classified as a rich catch. And she wasn't going to count on her minor title of baroness to aid her either.

Her thoroughbreds were the temptation she was counting on. Whomever she proposed to wouldn't just get a ready-made family; in all likelihood he'd get some wins at the racetracks as well. He'd have to want those wins, desperately, to accept her pregnancy, and her terms.

Deciding on a course of action was one thing, but implementing it was another. In that, Lady Beatrice helped immensely, obtaining invitations for her, spreading the word about her horses and that she was in the market for a husband. After only a few days, everyone was wondering about the Russian baroness who had come to London to find a husband.

As it turned out, her title was a bigger draw than she had supposed it would be, especially since she came with a guaranteed income from her breeding stock. But then, her looks alone turned out to be an equal enticement. She was attracting too many men who weren't horse fanciers, and although she would have discouraged them in her frank way, Lady Beatrice recommended that she not do so.

"Gossip, my dear," Beatrice explained. "Right now it is in your favor, but rejected suitors can turn it against you overnight."

"But won't too many suitors discourage the ones *I'm* interested in?"

Beatrice laughed. "Not at all. The ones you want will be even more intrigued by your popularity. If a girl has three men bussing about her, she'll soon have ten. It's human nature to see what all the fuss is about, and men *always* want what other men want."

That conversation took place, incredibly, on Alexandra's first evening out in London society, her acceptance by the *ton* was that quick. By the second evening she had met at least three gentlemen who fit her purposes exactly, and since she was in no position to waste time tiptoeing around the subject, she told each what her requirements were.

The first she took aside to speak with privately was apparently too shocked by her directness in doing the proposing to stick around to hear the rest of what she was offering, which was just as well. If he couldn't handle a simple thing like her proposal, he probably would have fainted when she got around to telling him about the baby.

After that experience, she was a little more careful with the second man, leading into the subject a bit more slowly, making sure that he was aware that she was seeking marriage before she asked if he was interested. He wouldn't give her an immediate answer, needed time to consider her proposal, though he hadn't counted on raising children so soon—he was only twenty-six.

The third man held the highest standing as a viscount, though he was the least attractive, a bit on the portly side. However, he fairly drooled when she mentioned how many horses she owned, and hardly batted an eye over the fact that she was pregnant. He did, in fact, give her a resounding yes, saying he would be delighted to marry her.

It was Alexandra's turn to be shocked. She really hadn't thought it would be this easy, or this quick, and she put him off, suggesting they spend a few days getting to know each other before they completely committed and set a wedding date. But at least the pressure was off. She'd solved her problem. Only now that she no longer had to worry about a father for her baby, her melancholy returned.

She spent a good portion of the next day with her viscount, Gordon Whately, which included riding through one of London's many parks. He brought one of his own thoroughbreds for her to ride—she had the impression it was a test of sorts, since the mare was high-spirited, which condition she had no difficulty controlling—and they ended up talking horses and nothing else. At least they would never lack for conversation as a married couple.

He was having no second thoughts—which

had been a possibility—and believed everything she claimed about her animals. She couldn't afford to have second thoughts herself.

Since it looked as if she would be staying in England, she would soon have to visit a dressmaker for clothing other than the completed, unclaimed dresses she had been able to buy with a minimum of alterations. That was how she had been surviving so far with her evening apparel, but she would soon run out of dressmakers who could accommodate her so quickly. And with all the invitations that Beatrice had lined up for her—which the older woman insisted Alexandra must still attend to broaden her acquaintances, even though she'd already accomplished her goal—she was going to need a much larger wardrobe.

That night there was a ball for which Beatrice was picking her up. Gordon wouldn't be attending, since he had a previous engagement he was unable to cancel, but Alexandra wasn't disappointed. Too much of his company gave her a headache.

She'd found a gown suitable for a ball late that afternoon, a fancy concoction in deep burgundy and black lace that showed off more of her bosom than she was used to, though she knew it to be the fashion. Still, she would have preferred not to go, having no more desire to socialize now than she'd had these past seven years.

But she went, and she even made an effort to enjoy herself. She wasn't succeeding very well, though, with visions of her future dampening her mood. Having spent so much time with Gordon today, she really couldn't imagine spending the rest of her life with him. And she certainly couldn't imagine making love with him. Yet what choice did she have?

She was dancing when the buzzing started, conversations everywhere picking up in volume, as if everyone were suddenly talking at once. Her partner was trying to look around to see what was happening, but he was no taller than she was, and he could find nothing amiss. She wasn't curious herself, although she couldn't help hearing some of the talk going on around her as they continued to twirl past the other couples on the dance floor.

"Is it the queen?"

"Over there by the . . ."

". . . never seen anyone so . . ."

"Good God, who is . . ."

". . . so handsome . . ."

". . . *so* handsome . . ."

". . . so *handsome* . . ."

Her partner had actually stopped dancing, even though the music continued to play. He didn't remember to apologize, he was so curious. But everyone else around them was doing the same thing, and the buzzing was getting even louder.

Alexandra sighed and excused herself to leave the floor. Whoever had so impressed these people was of no interest to her. So handsome? They'd have to go to Russia, to Cardinia to be exact, to see *really* handsome.

And then the crowd was suddenly parting before her, clearing a path for the man slowly walking across the room. And in the opened space she couldn't miss him, couldn't believe her eyes either, and couldn't take another step.

Vasili in London? Impossible. Yet there he was, coming straight toward her, his honey-gold eyes, as bright as she'd ever seen them, locked on hers. Everyone else saw an inscrutable expression, but she knew what that golden brightness indicated, that he was angry enough to throttle her, and she couldn't decide whether she ought to run, faint, cry—or laugh for the sheer joy that was over-whelming her senses at the very sight of him.

37

"We can discuss this for everyone's delectation, or you can come with me," Vasili said with forced evenness. "I have a carriage waiting outside."

That wasn't at all what Alexandra was expecting to hear. If she had been as angry as she suspected Vasili was, she wouldn't have held off whatever "this" was, just to avoid making an embarrassing scene. Of course, she was used to causing scenes and—and she'd better answer him before he made the decision for her.

"I was just about to leave anyway," she told him, her own tone carefully neutral.

It wasn't true, even if it was what she'd wanted to do ever since arriving. But she figured if she didn't go with him, he'd just become angrier, because then he'd be making that scene she knew he didn't want to make.

However, she nearly changed her mind about going anywhere with him. Although he had her compliance, she still felt as if he were dragging her out of there. But before she could make up her mind whether it would be in her best interest to remain where there were people, they were outside, and she was being shoved into his waiting carriage.

"Is it your intention to freeze me?" she asked, her tone sarcastic.

He hadn't stopped long enough to retrieve her

evening cloak, and the winter night air was damp and frigid. Inside the large, well-appointed carriage, it was not much warmer. But rather than go back for her wrap, he tossed a carriage blanket at her before he sat down.

The vehicle departed immediately with the slamming of the door, jerking Alexandra nearly off the edge of the seat. It wouldn't take much more for her to be losing her temper.

"Explain yourself, Petroff. If I had known you had a trip to England scheduled, I would have gone elsewhere."

"Would you? I doubt that."

He was sitting opposite her with his arms crossed, his legs stretched out and also crossed, his eyes still aglow as he stared at her. Whatever pleasure she had felt upon first seeing him was fast dissipating, irritation taking its place. And that he said no more after his sardonic remark left a silence that unnerved her.

She broke it, demanding, "Well? I assume there is some particular reason you have sought me out—or did we have the misfortune to turn up at the same function as well as in the same town?"

"We'll get to that in a moment, Alex. Right now I'm having a little trouble adjusting to seeing you, for all intents and purposes, looking like a lady. Or do you have your britches on underneath that gown?"

She couldn't imagine why that question made her blush, but it did. "If you failed to notice, that was a ball you dragged me out of. I do happen to know what the required dress is for such an occasion."

"No britches, then?"

She glared at him in answer. Vasili wasn't amused. He was, in fact, even more incredulous now than when he'd first spotted her on the dance floor. Silk and lace. He'd had fantasies of her wearing just that, but he could never have imagined anything like this. The artfully arranged coiffure, the long evening gloves, the deep scoop of her neckline—Jesus, her breasts, her magnificent breasts on display for any man who cared to look.

Even as that infuriated him, Vasili had to allow that he had never seen Alexandra looking more beautiful. And he resented that she had always denied him this soft, feminine side of her, that he hadn't known she even had a side like this— except in bed.

She could dance. She could apparently converse with her peers for a while without swearing or shocking them. And obviously she was careful not to attend gatherings where dinner was included, or she would very quickly become excluded from guest lists. But apparently she'd been able to fool these English into believing she was a lady, or that she knew how to act like one.

He was also furious that he hadn't been able to catch up with her before she sailed for England, that it had taken him more than a month to finally find her. They'd lost her trail twice, first when she had begun heading for the mountains, as if she were going home, then had changed directions to travel north. He'd sent home most of the men he had with him at that point, since it appeared they wouldn't be needed.

Then they had lost Alexandra again, when she switched her mode of traveling to a carriage. But between him and the eight men left in his party, it had taken only a few hours after their arrival in London to locate her hotel. And her maid, Nina, had obligingly told him where she could be found tonight.

And now he wasn't sure how to handle her. His first urge, as always, was to make love to her, and that urge was stronger than ever. Just being near her again had him hard and ready. His second urge was to throttle her for all the trouble she had put him through. But he had a third urge, just to hold her and tell her—what? That he'd been worried sick that she would marry Leighton before he found her? That he was in the lamentable position of finding himself in love for the first time in his life? She'd never believe it after the attitude he had demonstrated just for her.

And what about her Englishman? If he had found Leighton there with her, he probably would have challenged him on the spot. If she loved the man, if she *really* loved him, he wondered if he had the decency to bow out and let her have him. His jealousy said no, that he and the Englishman couldn't live on the same planet. But this damn love he was feeling wanted her to be happy.

The two feelings wouldn't reconcile. He supposed he ought to find out first if he had arrived too late.

"Is there a wedding planned, Alex?"

341

Alexandra drew in a sharp breath of surprise. How could he possibly have found out about her portly viscount? He couldn't know.

"What wedding?" she asked carefully.

"Between you and Leighton."

This was even worse. "How did you learn about Christopher?"

"From Lazar. *You* should have told me."

"It was none of your business—"

"We are to be married!" he cut in, his anger finally there between them. "It damn well is my business if you are in love with another man!"

"We are to be *what?*"

"Fickle after all, aren't you?" he sneered. "Or have you forgotten that you assured me you wouldn't break your word? A matter of honor, or so you claimed."

His attack had her hackles rising. "Didn't you get my note? Your mother said you couldn't possibly marry me, that I was a disgrace, hopeless—"

"My mother didn't arrange our marriage. She has no say in the matter."

"That wasn't the impression you gave the first time we discussed ending the betrothal," she said stiffly. "When she told me what she did, I assumed—"

"You assumed wrong, Alex, and you left without even confirming that assumption with me. And I repeat, it wasn't up to my mother. Whether we get married or not is up to us, and depends on whether or not we are going to honor what our respective fathers committed us to."

"You're saying we're still betrothed?"

"You're damned right we are." And before she knew what he was doing, he had her hand in his and was slipping the warm metal of her betrothal ring on her finger. "Don't remove it again, Alex. You belong to me. I want you wearing the proof of that."

The last was said as if it were a warning, and she heard some distinct possessiveness in his tone that confused and thrilled her at the same time. She sat back, assailed by relief and dread, and fought to ignore them both. She'd never get through this discussion if she didn't keep her emotions out of it. But, oh, how wonderful it felt to have that ring back! Tears had accompanied her removal of it. When she had left it behind with her note to him, it had felt as if she were leaving her heart behind, too. She wouldn't remove it again—but not because he'd told her not to.

"Would you mind explaining to me why?" she said, referring to his assertion that the betrothal was still on. "I gave you an out. And as I recall, you didn't want to marry me, so why didn't you take it?"

Because I love you!

Now was an excellent time to tell her. But she would laugh and scoff and probably say something sarcastic like "Sure you do, Petroff. You prove it to me every time you open your mouth." And since he was still having difficulty believing it himself, how was he going to convince her?

"You didn't give me an out, Alex. You ran off under a misconception. That didn't release me from the betrothal, it merely put me to the bother of bringing you back. However, if it *was* your intention to break your word, say so now and that will be the end of it."

"That was never my intention and you know it," she hissed at him.

"I didn't think so, so there you have your answer. We are still bound by that contract, still very much betrothed, and still going to be married. Or do you disagree with that?"

"No," she said in a low mumble.

"Then your coming to England hasn't changed your views about honor?"

"No," she said with more volume and a glare.

"I'm glad to hear it."

She snorted at that. "Careful, Petroff, or you'll almost have me thinking you *want* to get married now."

"Perhaps I do," he said softly.

"When pigs fly," was her retort.

He grinned. He just *knew* his Alex would say something like that.

"Actually . . ." He paused so she would think he was only just coming to this conclusion. "Since I have to get married eventually anyway—for an heir, you understand—it might as well be to you. After all, I've already devoted more effort to you than I ever have to another woman—and I absolutely adore your breasts, Alex."

He expected another hot retort, a blush, anything except the subdued expression he was getting. And he could have kicked himself for thinking that what he'd said would be more acceptable to her than the truth.

"Alex—"

"You don't have to explain," she interrupted him. "I've always known your position on the subject. And you've always known mine."

Reminding him that she hadn't wanted to marry him because she was in love with someone else worked to bring back the anger he'd displayed earlier, and to get his mind off telling her any more about how *wonderful* life was going to be with him. She could have told him about the baby now and he could start ignoring her before they were even married. But since that would probably delight him, she decided to be perverse and keep the news to herself.

He might have come after her, but obviously nothing had changed. So why did that "for an heir, you understand" make her feel like crying?

"You've seen Leighton?" he asked tightly.

"Yes."

"I'll kill the bastard if he touched you, Alex," he fairly growled.

What was this, jealousy by default? "Don't bother. He never wanted to marry me. He was waiting for me to marry someone else so he could then become my lover. He thought the same thing you did, except he knew I was a virgin and he was just waiting for me to change that fact."

"He's dead," Vasili said simply.

Alexandra sighed. "I'm the one who was insulted, Petroff, not you. Just because you're thinking of me as your wife now doesn't mean I won't still fight my own battles."

"He hurt you—"

"No, he didn't—which made me realize it was rather tepid, whatever I felt for him."

Vasili's smug smile at those words was irritating in the extreme, making her change the subject again. "Where, exactly, are you taking me?"

"To my ship. I didn't like this congested, over-crowded city the first time I visited it, and I still don't. We'll be leaving immediately."

"No, we won't. My people—"

"Should be aboard by now, I imagine, with some—friendly—persuasion."

"You're pushing it, Petroff."

"After all the trouble you've put me to, sweet-heart, I'd say I'm allowed."

38

The return to Cardinia seemed to take no time at all, but then, Alexandra was so sunk in her unhappiness that she barely noticed the passing of time. On the ship, she spent the entire week near a bucket, feeling half dead. She supposed she was fortunate, though, considering the stories she'd heard from other pregnant women, that during the sea voyage was the only time she was sick.

Once she was back on land, her health bloomed. In fact, she'd never felt better—physically. She didn't even catch the colds and coughs that the rest of her companions were suffering as they traveled through the worst part of winter, plagued by snow or freezing winds.

Her spirits picked up only when they were nearing Cardinia and she realized she would soon be back with her horses. It was then that she began to notice the unusual looks she was getting from Vasili, as if he might be regretting something. She could just imagine what.

However, he had told her earlier in the journey that he would give her time to get used to the fact that they *were* getting married. He seemed absolutely adamant about it now. And to give her that time to adjust, he had apparently decided that keeping their conversations down to a minimum would help. After all, it was a rare occasion when they could talk and not have their words progress into a heated exchange.

One time in particular should have been the argument of the century, the first time they came to an inn and ended up dining together. Alexandra had already decided there was no point in continuing her rustic ruse. It had never worked on Vasili anyway. And now that she was resigned to marrying him—just for the baby's sake—she was done with schemes to try to get out of it.

Vasili had raised his brows dubiously at the dresses she continued to wear since leaving England, though he didn't ask again if she had her britches on beneath them. But the night they sat at the same table, and he observed her normal eating habits for the first time, she thought he was going to go into shock.

Yet it didn't take long before his eyes had narrowed on her. "So all those horrid, disgusting manners were only for my benefit?" he guessed.

She didn't try to prevaricate, but answered simply, "Of course."

"The swearing?"

"I had help—and improvised."

"Your skill with a whip wasn't faked."

"Konrad taught me when we were children."

"And the threats you gave my women?"

She shrugged. "Sorry, but those were genuine. I never have been able to share what's mine."

He actually grinned at that point before telling her, "I've discovered I won't either, at least not where you're concerned."

She didn't take that declaration seriously. And she figured he had realized that he couldn't get angry over what she'd done to fool him because he had done the very same thing.

Tanya Barony had warned her, but she herself had been treated to Vasili's true character on the return trip for the proof of it. No more taunting, derisive remarks. No more contemptuous looks. And too many sensuous smiles for her heart to handle with any degree of indifference.

He was getting to her without even trying, and that frightened her. She could just imagine how painful it was going to be when he got around to ignoring her, and that would happen as soon as he figured out that she was already carrying his desired heir, which wouldn't be much longer. It also hurt her even more to discover that he really was likable when he wasn't deliberately trying to be otherwise, just as Tanya had claimed.

If she could only hate him, she could get through marriage to him with ease. But that wasn't the case, was so far from it that it was laughable. And too many times she came close to setting aside her pride and begging for his affection—at the very least, for his body.

It was deplorable how often those carnal feelings were assailing her these days. And she hoped that she would be married before her condition was discovered, because she was determined to have her wedding night, which was probably going to be the only night with him she would get. She would demand it, in fact, if necessary, because Vasili owed her that much after introducing her to the pleasures of the body, then leaving her yearning for more.

It was raining the day they arrived in the royal

city of Cardinia. Vasili and Lazar had chosen to join her in the carriage when it started. Vasili had supplied the vehicle for her three weeks ago, when he'd seen her leave the ship in a dress rather than her britches. She had been brooding too much at the time even to be aware that her dress wasn't suitable for riding.

But she hadn't objected to the carriage, or that, because of it, she wasn't supplied with a horse to do some riding. She wasn't sure that she *should* ride anymore, now that she was two and a half months into her pregnancy. Until a doctor could advise her on the matter, she preferred not to take any chances, no matter how much she might miss her daily rides.

Vasili had waited until the last minute, until they'd actually entered the city, to tell Alexandra she would be staying with his mother again. The way he said it led her to believe he was expecting an argument. She didn't give him one, despite the fact that she was dreading facing the countess again.

She supposed she owed the lady an apology. She would have seen to it when they arrived, and Maria met them no sooner than they had walked in the door, except Vasili had some things to say to his mother that momentarily surprised Alexandra.

"So you found her," Maria began.

"I told you I would, Mother. And since we will be married tomorrow, Alexandra will be staying here only tonight. But kindly do me the favor of not mentioning her previous behavior to her. It was all a pretense anyway, so you can stop worrying that—"

"Yes, yes, I know all about that," Maria cut in, surprising both him and Alexandra.

"How?" Vasili asked.

"Her father arrived not long after you left. He explained that although she is a trifle unconventional in certain areas—her horses, for one—she is every bit the lady we were expecting her to be. I was, of course, quite shocked. So was the baron when I related—"

"Let's *not* discuss it, Mother, if you don't mind. Did he return to Russia?"

"With his daughter missing?" she replied, her tone implying he should know parents weren't that cavalier. "He was going to go after her himself, until I assured him that you would bring her back. Of course, I offered him my hospitality."

"He's *here?*"

"Yes, upstairs, and you might as well know, Vasili, he confessed that there never was a . . ."

Alexandra didn't hear any more. She'd started backing up the moment Vasili's mother had mentioned her father, and soon she was out the door, heading for the stable. How could her father show up here after what he'd done to her? How could he pretend to care what— "Alex, where do you think you're going?"

Vasili had halted her with a gentle hand on her arm, but she kept her face averted from him until she could swipe at her eyes. She didn't want him to see the tears she'd been unable to hold back.

"I don't know," she admitted. "I just know I don't want to see my father—ever again."

Was that relief she heard in his sigh? "Then you won't have to. I'll take you to the queen. She'll keep you secluded until the wedding; then afterward, we'll retire to one of my country estates. But . . . might I ask why you don't want to see him?"

She was too upset to appreciate how helpful he was being, or to consider how he might take her answer. "Because he could have ended the betrothal before we even met, but he didn't. The hell we've put each other through is his fault, and I'm not forgiving him for that."

A few moments passed before he asked, "Alex, if he broke the betrothal now, would your word still stand?"

"Since I promised to marry you unless *you* cried off, I suppose it would."

"Even if there was no betrothal contract?"

She frowned up at him. "What kind of question is that?"

"A silly one, I suppose, but actually, it's related to something I've been meaning to do. I want to officially ask you to marry me."

The thrill of pleasure she experienced felt strange next to her pain, and was no more welcome. "You know that isn't necessary."

"Humor me, Alex, please. Will you marry me?"

"Yes."

"Will you give me your word?"

"You're pushing it, Petroff—"

"Please."

"All right, you have it, though it's the last time I'm promising anyone—"

He was kissing her before she'd finished, and Alexandra forgot what she'd gotten huffy about. When he let her go, she was breathless and not a little confused.

"What was that for?"

He grinned at her. "To thank you, because I *was* pushing it."

Her eyes narrowed. "Next time, just say the words, Petroff."

39

Vasili was waiting in the antechamber of the palace chapel for his bride to arrive, his friends keeping him company and ribbing him because he was there so early. He didn't say so, but he would have had the wedding yesterday if he didn't think Alexandra would question such haste. But it still couldn't happen soon enough for him, and he wasn't going to stop worrying until it was over.

He had managed to avoid Alexandra's father thus far. With any luck . . .

Instead of Tanya entering to say Alexandra was on her way, Constantin Rubliov appeared in the doorway, his expression thunderous, his voice nearly as thunderous. "Where have you hidden my daughter?"

Vasili sighed. Luck just hadn't been on his side, ever since he'd met the man's daughter. But he was determined to change that.

He glanced at Stefan pointedly. "Would you mind leaving us alone?"

Stefan looked from the angry father, whose identity was pretty obvious, back to Vasili, and he raised a black brow. "Must I?"

"Dammit, Stefan—"

His cousin chuckled, and with one arm around a curious Lazar and the other around a puzzled Serge, steered them out of the room.

Alone with Constantin, who was now flushing

with embarrassment because he had blustered in front of the King of Cardinia without realizing it, Vasili said, "Alex spent the night with the queen's ladies. We're about to be married."

"Wasn't she told I was here?"

"Yes," Vasili said, then added reluctantly, "But I'm afraid she doesn't want to see you, sir."

Constantin's embarrassment was abruptly forgotten. "Nonsense. My daughter and I happen to be very close. She—"

Vasili cut in. "Perhaps that's why she was so hurt by what you did."

Constantin's furious expression crumbled. "Then she knows there was never any betrothal?"

"No, she doesn't. She had already left when my mother told me about your confession. And I chose not to mention it to her. But the betrothal is no longer an issue. I've asked her to marry me, and she's accepted."

"Then she's happy with you now?"

"She will be."

This was said with such determination, Constantin couldn't help but believe him. But he had misunderstood.

"Thank God," he said. "After hearing what your mother had to say about her behavior, I was afraid Alex was never going to accept you, and that was why she finally left. But if she now wants to marry you—"

"I said she *will* be happy, Baron. At the moment, she's still brooding over finding out that her sweetheart, Leighton, was a worthless bastard who never intended to marry her. I've allowed her time to get over him, but once we're married, she'll damn well forget him, I promise you that."

Constantin was frowning by then. "Are you saying she is merely resigned to marrying you? After all the time you've had with her?"

"I'm afraid she and I didn't get off to a good start," Vasili admitted. "She didn't want to marry me; I didn't want to marry her. But after I changed my mind—I've spent my life seducing women, Baron. I couldn't bring myself to seduce the one I'm going to marry. But after we're married, I won't be so constrained."

"If she doesn't know that there was never any real betrothal, why doesn't she want to see me?"

"Apparently she hasn't forgiven you for throwing us together. I, on the other hand, couldn't be more grateful—at least now. You took a lot upon yourself, Baron. If I didn't feel the way I do about Alexandra, I would—"

Vasili didn't get to finish. Tanya had appeared, and said, "She's coming—oh, I beg your pardon."

"That's quite all right, Tanya. This is Alexandra's father."

The queen nodded, but asked, "And Stefan?"

"In the chapel," Vasili said.

"Shouldn't you be waiting at the altar yourself?"

"In a moment."

With another nod, she left through the door to the chapel. Vasili was now in the uncomfortable position of having to ask his future father-in-law to leave. He didn't want Alexandra upset again, if she should see him. But once again, his luck wasn't working.

She was suddenly there, looking so stunningly beautiful in the ivory silk wedding gown adorned with white Belgian lace and tiny seed pearls that he'd ordered made for her, she took his breath away. She had no such difficulty. Noticing her father, she turned around and left before he had seen her.

"Alex!" Vasili called out and started after her. But Constantin was ahead of him. And since the damage was already done, Vasili waited, allowing the baron the opportunity to at least try to make things right with his daughter, and wishing him success.

Alexandra wasn't going to stop. Those damn tears were threatening again, but she absolutely refused to let them fall this time. She wasn't going to talk to her father, wasn't going to . . .

Constantin caught up with her before she got halfway down the corridor. He tried to take her in his arms, but she drew hers back and up as if to say, "Don't touch me," and in fact, she said, "Don't!" And then, with a glare, she fumed, "I can't imagine why you've come here. You certainly don't care enough—"

"My God, you know that isn't true, Alex."

His stricken look was choking her, but she wasn't going to be swayed. "That I am here shows how much you cared. I don't think I've ever been more unhappy, and I have you to thank for it."

"I don't understand. You and Vasili were extremely well suited. You were greatly attracted to him. Why didn't you give it a chance?"

"Because I was in love with someone else—or thought I was. You, of course, will be delighted to know what a mistake that was, just as you always maintained," she said bitterly. "But even if that weren't so, it would have made no difference between Vasili and me, since he was against the marriage from the start. The only reason he's reversed his opinion is because he figures he has to marry someday anyway, and he doesn't want to have to bother courting some other woman— not that he ever bothered to court me."

"That isn't the impression—I don't think that's why he's marrying you, Alex. But what is more important here is, how do you feel about him now?"

"What difference can my feelings make when he doesn't love me?"

"Then you don't have to marry him," Constantin said. "I'll talk to him—"

"Don't bother. His own mother told him he couldn't marry me, but he wouldn't listen. He's completely reversed his stand. And besides, it's too late for you to break the betrothal, as you *should* have done. I gave him my word I'd marry him, so the betrothal no longer has anything to do with it. And I will marry him—just as soon as you leave."

"Alex!"

"I'm sorry, but I can't forgive you for doing this to me. And—and I have nothing more to say to you."

She turned her back on him and closed her eyes against the pain welling up inside her. For a long moment there was silence, then his footsteps receding, and that was when the tears started streaming down her cheeks. The lump in her throat felt as if it were going to burst, it was so huge. Oh, God, it was killing her!

Vasili was suddenly there, his arms gathering her against his chest, his voice at her ear, telling her, "I promise you, Alex, I *swear* it, you will be happy with me. And you're going to want to thank your father one day for bringing us together, so forgive him now. Tell him you forgive him. You won't regret it."

She was crying loudly by then, and leaning back, she could barely see Vasili through the tears, but what she saw was such concern and caring and sincerity and . . . oh, God, what had she done?

She wrenched herself away from him to run down the corridor, shouting for her father to wait—he had nearly reached the end. And when he finally heard her and turned, she saw that he'd been crying, too, and it tore a sound of anguish from her as she closed the distance and threw herself into his open arms.

"I'm sorry, Papa, I didn't mean it—I didn't mean any of it!" she wailed.

"I know, I know. Hush, Alex, it's all right—"

"It's not. I wanted to hurt you because I hurt, but it's not your fault that he doesn't love me."

"I think he does, Alex," Constantin murmured as he wiped the tears from her cheeks.

"He doesn't—but he will," she said fiercely. "I've been feeling sorry for myself when I should have been fighting for what I want."

Constantin couldn't help it; he laughed at that

point. "That's my girl." And all the pain drained out of Alexandra, hearing it.

She glanced back to see Vasili standing where she'd left him, her golden Adonis, more handsome than words could describe—and he'd just promised to make her happy.

Her smile was nearly blinding when she looked back at her father. "Will you give me away, Papa?"

"Then you do love him?"

"Oh, yes, more than I can say." And with a grin: "Certainly more than he deserves."

"Then let's not hold up this wedding any longer."

40

Soft candlelight, silk sheets, an extremely thick fur rug before the fireplace. The more Alexandra observed the seductive atmosphere of Vasili's bedroom, the more annoyed she became as she waited for him to join her. Nervousness, possibly, already had her on edge.

She'd told her father earlier today that she was going to make Vasili love her; however, she didn't expect miracles overnight. But at least she didn't feel hopeless about it anymore. Talking with her father had restored her confidence, and also made her realize how completely it had deserted her for a while. She wondered now if her pregnancy wasn't responsible for some of her moodiness.

She turned away from staring at the fire and found that Vasili had come silently into the room. He was leaning against the foot of the bed, his arms crossed over a maroon robe, staring at her. As usual, his handsomeness made her sigh, the lean lines of his face so perfect, his golden hair in disarray, the hard planes of his body in evidence. Just how was she going to make this beautiful man love her?

"What did you do with all those mistresses you had spread around this city?"

He lifted a brow curiously. "Are we about to have a fight, sweetheart?"

"It's quite possible."

"Can't you think of something more . . . interesting to do, since this happens to be our wedding night?"

"If you mean making love, Petroff, believe me, we'll get to that."

He burst out laughing. "In that case, you might as well know that I visited each and every one of them while you were endeavoring *not* to become a lady under my mother's tutelage. And imagine my amazement when not one of them was able to tempt me into her bed. There was nothing left for me to do but pay them off."

"I'm supposed to believe that?"

His expression turned sensually serious. "You'd better, sweetheart, since the last woman I made love to was you, and considering how long ago that was, I'm rather ravenous."

Her blush was instantaneous and all the more apparent beneath her white negligee. And she remembered thinking that she was going to demand her rights tonight. She didn't feel like demanding now, but the stirrings his confession caused insisted that she ask.

"Do you—do you think we could—?"

"God, yes," he said hoarsely as he took the few steps that separated them and gathered her in his arms. But he didn't kiss her immediately as he usually did, and his eyes were a soft golden glow as they searched hers. "Alex, there is something I probably should have told—"

"This isn't the time for talking, Petroff," she said as she put her arms around his neck and drew his mouth down to hers.

His groan thrilled her. His arms crushed her.

And his mouth, his divinely erotic mouth, moved over hers in heated play, his tongue delving, hiding, forcing hers to seek, and she did. Oh, yes, she did. By the time his kisses had moved down her neck on a path to her breasts, her desire was already so hot she could have dragged him to the bed.

For all his being ravenous, he was showing remarkable restraint. Alexandra just didn't know what it cost him. But he was determined to give her a night she would never forget. And she was determined to get him inside her before she exploded.

They ended up compromising, because he was undone by her saying, "Make love to me now."

Her gown was divested before he carried her to the bed, and with her hands urging him, urgently guiding him, she had her first climax in moments, with Vasili following her to that coveted pinnacle so swiftly, it left them both breathless and clinging.

And then he had *his* way, and she found out what being lavished with kisses on every part of her body was like—unbelievably nice. His hands were so gentle, almost loving in his caresses. And her breasts, God, they were even more sensitive because of her pregnancy, and he really did adore them, fairly worshiped them with his hands and mouth, until she thought she would scream with pleasure.

She came again with his fingers inside her, because she was aroused so quickly by him, and climaxed so easily to his touch. And when he finally entered her again, it was so very different, so very tender and slow, and all the more glorious when they reached the ecstasy together.

He was incredible, and she pitied all those women who would have to do without him now. She wasn't going to share this man, not even a little. And as they lay there together, her head on his shoulder, his hand still softly caressing her arm slung across his chest, she wanted to thank him for tonight; and for her, that meant giving from the heart what would please him the most and mean the most to her, and she knew of only one thing that would.

Softly, she said, "I'm giving you Prince Mischa for a wedding gift." And then, because tears were already gathering in her eyes, she added, "But if you ever hurt him, I'll take my whip to you."

He saw the tears before she turned her face into his shoulder. "Alex, you don't have to do this."

"I want to."

He hugged her fiercely. "Thank you," he said humbly. "I'll care for him as if he were my own baby."

He realized she must have heard him talking to Stefan that time in the stable. But he also realized something else that filled him with joy. There could be only one reason that she would give up one of her beloved horses.

"Why didn't you tell me, Alex?" he asked gently.

"What?"

"That you love me."

Her head reared up so she could scowl at him. "Whatever gave you that—"

"Admit it, you love me."

"I'd be a fool to—"

"You love me! Say it!"

"Why? So you can gloat? So you can—"

"So I can tell you I love you, too. I loved you before you showed your true colors, sweetheart. Why do you think I came after you?"

"I recall what you said at the time, and it had nothing to do with love."

"Would you have believed me then? I didn't think so, but you have to believe me now, Alex."

She was suddenly smiling at him, and he'd never been so dazzled in his life. "I do," she said, and leaned over to give him a sweet I-love-you kind of kiss, then ruined it by adding, "It's lucky for you I told my father I was going to make you love me."

"Why?"

"Because I prefer quick successes—otherwise it would have taken you all night to convince me."

He wasn't sure if she was serious or not, so he grunted and said, "As long as we're having these confessions, when were you going to get around to telling me about the baby?"

She gasped. "Dammit, Vasili, you weren't supposed to guess this soon!"

He laughed at that. "I should have known the first time you ever used my given name, it would be in a complaint."

She ignored that to demand, "When did you guess?"

"Tonight." He was smiling with pleasure over her confirmation. "Considering how much I adore your breasts, Alex, did you think I wouldn't notice the slight change in them?"

There was that blush again. "Don't think you're going to ignore me just because you've got your heir on the way."

He winced. "You *would* have to remember I said that."

"I remember everything you've ever—"

"You can't hold me accountable for whatever I said then, because I was in a state of panic. I really didn't think marriage would agree with me."

"And now?"

"And now I don't think I can do without it—or you. Ignore you, sweetheart? I think it would be easier to stop breathing."

She smiled and hugged him, then got the sudden urge to find out what teasing him would be like. "You know, I left a fiancé back in England."

"You did *what?*"

"A rather chubby viscount who was willing to marry me, baby and all, just to get his hands on my horses. Are you sure that's not why you married me?"

"Why else?" he retorted. "And how dare you even think about giving my son to another man?"

"Your *daughter* needed a father."

"My *son* already had one."

"But you were taking your sweet time finding me."

"And you were staying in out-of-the-way places so I'd keep losing your damn trail."

She hid her face in his shoulder again before saying, "Is that what I was doing?"

He looked down at her suspiciously. "Are you laughing, Alexandra?"

She couldn't conceal it any longer. "It feels so good, fighting with you again."

"You little witch." He grinned. "Remind me not to be so gullible in the future."

"Oh, no, I like you gullible. And I like that little streak of jealousy you have. And I love you flat on your back, naked, where I can—"

"Jesus, Alex, that's going to get you flat on *your* back again."

"So what are you waiting for?"

"How about a pretty please?"

"You're pushing it, Petroff."

"No," he said as he came over her, entered her, then grinned down at her. "But now I am."

Her laughter joined his before their bodies once again rejoiced in finding each other—due to a betrothal that never was.

IF YOU HAVE ENJOYED READING THIS
LARGE PRINT BOOK AND YOU
WOULD LIKE MORE INFORMATION
ON HOW TO ORDER A WHEELER
LARGE PRINT BOOK, PLEASE WRITE
TO:

WHEELER PUBLISHING, INC.
P.O. BOX 531
ACCORD, MA 02018-0531